D1498732

GRAND HOTEL

Books By
VICKI BAUM

Bubenreise

Die Tanze der Ina Raffay

Feme

Hell in Frauensee

Menschen im Hotel

Vicki Baum

GRAND HOTEL

TRANSLATED BY
BASIL CREIGHTON

DOUBLEDAY, DORAN & COMPANY, INC.
GARDEN CITY 1931 NEW YORK

PRINTED AT THE *Country Life Press*, GARDEN CITY, N. Y., U. S. A.

GRAND HOTEL

THE hall porter was a little white about the gills as he came out of No. 7 box. He went for his cap which he had left on the radiator.

"What was it?" asked the operator at the switchboard, earphones over his head and the red and green stops between his fingers.

"They've taken my wife to the hospital all of a sudden. I don't know at all what that means. She says it's beginning. But, good heavens! it can't have got that far."

The operator was only half listening. He had a call to put through. "Well, don't worry, Herr Senf," he said. "You'll have a fine boy first thing in the morning——"

"Thank you, anyway, for calling me to the phone here. I can't go shouting about my private affairs over there at my desk. Duty is duty."

"Just so. And when the baby's there I'll ring through," said the operator absentmindedly, and carried on with his calls. The porter took his cap and went off on tip-toe. He did this unconsciously because his wife had been brought to bed and was about to have a child. As he crossed the passage, where the silent reading and writing rooms had half their lights switched off, he let out a deep breath and ran his fingers through his hair. He was surprised to find them wet, but there was no time to wash his hands. After all, the routine of the hotel could not be

1

upset because Hall Porter Senf's wife was expecting a baby.

The music from the tea room in the new building beat in syncopation from mirror to mirror along the walls. It was dinner time and a smell of cooking was in the air, but behind the closed doors of the large dining room there was still silence and vacancy. The chef, Mattoni, was setting out his cold buffet in the small white room. The porter felt a strange weakness in his knees and he stopped a moment in the doorway, arrested by the bright gleams of the colored lights behind the blocks of ice. In the corridor an electrician was kneeling on the floor, busied over some repair to the wires. Ever since they had had those powerful lights to illuminate the hotel frontage there had always been something going wrong with the overworked installation of the hotel. The porter pulled himself together and went back to his post. Little Georgi meanwhile had taken charge. Georgi was the son of the proprietor of a large hotel business who wanted to see his son work his way up from the ranks. Senf, feeling somewhat oppressed, made his way straight across the lounge, where there was now a throng of movement. Here the jazz band from the tea room encountered the violins from the Winter Garden, while mingled with them came the thin murmur of the illuminated fountain as it fell into its imitation Venetian basin, the ring of glasses on tables, the creaking of wicker chairs, and, lastly, a soft rustle of the furs and silks in which women were moving to and fro. A cool March air came in gusts through the revolving doors whenever the page boy passed guests in or out.

"*All right*," said little Georgi in English as Senf finally dropped anchor at the porter's desk. "Here's the seven o'clock post. Sixty-eight has been making a row because her chauffeur wasn't there on the tick. Rather a hysterical lady, eh?"

"Sixty-eight—that's Grusinskaya," said the hall porter, and began to sort the letters with his right hand. "That's the dancer. We know her—for eighteen years past. She gets a fit of nerves every night before she goes on the stage, and then she makes a row."

A tall gentleman in the lounge got up stiffly out of an easy chair and came with bent head towards the porter's desk. He loitered for a bit round the lounge before approaching the entrance hall. The impression he made was emphatically one of listlessness and boredom as he glanced at the magazines displayed on the little bookstall and lit a cigarette. Finally, however, he fetched up beside the porter and asked casually, "Any letters for me?"

The porter knew his cue in this little comedy. He looked in pigeon hole No. 218 before he replied: "Not this time, Herr Doktor." Whereupon the tall gentleman slowly set himself in motion again. After coasting round to his chair he sank down into it stiff-legged, and then stared blindly out into the lounge. His face, it must be said, consisted of one half only, in which the sharp and ascetic profile of a Jesuit was completed by an unusually well-shaped ear beneath the sparse gray hair on his temples. The other half of his face was not there. In place of it was a confused medley of seams and scars, crossing and overlapping, and among them was set a glass eye. "A souvenir from Flanders," Dr. Otternschlag was accustomed to call it when talking to himself.

He sat there for a while surveying the gilded stucco capitals of the marble pillars, a sight he was heartily sick of, and staring his fill with unseeing eyes into the lounge, which was now emptying fairly quickly as the theaters opened. Then he got up once more and stumped across with his marionette gait to the porter's desk, where Herr Senf, putting aside his private affairs, was now officiating with zeal.

"No one asked for me?" Dr. Otternschlag inquired as he glanced at the glazed mahogany board where the porter pasted notes and messages.

"No one, Herr Doktor."

"Telegram?" asked Dr. Otternschlag after a moment. Herr Senf obligingly looked once more in pigeon hole 218, though he knew very well there was nothing in it.

"Not to-day, Herr Doktor," and added, with a touch of human kindness, "Perhaps Herr Doktor would like to go to the theater. I have a stall for Grusinskaya—at the Theater des Westens."

"Grusinskaya? No thanks!" said Dr. Otternschlag and wandered off through the entrance hall and back round the lounge to his chair. So Grusinskaya doesn't sell out any more, he thought meanwhile. Not surprised. Know *I'll* never go to see her again. He settled down miserably in his chair.

"That man's enough to drive one silly," said the porter to little Georgi. "Everlastingly asking for letters. Every year for ten years he's spent a month or two here, and not a letter has he ever had and not even a dog has ever asked for him. And there he sits about just the same and waits..."

"Who's waiting?" asked Rohna, the head reception clerk, from the bureau near by, sticking up his bright red head over the low glass partition. But the porter did not reply. He thought he had just heard his wife cry out and he strained his ears. Then he had to dismiss his private cares again, and help little Georgi unravel some complicated train connections in Spanish for the Mexican gentleman in room No. 117. Page boy No. 24, with red cheeks and well-plastered hair, shot across from the lift and called out excitedly—too loud for the dignity of the lounge— "Baron Gaigern's chauffeur!" Rohna raised an admonitory and repressive hand like a conductor. The porter passed on the order for the chauffeur by telephone. Georgi

opened eyes of boyish expectation. There was a smell of
lavender and expensive cigarettes, immediately followed
by a man whose appearance was so striking that many
heads were turned to look at him. He was unusually tall
and extremely well dressed and his step was as elastic as
a cat's or a tennis champion's. He wore a dark blue trench
coat over his dinner jacket and this was scarcely correct
perhaps, but it gave an attractively negligent air to his
appearance. He patted page boy No. 24 on his sleek head,
stretched out his arm without looking over the porter's
table for a handful of letters which he put straight into his
pocket, taking out at the same time a pair of buckskin
gloves. With a friendly nod to the head reception clerk he
put on his dark felt hat, took out his cigarette case and
put a cigarette between his lips. The next moment he removed his hat and stood aside to allow two ladies to pass
before him through the revolving door. It was Grusinskaya,
a small slim figure in a fur coat, followed by a vague and
self-effacing being with two cases in her hands. When the
commissionaire at the entrance had stowed these two in
their car the engaging gentleman in the blue raincoat lit
his cigarette, put his hand in his pocket for a coin to give
page boy No. 11 who was working the revolving door, and
disappeared through its whirligig of reflected lights with
the blissful air of a young fellow going out on the spree.

As soon as this charming Baron Gaigern had forsaken
the lounge it suddenly became still, and the illuminated
fountain could be heard falling into its Venetian basin
with a cool and gentle murmur. The reason was that the
lounge was now empty, the jazz band in the tea room had
stopped, the music in the dining room had not begun, and
the Viennese Trio in the Winter Garden was having a
pause. The sudden stillness was broken only by the agi-
tated and persistent hooting of cars as they passed the
hotel entrance and were lost again in the night life of the

town. Within, however, the lounge was as still as if Baron
Gaigern had taken the music, the noise, and the murmur
of voices away with him.

Little Georgi jerked his head towards the revolving door
and said: "He's all right. Nothing wrong with him."

The hall porter shrugged his shoulders with the air of a
man who knows his fellowmen. "Whether he's all right
remains to be seen. He's a bit—I don't know. He's too
much of the fine fellow for me. The side he puts on and
the tips he gives. It seems a bit queer to me. And whoever
travels nowadays to throw his money about, unless he's a
swindler? If I were Pilzheim I'd keep my eyes open."

Rohna, the head reception clerk, whose ears were always
on the alert, looked up again over the glass partition. The
blue-white skin of his head gleamed beneath his thin red-
dish hair. "That will do, Senf," he said. "Gaigern's all
right. I know him. He was at school with my brother at
Feldkirch. There's no need to put Pilzheim on to *him*."
(Pilzheim was the detective employed by the Grand
Hotel.)

Senf saluted and was respectfully silent. Rohna knew
what he was talking about. Rohna was a count himself,
one of the Silesian Rohnas, an ex-officer, and a good fellow.
Senf saluted once again, and Rohna's greyhound face was
withdrawn. It was now to be detected only as a shadow
behind the frosted glass.

Dr. Otternschlag behind in his corner had sat almost
erect as long as the Baron was to be seen in the lounge.
Now he was hunched together again, more forlorn than
before. He raised his elbow to empty half a glass of cognac
without even a glance at it as he did so. His thin tobacco-
stained hands hung down between his parted knees as
though they were encased in lead. He looked between his
long patent-leather shoes at the carpet that everywhere
covered the stairs, passages, and corridors of the Grand

Hotel; he was sick of its straggling pattern of yellow pine-apples mingled with brown foliage on a raspberry-red ground. Everything was so dead. The lounge was dead. Everyone had gone out to his business or pleasures or vices, and had left him to sit there alone. The woman attendant in the cloakroom suddenly came into view across the deserted lounge. She stood behind the empty racks in the entrance hall and combed back the thin hair on her old head with a black comb. The porter left his compartment and shot straight across with unseemly haste to the tele-phone room. He appeared to have something on his mind —this porter. Dr. Otternschlag looked for his cognac and found it gone. "Shall we go up and lie down for a bit?" he asked himself. A light flush came into his cheeks and dis-appeared again as though he had betrayed a little secret of his own. "Yes," he replied to his own question, but he did not get up. Even for this he was too listless. He merely raised one yellow-stained finger. Rohna from the far side of the lounge observed it and with a scarcely visible nod wafted a page boy to the doctor.

"Cigarettes, newspapers," Otternschlag said dully. The page boy darted across to the cataleptic lady at the book-stall (Rohna looked with disfavor at this lively exhibition of youthful exuberance), and then Otternschlag took the papers and cigarettes that the page boy had selected for him. When he paid he put the money on the plate, not into the boy's hand. He always set a distance between himself and others, though he was not aware of it. The half of his mouth that was still intact even smiled after a fashion as he unfolded the papers and began to read. He expected something of them that never came, just as no letter, telegram, or caller ever came; he was dismally alone, empty, cut off from life. Sometimes when he was alone he confided this fact to himself aloud. It's a ghastly business, he often muttered, gazing on the stretches of raspberry-red carpet and shuddering at himself. It's ghastly, This is no life. No life at all. But where is there any life? Nothing happens. Nothing goes on. Boring. Old. Dead. Ghastly. Every object around him was a sham. Whatever he took up turned to dust. The world was a crumbling affair not to be grasped or held. You fell from vacancy to vacancy. You carried about a sack of darkness inside you. Dr. Otternschlag lived in the most utter loneliness—although the earth is full of people like him. . . .

He found nothing in the papers to satisfy him. A typhoon, an earthquake, some petty war between blacks and whites. Arson, murder, political strife. Nothing. Too little. Scandals, panic on the Bourse, colossal fortunes lost. What did it matter to him? How could it affect him? Ocean flights, speed records, sensational headlines. Each page screamed louder than the last till finally you heard none of them. The noise and bustle nowadays made you blind and deaf and deadened all sensation. Pictures of nude women, of legs, breasts, hands, teeth, surged up before him. Dr. Otternschlag had had women in his earlier days. He still remembered it; but without emotion; the memory occasioned only a faint creeping chill in his spine. He let the papers fall in disorder from his tobacco-stained fingers on to the pineapple carpet—so boring and utterly meaningless were they. No, nothing happens, nothing at all, he muttered. He had once possessed a little Persian cat, called Gurba. Ever since she forsook him for a common street tom he had been obliged to carry on his dialogues with himself.

Just as he was steering a roundabout course for the porter's desk to get the key of his room, the revolving door discharged an extraordinary individual into the entrance hall.

"Heaven help us, here he comes again!" the hall porter said to little Georgi, and turned his best N. C. O.'s gaze upon the new arrival. He was certainly not the sort of person you would expect to see in the hall of the Grand Hotel. He wore a cheap new bowler hat that was too large for him and only prevented by his projecting ears from coming even farther down over his face. His face was yellowish, and he had a thin and timid nose which was retrieved by an aggressive mustache. He was clothed in a tight, much-worn, and sadly unfashionable overcoat of a gray-green shade, blacked boots that looked too large for his small stature and showed too much of their tops below his short black trousers. He wore gray cotton gloves and grasped a suitcase. It was much too heavy for him and he held it against his stomach with both hands. Besides this he had a bulky brown-paper parcel clapped under one arm. His whole appearance was comic and pitiful, and he was clearly in the last stages of exhaustion. Page boy No. 24 certainly made an attempt to relieve him of his imitation-leather suitcase, but the man would not give it up and his embarrassment seemed to be increased by this officious attention. He did not put his case down till he had reached Herr Senf's box, and then after pausing to get his breath he made a sort of bow and said in a high-pitched, rather pleasant voice: "My name is Kringelein. I've been here twice already. I want to inquire again."

"Will you please inquire over there; but I don't think there is a room free," said the porter, and pointed towards Rohna. "The gentleman has been waiting two days for a room here," he said in explanation over the glass partition. Rohna, who had taken in the whole situation without a glance, made a polite and fleeting pretense of looking through the pages of his register, and then said: "Unfortunately we are full for the moment. Extremely sorry——"

"Still full? I see. Well, where am I to find a room, then?"

"You might look round near the Friedrichstrasse Station. There are a number of hotels there. . . ."

"No, no, thanks." He took a pocket handkerchief and wiped the moisture from his brow. "I went to one of those on arriving. That's not what I want. I want a really first-class hotel." He took a damp umbrella from under his left arm and at this the bulky parcel slipped from the grasp of his right and disclosed a few dry and crumbling pieces of bread and butter. Count Rohna suppressed a smile. Georgi turned away and gazed at the keys hanging on the board. Page boy No. 17 gathered up the parched fragments with irreproachable composure, and with trembling fingers the man stuffed them into his pocket. He took off his hat and put it down in front of Rohna on the office counter. His forehead was high and wrinkled and his temples pinched and blue. For a moment he blinked with very clear blue eyes behind the pince-nez that looked as though it would slip off his thin nose. "I want a room here. There must be rooms free here sometimes. Will you please reserve me the first one that's vacant? This is the third time I have come, and you will agree that that is not very pleasant. You can't always be full up."

Rohna shrugged his shoulders with an air of regret. For a moment there was silence. The music could be heard in the red dining room; also the jazz band, now performing in the yellow pavilion. A few of the guests had re-assembled in the lounge and some of them looked across at this strange personage with a mixture of amusement and surprise.

"Do you know Herr Generaldirektor Preysing? He always stops here when he comes to Berlin. Well, I want to stop here, too. I have something important—an important conference with—with Preysing. I was to meet him here as a matter of fact. He particularly recommended me to take a room here. I was to refer you to him. I refer you to Herr Generaldirektor Preysing. So now please, when will there be a room vacant?"

"Preysing? Generaldirektor Preysing?" asked Rohna, looking across to Senf.

"From Fredersdorf. Of the Saxonia Cotton Company. I'm from Fredersdorf too," the man put in.

"Why, yes," said the porter, consulting his memory, "there is a Herr Preysing who's been here once or twice."

"I believe he has a room booked for to-morrow or the day after," Georgi whispered officiously.

"Perhaps you would be good enough to look in again to-morrow, when Herr Preysing is here. He arrives to-night," said Rohna after he had turned the pages of his register and come upon the reservation of the room.

Very surprisingly this news seemed to fill the man with some consternation.

"Arrives to-day?" he exclaimed as though in alarm, and his voice grew a little shriller. "Good. Then he comes to-night. Good. And there's a room for him. Then there are rooms to be had. Yes, and why should Herr Generaldirektor have a room and not I? What does that mean? I shall not put up with it! What's that? Reserved in advance, you say? Well, so did I. This is the third time I have been here. The third time, if you please, I have lugged this heavy bag along here. It's raining. Every bus overcrowded. I am not in good health, I may tell you. And how many more times am I to make this journey? What's that? That's no way to talk. Is this the best hotel in Berlin? Yes? Well then I want to stop in the best hotel in Berlin. Is it forbidden?" He looked from one to another. "I'm tired," he added. "I'm tired out." His fatigue was obvious, and so was his ridiculous effort to express himself in correct style.

Suddenly Dr. Otternschlag intervened in the discussion. He had been standing near by all this while, with the key of his room in his hand, resting his sharp elbows on the ledge of the porter's desk.

"The gentleman can have my room if it's a matter of such importance," said Otternschlag. "It is utterly indifferent to me where I stay. Send his things up. I can move out. My boxes are packed. They're always packed. Do as I say, please. You can see the man's dead beat and ill," he added, to forestall an objection which Count Rohna was about to bring forward with the eloquently gesticulating hands of a conductor.

"But, Herr Doktor," said Rohna quickly, "there can be no question of your giving up your room. Let me have another look. Let me see—— If the gentleman will be so good as to enter his name. Thank you—No. 216, then," he said to the hall porter.

The hall porter gave page boy No. 11 the key of No. 216. The newcomer took the pen which was handed to him and in a curiously flowing handwriting wrote his name in the visitors' book.

"Otto Kringelein, Bookkeeper. Fredersdorf, Saxony, born at Fredersdorf, 14–7–1882."

"There we are then," he said with a sigh of relief as he turned and blinked with wide-open eyes into the lounge.

So there he stood in the lounge of the Grand Hotel— Otto Kringelein, bookkeeper, born at Fredersdorf and residing in Fredersdorf. He stood there in his old overcoat, and the glasses of his pince-nez eagerly devoured it all. He was as dead beat as the winner of a race when he breasts the tape, but he saw the marble pillars with stucco ornament, the illuminated fountain, the easy chairs. He saw men in dress coats and dinner jackets, smart cosmopolitan men. Women with bare arms, in wonderful clothes, with jewelry and furs, beautiful, well-dressed women. He heard music in the distance. He smelt coffee, cigarettes, scent, whiffs of asparagus from the dining room and the flowers that were displayed for sale on the flower stall.

He felt the thick red carpet beneath his black leather boots
and this perhaps impressed him most of all. Kringelein
slid the sole of his boot gingerly over its pile and blinked.
The lounge was brilliantly illuminated and the light was
delightfully golden; also there were bright red-shaded
lights against the walls and the jets of the fountain in the
Venetian basin shone green. A waiter flitted by carrying a
silver tray on which were wide shallow glasses with a little
dark-gold cognac in each, and in the cognac ice was float-
ing; but why in Berlin's best hotel were the glasses not
filled to the brim?

One of the porters carrying the wretched suitcase woke
Kringelein from his trance. Page boy No. 11 conducted
him to the morose one-armed man who worked the lift
and he was conveyed upwards.

Rooms No. 216 and No. 218 were the worst in the hotel.
Dr. Otternschlag occupied No. 218 partly because he was
staying *en pension*, partly because his means were moderate,
chiefly, however, because he was too apathetic to demand
a better. No. 216 was at right angles to it, and the two
rooms were wedged in between the service lift by the back
stairs and the bathroom of the third floor. The waterpipes
sucked and bubbled in the wall. Kringelein, after being led
past groups of palms in pots, bronze chandeliers, and pictures of dead game into ever drearier recesses of the hotel,
slowly and dejectedly entered the room that an old and
ugly chambermaid unlocked. "No. 216," said the page
boy as he set the case down and waited for a tip. Receiving
none, he abandoned the speechless Kringelein. Kringelein
sat on the edge of the bed and surveyed the room.

The room was long and narrow. It had one window. It
smelt of stale cigar smoke and damp cupboards. The carpet was thin and worn. The furniture—Kringelein ran his
fingers over it—was just polished nutwood. There was
furniture like that in Fredersdorf. A portrait of Bismarck

hung over the bed. He had nothing against Bismarck, but he too was on the walls at home. He had expected other pictures over the beds in the Grand Hotel—gay, luxurious, something out of the common, something cheerful. He went to the window and looked out. There was a blaze of light below, for the glass roof of the Winter Garden spanned the court. Opposite a blank wall shut off the sky. A luke-warm and distressing smell of cooking steamed up. Kringe-lein felt a sudden nausea and supported himself on both hands over the washstand. The fact is, I'm not quite well, he thought sadly.

He sat down again on the faded bed cover and his sense of oppression increased with every moment. I shall not stay here, he thought. No, I shall not stay here in any case. This is not what I came for. It would not be worth while doing all I've done for this. This is no way to begin. I should be wasting my time in a room like this. They are deceiving me. They have plenty of better rooms than this in their hotel. Preysing does not have a room like this. Preysing would not stand it. He would make a row and they'd soon sit up. Fancy giving Preysing a room like this. No, I shall not stay here. Kringelein broke off his reflec-tions and collected himself. He waited a few minutes. Then he rang for the chambermaid and made a row.

When it is considered that this was the first time in his life he had ever made a row, it must be admitted that he did not do so badly. The white-aproned chambermaid, in alarm, brought on to the scene a superior with no apron. The floor valet stood by in the offing and a bedroom waiter, balancing a tray of cold food on the palm of his hand, listened at the door. Rohna was consulted by telephone and requested Herr Kringelein's presence in the office. A director, one of the four directors, had to be summoned. Kringelein, obstinate now he had run amok, insisted that he required a superior and beautiful and expensive room,

at the very least a room like Preysing's. He seemed to think
the name of Preysing was a name to conjure with. He had
not yet taken off his overcoat. His trembling hands
clutched the old crumbling Fredersdorf provisions, while
he blinked his eyes and demanded an expensive room. He
was exhausted and ill and ready to cry. For some weeks
past he had begun to cry very easily for physical reasons
connected with his health. Suddenly, just as he was about
to give in, he won the day. He was given No. 70, a first-
floor suite with sitting room and bath, fifty marks a day.
"Good," he said, "with a bathroom? Does that mean that
I can have a bath whenever I like?" Count Rohna without
a tremor said that that was so. Kringelein moved in for
the second time.

No. 70 was the right thing. It had mahogany furniture,
a cheval glass, silk upholstery, a carved writing table, lace
curtains, and a picture of pheasants on the wall. Also a silk
down quilt on the bed. Kringelein incredulously felt its
lightness, its smoothness, and its warmth three times in
succession. On the writing table stood a most superior
bronze inkstand in the form of an eagle whose jagged outstretched wings sheltered two empty inkpots.

Outside the window there was a chill March rain, a
smell of soline and the sound of motor traffic. Opposite an
electric sign in red, blue, and white letters occupied the
whole façade. As soon as it had run along to the end it
began again at the beginning. Kringelein watched it for
six minutes. Down below in the street there was a medley
of black umbrellas, light-colored stockings, yellow buses,
and arc lights. There was even a tree that spread its
branches not far from the hotel, but its branches were very
different from those in Fredersdorf. This Berlin tree had a
little island of soil in the midst of the asphalt and round
the plot of soil there was a railing as though it needed some
protection against the town. Kringelein, surrounded by

so much that was strange and overwhelming, found something friendly in this tree. Next he stood for a while in perplexity over the unfamiliar mechanism of the nickel bath taps, but suddenly it began to work and warm water shot out over his hands. He got undressed. He found it rather disconcerting to bare his delicate wasted body in the full light of the brightly tiled room. But finally he lay for over a quarter of an hour in the water and felt no more pain. The pains that had pursued him for weeks past had suddenly left him; and he certainly wanted no more of them during the time that lay ahead. . . .

At about ten o'clock in the evening Kringelein was strolling round the lounge, resplendent in a black coat, tall stiff collar, and a ready-made black tie. He was not at all tired now. On the contrary he was possessed by a feverish excitement and impatience. Now it's beginning, he kept thinking to himself, while his slender shoulders twitched like those of a restless dog. He bought a flower and stuck it in his buttonhole, slid his feet blissfully over the raspberry-colored carpet, and complained to the porter that there was no ink in his room. A page boy conducted him to the writing room. Kringelein was no sooner confronted by the rows of vacant writing tables, discreetly lighted by green-shaded electric lamps, than his confident bearing deserted him. He took his hands from his trouser pockets and looked rather forlorn. From force of habit he pushed his white cuffs up into the sleeves of his coat before he sat down and began to write in the flowing copper-plate handwriting of a clerk.

"To the Management of the Saxonia Cotton Company, Fredersdorf.

"SIRS—The undersigned begs leave to say that in conformity with the enclosed medical certificate (enclosure A) he is unfit for duty for the ensuing four weeks.

The undersigned requests that his salary for March due on the last of the month may in conformity with his written authority (enclosure B) be paid to Frau Anna Kringelein, 4 Station Road. Should it be impossible for the undersigned to return to duty at the end of four weeks, a further communication will follow.

"Your obedient and respectful servant,

"OTTO KRINGELEIN."

"To Frau Anna Kringelein, 4 Station Road, Fredersdorf, Saxony," Kringelein wrote next, and he wrote the A with a large and rounded flourish.

"DEAR ANNA—I have to tell you that the result of Professor Salzmann's examination was not very hopeful. I am to go direct from here to a sanatorium, costs to be borne by the sick fund, for which there are a few formalities still to be seen to. For the moment, am putting up very reasonably here at the recommendation of Herr Generaldirektor Preysing. Sending further news in the course of a day or two, as must be X-rayed again before anything definite can be said.

"Yours,

"OTTO."

"Herr Kampmann, Solicitor, Villa Rosenheim, Mauerstrasse, Fredersdorf, Saxony.

"MY DEAR FRIEND," Kringelein wrote thirdly. "You will be surprised to receive a lengthy letter from Berlin, but I have important developments to communicate and count on you to understand and to maintain a professional silence. It is not easy unfortunately for me to express myself in writing. However, I hope that your superior education and knowledge of the world will enable you to put the right construction on my letter. As you know I have never been myself since my operation last summer and have not great confidence in our hospital and doctor. Hence I have availed myself of the inheritance from my father to come here so as to be examined and know what is wrong. Unfortunately, my dear friend, there is something seriously wrong, and, in the specialist's opinion, I have not long to live."

Kringelein paused after this for perhaps a minute with his pen in the air. He forgot to put a full stop at the end of the sentence. His mustache, that absurdly large mustache, trembled slightly, but he bravely resumed.

"Naturally such a piece of news as that makes one think and I have not slept for several nights, but only kept thinking things over. The result is that I have come to the conclusion not to return to Fredersdorf, but to enjoy life a little during the few weeks I have to live. It is not very nice to go to one's grave at forty-six without having lived at all and only been harassed and starved and bullied by Herr P. at the works and by the wife at home. It seems all wrong that this should be the end of it all when one has never had a single real pleasure. Unfortunately, dear friend, I cannot express myself properly. So I can only add that the will I made in the summer before my operation remains in force though the conditions have now altered. I have, for example, had all my savings transferred here from the bank, also I have borrowed a considerable sum on my life policy, also I have brought the legacy from my father of 3,500 marks with me in cash. In this way I can live for a few weeks as a rich man and such is my intention. Why should only the Preysings get anything out of life while fools like us do nothing but pinch and save? In all I have taken 8,540 marks. Anna can have what is left over, and in my opinion I don't owe her any more. She has given me a wretched life of it with that tongue of hers and no child either. I will keep you apprised of how I go on, but I must request your professional secrecy. Berlin is a fine town and greatly increased in size, when one has not been here for years. I think of a trip to Paris, too, as I know French pretty well from business correspondence. As you see I am keeping the flag flying and feel better than for a long time past.

"Hearty greetings from your moribundus,

"OTTO KRINGELEIN.

"P.S.—Tell our friends at the musical society that I have gone to a sanatorium."

Kringelein read the letters through. He had composed them in the course of two sleepless nights. He was not quite satisfied. It seemed to him that something essential was left unsaid in the one to the solicitor, but he could not find out where the omission lay. Kringelein, though he was of a diffident and modest nature, was not actually stupid. He had idealism and aspirations. For example, he called himself "moribundus" as a joke and this expression was one he had encountered in a book from the lending library, which he had read with some trouble and often discussed with the solicitor. Kringelein had lived from childhood the ordinary life of a small provincial town, the rather dreary, uninspired, and pointless life of a petty clerk. Early in life and without any strong impulse he had married Fräulein Anna Sauerkatz, the daughter of Sauerkatz, the grocer. During the time between their engagement and marriage she seemed to him attractive, but very soon after the marriage he found her hateful. She was disagreeable and parsimonious and obsessed by petty cares. Kringelein had a fixed salary with a small rise every five years, and, as his health was not robust, his wife and her family pinned him from the first day to a rigid economy in the vague prospect of his becoming a charge on them later on. For example, he was denied the piano that he had longed for all his life. Also he had to sell his little dog, Zipfel, as soon as a tax was put upon dogs. He always had a sore place on his neck from the frayed edges of the old collars he was forced to wear. Now and then it occurred to him that something was not quite right with his life, but what it was he did not know. Often at the meetings of the musical society, when the high tremolo of his tenor voice climbed above the other voices, he had a soaring, blissful feeling as though he himself escaped on wings. Often in the evening he went out along the road to Mickenau, and then leaving the road and climbing across the wet ditches, he wandered into the country along the balks dividing field from field. There was a soft murmur between the stalks of the corn and when the ears stroked his hand he felt a strange pleasure. He had also had some remarkable and happy experiences under chloroform in the hospital, though he had forgotten them. It was only in little things that Otto Kringelein, the bookkeeper, differed from his fellows. But these little things, combined perhaps with the bewildering dose of death in his veins, had brought this "moribundus" to Berlin's most expensive hotel, and set him down before those sheets of notepaper to which he had confided his strange resolve and its pitiful causes.

Kringelein rose rather unsteadily to his feet and as he went with his three letters through the reading room he met Dr. Otternschlag. He had a violent shock when he found the mangled side of the doctor's face turned inquiringly towards him.

"Well? Settled in?" Otternschlag asked listlessly. He wore a dinner jacket and looked down at the toes of his patent-leather shoes.

"Yes, rather. First class," Kringelein answered with embarrassment. "Thanks. Indeed it is you I have to thank, sir. You were so extremely kind——"

"Kind? I? Not at all. Oh, about the room? Not a bit. Y'see, I've been wanting to move on for a long time, only I'm too lazy. Miserable pub, this hotel. If you'd taken my room, I'd have been in the wagon-lits train now for Milan or somewhere. Been very nice. Well, it's all one. Beastly weather everywhere in March. Same wherever you stick it out. May just as well stay here."

"You travel a great deal, sir, no doubt?" Kringelein asked shyly. He was ready to attribute immense wealth or high birth to every visitor in the hotel. He made a bow of the utmost Fredersdorfian elegance as he went on to say timidly: "Allow me to introduce myself—Kringelein. You have seen a lot of the world, sir?"

Otternschlag turned aside the "souvenir from Flanders." "Oh, pretty well," he said. "Been everywhere everyone else goes—India and a few places besides." He smiled faintly at the inordinate hunger for such experiences that shone in the blue glint behind Kringelein's glasses.

"It is my intention to travel, too," said Kringelein. "The head of our firm, Preysing, for example, goes abroad every year. A short time ago he was at St. Moritz. Last Easter he took his whole family to Capri. That sort of thing must be wonderful."

"Have you any family?" asked Dr. Otternschlag, laying aside his paper. Kringelein took five seconds to consider the matter and then replied:

"No."

"No," returned Otternschlag, and in his mouth the word had something irrevocable about it.

"First I should like to go to Paris," said Kringelein. "Paris must be a beautiful city?"

Dr. Otternschlag, who up to now had shown a glimmer

of warmth and interest, seemed to be falling asleep. He frequently had such moments of enervation in the course of the day, and the only resource he had against them was of a secret and vicious kind. "You must go to Paris in May," he murmured.

"I shan't have time for that," Kringelein said quickly.

Dr. Otternschlag got up abruptly and left him. "I'm going up to my room to lie down a bit," he said, more to himself than to Kringelein, who was left standing with his three letters in the reading room. The newspaper that Otternschlag had been glancing through fell to the ground. It was penciled over with scribbles of little men and over each little man was a thick cross. Kringelein, slightly dashed, left the reading room too, and timidly went in search of the dining room. Sounds of music issued from it, insistent though subdued, and the alternating drag and beat echoed all through the big hotel.

T HE curtain came down. It met the stage with the dull thud of heavy iron. Grusinskaya, who but a moment before circled as light as a flower among her troupe of girls, crept panting into the nearest wing. Utterly dazed, she grasped the brawny arm of a scene shifter. Her hand shook and she gasped for breath like a wounded animal. Sweat ran along the wrinkles below her eyes. The clapping made no more noise than distant rain and then it came suddenly near—a sign that the curtain had gone up. A man in the wings opposite was laboriously winding it up with great swings of the crank handle. Grusinskaya adjusted her smile like a cardboard mask and danced forward to make her curtsey before the footlights,

Gaigern, whose boredom had been immeasurable, clapped feebly three times merely from good nature and left the stalls for one of the crowded exits. In the front rows and in the gallery a few stalwarts shouted and clapped. Farther back there was a general stampede for the cloakrooms. To Grusinskaya on the stage it looked like a rout, a panic. All the white shirt fronts and dress-coated backs and theater cloaks streamed on in one direction. She smiled. She threw up her head on her long thin neck. She made a skip to the right, then to the left. She flung out her arms in greeting to the public that was now in full retreat. The curtain came down, rose again. The ballet stood its ground rigidly posed and disciplined. "Curtain! Curtain up!" shouted Pimenov, the ballet master, hysterically. He took charge of the curtain. Slowly it went up while the man at the crank worked like mad. One or two people in the stalls, who were just leaving, stopped and turned round, smiling vacantly and clapping. There was some applause too from a box. Grusinskaya pointed to the girls in gauze, who were grouped around her. Modestly she diverted the meager applause from herself to these unimportant young creatures. And now a few more came back with their coats and cloaks on and surveyed the scene with an air of amusement. Witte, the old German conductor, down below in the orchestra, was exerting his authority with frantic gestures—for the musicians were already packing up. "No one is to go," he whispered nervously. He too was trembling and perspiring. "No one is to go, gentlemen, please. Perhaps the Spring Waltz will have to be repeated."

"No bally fear," said a bassoon. "No encores to-day. Finished for to-day. There, what did I say?"

In truth the applause died down. Grusinskaya caught sight of the laughing musician's cavernous black mouth just as the curtain separated her from the house. The applause abruptly terminated and the sudden silence on the other side of the curtain gaped ominously. In the silence the tips of the ballet girls' silk shoes could be heard scraping the stage.

"May we go off?" whispered Lucille Lafitte, the *première danseuse*, in French, to Grusinskaya's trembling powdered back.

"Yes, off. Everyone off. Go to the devil!" Grusinskaya answered in Russian. She meant to shout it, but it died in her throat like a sob. All the gauze rustled off in a scare. The footlights went out and Grusinskaya stood alone for a moment on the stage freezing in the gray light as though at a rehearsal.

Suddenly a sound was heard like the snapping of a branch or the ring of a horse's hoofs. It was unmistakable. One man was clapping by himself in the empty house. Not that there was anything extraordinary in this. It was only the impresario, Meyerheim, making a desperate and courageous attempt to retrieve the day. He struck his resounding palms together with all his might as though in frantic enthusiasm and at the same time threw up an angry glance at the seats that an undutiful *claque* had too quickly deserted. Baron Gaigern was the first to hear this solitary outburst. He came back to see what was going on and to join in the fun, and hurriedly pulling off his gloves swelled the applause. He even stamped his feet like an excited student, as some of the *claque* and a few more inquisitive persons came in again from the cloakrooms. They were joined delightedly by others. It grew to a small spontaneous ovation and at last there were about sixty people, all clapping and calling for Grusinskaya.

"Curtain! Curtain!" shouted Pimenov at the top of his voice. Grusinskaya danced hysterically on to the stage and off again. "Michael! Where is Michael? Michael must come on too," she cried, laughing. Blue paint, perspiration, and tears were mingled round her eyes. Witte pushed the dancer Michael on from the wings. Without looking, Grusinskaya took his hand. It was so moist and slippery that she could scarcely grasp it. Then, standing just in front of the prompter's box, they made their bows with the beautiful harmonious grace of bodies trained to match each other. No sooner had the curtain fallen than Grusinskaya gave vent to her excitement by making a scene. "You bungled everything. It was all your fault. You went to pieces in the third arabesque! Such a thing would never have happened to me with Pimenov."

"For mercy's sake—I? But, Gru!" Michael whispered despairingly in his comical Baltic speech. Witte quickly drew him away behind the third wing and put his aged hand on his lips. "For God's sake, don't answer her back. Leave her alone," he whispered. Grusinskaya took the curtain alone. In between, while the curtain was down, her rage broke out. She cursed them all unmercifully. She called them swine, hounds, rotten slackers, one and all. She accused Michael of drunkenness and Pimenov of worse. She threatened the departed ballet with dismissal and accused Witte, the conductor, who was still there, sad and silent, of driving her to suicide by his murder of the *tempo*. All the while her heart fluttered in her breast like a lost and weary bird and tears streamed down over her waxen painted smile. At last the man in charge of the lighting made an end by turning off the light. The theater was in darkness and an impatient attendant spread gray cloths over the rows of seats. The curtain remained down and the man who worked the crank went home.

"How many curtains, Suzette?" Grusinskaya asked the elderly woman who threw a worn old-fashioned woollen cloak over her shoulders before opening the iron door that led off the stage. "Seven? I counted eight. Seven, you say? Even so that was not bad. But was it a success?"

She listened with impatience to Suzette's protestations, according to which the success had been immense, almost as immense as at Brussels three years before. Madame remembered? Madame did remember. As though one forgot a great success! Madame sat in the little dressing room, staring at the electric bulb that hung in a wire cage over the looking glass, and consulted her memory. No, she thought gloomily, it was not such a success as at Brussels. She was tired to death. She stretched out her moist limbs. She sat there, like a boxer who lies in his corner after a hard round, and let Suzette rub her down and chafe her and remove the paint. The dressing room was overheated, dirty, and small. It smelt of old dresses, of glue, of paint, of a hundred exhausted bodies.

Perhaps Grusinskaya fell asleep for a few seconds, for she saw herself in the stone-paved entrance hall of her villa on Lake Como, but in a moment she was back again with Suzette and her gnawing and feverish dissatisfaction over the performance. It had not been a great success. No, it had not been a great success. And what a wretched, incomprehensible world to deprive a Grusinskaya of a great success.

No one knew how old Grusinskaya was. There were old Russian aristocrats in exile, living in furnished rooms in Wilmersdorf, who asserted that they had known Grusinskaya for forty years. This assuredly was an exaggeration. But there was none in putting twenty years as an international celebrity to her credit, and twenty years of celebrity and success are an age. Sometimes Grusinskaya said to old Witte, who had been her friend and accompanist since the beginning of her career: "Witte, it is my fate to support a weight far too heavy for me, on and on, all my life long." And Witte answered earnestly: "Please let no one observe it, Elisaveta Alexandrovna. Do not speak of heaviness. The world has grown heavy. It is your mission, Elisaveta, if you will allow me to say so, to be lightness. Please do not alter. That would be the world's misfortune. . . ."

Grusinskaya did not alter. She had weighed ninety-six pounds since the age of eighteen and in this lay part of her success and her capabilities. Her partners, once accustomed to this lightness, could not dance with anyone else afterwards. Her neck, her figure that seemed to be all joints, the beautiful oval of her face never changed. Her arms obeyed her will like wings. The smile that shone out beneath her long eyelashes was in itself a work of art. Grusinskaya bent all her force to one aim, to be as she had been. And she did not observe that it was exactly this of which the world began to tire.

Perhaps the world would have loved her as she really was, as she looked now, for example, sitting in her dressing room—a poor, delicate, tired old woman with worn-out eyes and a small care-worn human face. When Grusinskaya did not have a success—and this sometimes happened nowadays—she shrank into herself and became very aged in an instant, seventy years old, a hundred years old, older even than that. Suzette in the background muttered her complaints in French as she stood over the grimy wash-hand basin and the hot water would not flow properly. Finally, however, she succeeded in producing the steaming compresses and Grusinskaya resigned her face to the tingling heat, while Suzette loosed her pearls from her neck, those world-famed, almost fabulously beautiful pearls that came from the days of her grand duke.

"You can put the pearls away. I shall not wear them any more to-day," said Grusinskaya, catching sight of their rosy shimmer from beneath her half-closed eyelids.

"Not the pearls? But Madame ought to look her best for the banquet."

"No. There, that's enough. Make the best of me without the pearls, Suzette," Grusinskaya said, and gave herself up with a resigned air to the finger tips and the compresses and the rouge of her self-effacing factotum. She had to go to a supper given in her honor by the Stage Society and for this she must be painted in as deadly earnest as an Aztek warrior before he went to meet his enemies.

Witte walked to and fro in the passage outside the dressing room as patiently as a sentry. He tapped the case of his watch which he wore in the old-fashioned style in the pocket of his white waistcoat. His old musician's face betrayed anxiety and sadness. After a while, Pimenov, the ballet master, joined him, and then finally Michael came along. His eyelashes shone with vaseline and he was heavily powdered.

"Are we waiting for Gru?" he asked cheerfully. "Are we all going together?"

"I would advise you to vanish, my boy," said Witte, "however little you may have gone to pieces."

"But I didn't go to pieces. Pimenov, did I go to pieces?" he exclaimed almost in tears. Pimenov merely shrugged his shoulders. He too was an old man. He had a large nose that was full of character, and he loved to wear the old-fashioned cravats of the time of Edward VII. He did not dance any longer but only conducted the rehearsals and composed Grusinskaya's *divertissements* in the severe style of classical choreography full of birds and flowers and allegories, danced on the point of the toe. "Go to bed, don't face Gru to-night. Lucille has disappeared already," he said sagely.

Michael's youthful face rose in revolt, and he knocked on the dressing-room door. "Good-night, madame," he called out. "I am not coming with you. What time is the rehearsal to-morrow morning?"

"Of course you're coming. You must sit next to me," Grusinskaya called back. "Don't make me so unhappy, *chéri*. We can talk about the rehearsal later. Wait for me. I'm just ready."

"*Tiens*—she's had her cry out," Witte whispered with the air of a conspirator.

"*Larmes, oh, douces larmes,*" Pimenov declaimed, with his chin sunk in his collar.

"I wouldn't condemn my worst enemy to dance a *pas de deux* with Gru—if you'll pardon me, my dear fellow," Michael affirmed in his comical Baltic German.

On the other side of the door Grusinskaya was dabbing
powder behind the lobes of her ears in the brilliantly lighted
mirror of the dressing room. Michael must be there, she
thought, I always have old people about me—Pimenov,
Witte, Lucille, Suzette. She had a sudden spasm of hatred
for the worn-out hat that Suzette behind her was putting
over her gray hair. She pushed her aside with an abrupt
movement and went out into the passage carrying her
cloak of black and gold and ermine over her arm. She
turned her shoulders to Michael to have her cloak put on.
He did this with feminine delicacy, as he did everything.
It was a little ceremony of reconciliation. But it was something more. It was an unspoken pleading on Grusinskaya's
part for the freemasonry of youth. Michael was young; for
Grusinskaya frequently changed her dancer. She was sus-
ceptible and exacting when it came to her partner. The
rest had grown old with her in her service.

Now, at any rate, she looked dazzling. She was beautiful,
distinguished, flower-like, resilient. "Elisaveta looks enchanting," said Witte, with a bow from a past century.
He had accustomed himself to the use of studied expressions, firstly in order to conceal his love for Gru, to whom
he had been devoted since his youth, and secondly, from
the necessity of translating his speeches now into Russian,
now into French. Grusinskaya herself slipped continually
from one language into another, from the Russian "thou"
into the French and English "you." She could speak German too. She was as fluent in the one as the other, however
abusive or however amiable it was necessary to be. It was
not always easy to follow her. For example, she was no
sooner in her motor car than she asked: "Do you think,
Witte, it was the fault of the pearls?"

"In what sense the pearls? And the fault for what?"
asked Witte in dismay—for the second of his questions
arose from pure sensibility. He knew well enough what

Grusinskaya meant. "*Mon Dieu*, how do you mean—the pearls?" Pimenov asked too.

"Certainly I mean the pearls. They bring me bad luck, those pearls," she said with childish insistence. Witte folded one old-fashioned glacé kid glove in the other. "But, my dear." He was disconcerted.

"What!" exclaimed Pimenov. "Why, the pearls have brought you luck all your life. They were your mascot, your talisman. And are you going to say now that they bring bad luck? What an idea, Gru!"

"They do bring bad luck all the same. I see it," Gru said with a self-willed frown between her artificially emphasized eyebrows. "I cannot explain it, but I have been thinking over it a great deal. They brought me luck as long as the Grand Duke Sergei was alive. *Voilà!* Ever since he was murdered nothing but bad luck have they brought me. In London last year there was the sinew I broke in my ankle. At Nice—a deficit. And altogether nothing but bad luck. I shall not dance in them any more. So now you know."

"Not dance in them! But, dear, dearest Gru, you cannot possibly go on without your pearls. All your life long it has been your firm belief that you could not go on without the pearls, and now suddenly——"

"Yes," Grusinskaya said, "it was just a superstition."

Witte began to laugh. "Lisa," he cried, "my dove, my dear little one, why you're a child!"

"You don't understand me. You don't understand me in the least, Witte. The pearls are no longer suitable. I shall not wear them any more. In the old days, in Petersburg, in Paris, jewels were *de rigueur*. A dancer had to possess jewels and display them. But now—who wears real pearls today? I am a woman. I have a sense of these things, I have the flair. Michael, are you asleep? Say something."

Michael, without moving his graceful limbs, said in

clumsy French: "If you wish to know, madame, you ought
to give your pearls away for poor children and cripples, to
give them away for charity, madame."

"What do you say? Give them away, my pearls?" Grusinskaya cried out in Russian and the word *Pozertwowatj*
rang out like a song.

"Here we are," Pimenov said as the brake was suddenly
applied.

"*En avant*," Grusinskaya commanded. "We must be
beautiful—and enjoy ourselves!"

The door of the house was thrown open; Witte, as he
went up the steps behind the dancer, remarked: "Elisaveta
Alexandrovna has only one fault. She is in love with the
categorical imperative."

Grusinskaya began to smile and to beam like a light
suddenly turned on, and thus beaming and smiling she
entered the club where thirty gentlemen in evening dress
stood awaiting her entry.

Baron Gaigern was the very last to stop clapping; but
as soon as he was sure that the curtain would not go up
any more, he left the theater with the set face of a man
in a hurry. The rain had stopped. White and yellow lights
were reflected in the wet surface of the Kantstrasse; policemen were regulating the traffic; the destitute were eagerly
opening the doors of motor cars for those in fur coats to
step in. Gaigern threaded the crowd, disregarding traffic
regulations at the risk of his life, and hurried into the
comparative obscurity of the Fasanenstrasse, where his car
—an unobtrusive four-seater—was parked. The chauffeur
was smoking a cigarette.

"Well?" asked Gaigern with his hands in the pockets
of his blue coat.

"She's changed her chauffeur again," said the chauffeur.
"It's an Englishman this time. She picked him up at Nice.

His employer went bankrupt and left him stranded there. I've had a meal with him, but I can't get anything out of him."

"I've told you a hundred times not to smoke when I'm speaking to you," Gaigern said.

"Right," said the chauffeur, and threw away his cigarette. "He's driven round to the theater now to take her to the Stage Society. He doesn't know yet when he has to take her back."

"He doesn't know?" Gaigern replied, and struck the palm of his hand reflectively with his gloves. "Right. Then I'll go across there again. Bring the car round to the theater and wait there."

Gaigern returned to the front of the theater with the same set expression of a man intent on business. He found it dreary and deserted. The electric signs were dark and the placards looked as if they had nothing further to say. The stage door did not open on to the street, but into a courtyard where blank walls gleamed with wet ivy. Gaigern wedged himself among the little crowd of loungers who were waiting for Grusinskaya to emerge. Their eyes were fixed on the frosted-glass panels of the door through which a light was shining. First a detachment of the fire brigade marched out. Next came the scene shifters— brawny fellows with pipes in their mouths. Then there was a pause before the door opened once more and out came the ballet in twos and threes. Their slim figures were concealed in cheap fur coats, scraps of French, Russian, and English eddied around them as they went. Gaigern looked after them and smiled. He had known several of them in Nice and Paris. His upper lip shortened when he laughed, like a little child's. It was charming. Many women at least found it so.

My God, what a time it's going to be—as usual, he thought impatiently, as the courtyard fell asleep again.

Nearly a quarter of an hour went by. Then the chauffeur in Grusinskaya's motor car stirred like a dog in its sleep and started up the engine. Gaigern had been waiting for this signal. He pressed into the shadow against the wall. When Grusinskaya finally appeared he was invisible. She turned back into the doorway. "Wait here, Suzette," she said. "I'll send Berkeley straight back and he will take you to the hotel." She was cloaked above the chin in an extremely decorative evening wrap of gold and black and ermine and looked every bit as beautiful at this moment as her photographs in the world's illustrated papers. Gaigern fixed her with his eyes from his hiding place in the shadow. As she put her silver foot on the running board she opened her ermine collar and Gaigern could see the world-famed long white neck. It looked peculiarly naked and flower-like this evening. Gaigern drew his breath through his teeth in a spasm of delight. He had desired nothing more eagerly than to see this bared neck.

She had scarcely driven off when Suzette appeared in the dark and deserted courtyard. The porter followed and shut the stage door behind him. Suzette always looked like an old and faded copy of her mistress, and the reason was that she wore Grusinskaya's old clothes and hats when they had long ceased to be the fashion. On this occasion she shuffled across the courtyard in a long bell-shaped skirt over which she wore a buttoned-up cloak with a kind of Byronic collar. Both her hands were laden. In the left she carried a fair-sized flat suitcase, and in the right a small one of black patent leather. Thus encumbered she made her way slowly as far as the iron gateway that parted the theater yard from the street, and there she strolled to and fro in the full light of the arc lamps. Wild thoughts sprang to the surface of Gaigern's mind during these seconds. He stood in his shadowed corner on the tiptoe of suspense, as though making ready for a jump or to start forward at the pistol shot. But he attempted nothing, for at that moment that damned fellow Berkeley drew up at the curb on a masterly turn. Suzette got into the gray car just as it struck half-past twelve from the Gedächtniskirche, and Gaigern, who for the space of a minute had forgotten to breathe, took in a deep breath. He whistled. His little four-seater came up. "Straight after them to the hotel." He jumped up beside the chauffeur.

"Well, any hopes to-day?" asked the chauffeur. Again he had a cigarette between his lips as he spoke.

"Wait," Gaigern replied.

"Another whole night to stand by with the car, eh? All the same to you if I ever get another night's sleep or not, I suppose?"

Gaigern pointed his finger at the gray car, which was taking the little bend round the traffic sign at the Hitzig-brücke Bridge. "Overtake it," was all he said. The chauffeur accelerated. There was no policeman now on point duty at the bridge. The night life of Berlin thronged the streets beneath a red vault, where not a star showed in the cloudless spring sky.

"It's enough to feed one up," the chauffeur went on. "The game's not worth the candle. The end will be that we'll go bust."

"If you don't like it, you know what to do," the Baron answered amiably, and his upper lip curled. "If you're not pleased you can take your pay and go."

"I mean no harm," said the chauffeur.

"Nor I," said the Baron.

There was silence till they reached the hotel.

"Park at entrance No. VI," said Gaigern as he jumped out. In the revolving door that led from the small entrance lobby into the hall of the hotel, he came upon a comical gentleman. It was Kringelein who had got stuck there owing to the mistake he made in trying to revolve the door in the opposite direction. Gaigern gave it an impatient kick and sent the glass whirligig, together with its contents, round in the right direction. "That's the way round," he said to Kringelein.

"Thank you. Thank you very much," replied Kringelein, who had wanted to go out and now found himself shot inside the hotel again. Gaigern went quickly for his key, and as quickly to the lift. Arrived at the first floor, he told the one-armed lift attendant to wait a moment. He would be back in one second. He ran along the passage to his room, No. 69, threw down his hat and coat, snatched up a fine orchid spray from a vase, and ran along the passage again. "Tell the lift attendant, please, that I shan't need him," he said to the chambermaid, who, half asleep, sidled along past door after door. She gave the message and the man grumbling took the lift down again. When he reached the ground floor, Suzette was there waiting with her two cases to be taken up. And this was precisely what Gaigern had intended. . . .

When Suzette arrived at the door of No. 68, the room occupied by Grusinskaya, she saw a charming young man standing behind a palm. His bashful and ingratiating features seemed not unfamiliar to her.

"Good-evening, mademoiselle. Permit me to say one word," he said in his charming and rather old-world French, the French that is taught in a Jesuit seminary. "Only one word. Madame is not in her room?"

"I do not know, sir," replied the well-trained Suzette.

"It is only—forgive the presumption—that I should like so much to lay a little flower for Madame in her room. I have so great a veneration for Madame. I was at the theater to-night. I never miss an evening when Madame dances. I have read in the papers, you see, that Madame loves these Cattleias—is it true?"

"Yes," said Suzette, "she loves orchids. We have started

the cultivation of orchids in our hothouses at Tremezzo."

"Ah! Then may I give you my spray and ask you to leave it in Madame's room?"

"We have had a lot of flowers to-day. The French ambassador sent a whole basketful," said Suzette, who was still smarting from the evening's doubtful success. She looked at the bashful young man with considerable friendliness. But she could not take the spray because she had both her hands full. It was difficult even to get the key into her right hand in order to open the door of No. 68. Gaigern, who saw her embarrassment, went quickly up to her. "Allow me," he said, and put out his hands to take the two cases. Suzette surrendered the larger one, but she drew back instinctively as she maintained her grasp of the smaller one. So the famous pearls are in that one, Gaigern thought, though he kept his thoughts to himself. He opened the door for her and the inner one as well, and with shy and at the same time enraptured steps crossed the threshold of the room where Grusinskaya slept.

The room had the same banal and tawdry elegance as all the others. The cool air inside smelt of a curious aromatic scent as well as of the bouquets of flowers, and the window on to the small balcony stood open. The bed was turned down, and a pair of little bedroom slippers were by the bed. They were rather trodden down and shabby— the slippers of a woman who is accustomed to sleep by herself. Gaigern, as he stood by the door, felt a fleeting tenderness of pity at the sight of these little tokens of resignation on the part of a famous and beautiful woman. He stood in the door, holding out his orchids as though beseeching the acceptance of them. Suzette put down the smaller suitcase on the dressing table between the three mirrors and at last took the flowers.

"Thank you, monsieur," she said, "what name shall I say?"

"What an idea! I am not so presumptuous," said Gaigern. He looked observantly at Suzette's wrinkled face and saw a strange resemblance to the face of her mistress. "You are tired," he said, "and no doubt Madame will be late. Have you to wait up for Madame?"

"Oh, no, Madame is good. Madame says every night, 'You can go to bed, Suzette.' But Madame needs me all the same. So I wait up for her. Madame is never later than two o'clock because she has to start work every morning at nine. And how she works, monsieur. Oh, *mon Dieu!* No, Madame is very good."

"She must be an angel," said Gaigern ecstatically. (So there is only a bathroom without a window between 68 and 69, he thought, as he said it.) His wandering gaze returned to Suzette's cavernous yawn.

"Good-night and a thousand thanks, mademoiselle," he said politely, and with a smile disappeared.

Suzette shut both doors behind him and after putting the orchids in a glass of water sank, a little shivering heap, into an armchair—to wait.

Before one o'clock at night there were very few pairs of shoes to be seen in front of the bedroom doors of the Grand Hotel. Everyone was out and about, eagerly savoring the hectic pleasures of the great city in its blaze of electric light. At the end of each passage on every floor a dead-tired chambermaid, faded and virtuous, yawned in her little office. The page boys came on night shift at ten, but they too, under their jaunty flat-topped caps, had the feverishly bright eyes of children who ought to have been put to bed long before. The ill-tempered one-armed man at the lift was relieved at midnight by another equally ill-tempered one-armed man. The hall porter Senf, too, was relieved by the night porter at about eleven, and went off half dazed to the hospital, in such a state of anxiety that his teeth chattered. On arriving there he was sent back home by an unamiable night nurse, who told him that it would be twenty-four hours till the baby was born, but this, of course, was his own affair and did not concern the hotel. The hotel, meanwhile, was in all its glory. There was dancing in the yellow pavilion and great inroads had been made on Mattoni's cold buffet. Mattoni's nigger-like eyes were smiling as he shaved off slices of cold beef, or mixed maraschino in iced fruit salads. The electric fans whirred and spewed out the bad air into the courtyards of the hotel, and down below in the servants' quarters the chauffeurs sat and talked scandal about their masters. (They are an irritable lot, these chauffeurs, because they are not allowed to drink.) In the lounge, visitors up from the provinces sat in amazement and mild vexation over the Berlin men who wore their hats on the backs of their heads and waved their hands about, and over the Berlin ladies with their painted faces. Rohna, spruce and refreshed by a *friction* of toilet vinegar, as he crossed the lounge, was thinking: It is true that our night-time *clientele* is not of the first order. But—*que voulez vous?* nowadays only a vulgar *clientele* puts money in the till.

Just before one o'clock Herr Kringelein landed in the bar. He was tired, and he sank down at a small table and surveyed the world about him with watery eyes. To tell the truth, this Kringelein was utterly tired out, but he had the obstinacy of children on their birthdays—he simply would not go to bed. Moreover he felt that he was asleep already, for everything entered his brain like a confused and feverish dream and the noise, the perpetual movement, the voices, and the music seemed at one moment quite close and at the next moment very far away and entirely unreal. The world hummed most strangely about his ears and everything combined to produce in him a mysterious state of intoxication. Once, when he was ten years old,

Kringelein had played truant from school. In a panic at
the thought of a dictation lesson, he had gone out into the
warm morning mist along the road to Mickenau. Then he
had left the road and lain down in the heat of the day and
slept with his head on a cushion of clover. Later he had
got into a grassy hollow by the river and feasted on the
raspberries that grew there in immense profusion. All
his life he had never forgotten the buzzing of the great
gnats that had fastened on his bare legs and his red juice-
stained fingers as he pressed in among thorns and nettles
to gather handful after handful of raspberries. He felt
again, here in the bar of Berlin's most expensive hotel,
the same intoxicated feeling, a sense of exuberant plenty
as well as of anxiety and alarm, the faint threat haunting
the wicked joy of wrongdoing, the excitement of an esca-
pade. It all came back to him as he sat there between one
and two in the morning. The stinging gnats were there too
in a sense. They had taken on the likeness of figures
that tormented his brain, the brain of a bookkeeper who
had kept accounts all his life long and now could not
stop.

Caviare, for example, cost nine marks. Caviare was a
delusion, Kringelein decided. It tasted like herring and
cost nine marks. Kringelein had gone hot and cold under
the supercilious gaze of three waiters while he stared at
the wagon of hors-d'œuvres which had come to a stop in
front of him. He had had to miss out the *prix fixe* supper—
at twenty-two marks—out of consideration for his ailing
stomach. Burgundy was a heavy, sour wine that lay in a
kind of cradle, like a baby. The rich had odd tastes, it
seemed. Kringelein was by no means stupid; he was very
willing to learn; and it had not taken him long to see that
he had been badly brought up and did not know how to
make proper use of the array of knives and forks before
him. During the whole evening he could not rid himself

of a horrible nervous tremor. Embarrassment over tips
and wrong doors and puzzled inquiries kept him in a constant state of painful confusion. But this first evening as a
man of wealth had its great moments. The shop windows,
for example. In Berlin, the shop windows are lighted up
at night, and the riches of the whole world are displayed
there. I can buy what I like, is a novel and enchanting
thought for a man like Kringelein. Then again he had been
to the cinema. In Berlin you can go to the cinema as late
as half-past nine. He had treated himself to one of the
best seats. There is a cinema in Fredersdorf, too. You went
three times a week to Zickenmeier's Rooms, where the
music club also held its rehearsals. Kringelein had been
two or three times with his stingy Anna in the cheapest
seats, right in front among the factory hands, and there
he had sat with his head screwed back staring straight up
at the gigantic and distorted figures on the screen. It was
one of the revelations of the evening to find that the film,
when seen from an expensive seat, had a totally different
appearance. If you could only pay enough, it became as
living as life itself. Incidentally, this film of St. Moritz
opened up a wonderful and scarcely believable world.
Kringelein decided then and there that he would go to
St. Moritz. Those mountains and lakes and valleys were
not put there only for the Preysings, he thought to himself,
and at the thought, as it recurred again and again, his
heart beat. There is a sweet, a bitter, and triumphant sense
of freedom in those for whom death is decreed. Kringelein
could find no word for it; but, whenever it came over him,
he was forced to catch his breath in a heavy sigh.

"Excuse me——" said Dr. Otternschlag, in the midst
of these whirling thoughts, as he pushed his bony knees
under Kringelein's table. "There is not another seat left
in this cursed bar. Rotten accommodation. Louisiana flip,"
he said to the waiter, and laid his skeleton fingers on the

table between himself and Kringelein, like ten cold, heavy metal bars.

"Delighted," Kringelein said in his politest manner. "I am delighted to meet you again. You were so very kind to me, sir—believe me, I don't forget it. No, indeed."

Otternschlag, who had never, over a stretch of untold dreary years, heard anyone describe him as kind, and who for ten years had scarcely spoken to a living soul, felt a slight scorn mixed with a certain gratification at this repeated expression of thanks on the part of the gentleman from Fredersdorf. "Well, here's the best," he said, and tossed down his flip. Kringelein, who had ordered something at random that he now scarcely dared to drink, took a sip of the copper-coloured fluid in the shallow metal cup.

"The life here is a little confusing at first," he said timidly.

"Hm," replied Dr. Otternschlag. "At first, yes. Doesn't improve on acquaintance either, when you live here as I do. No. Bring me another Louisiana flip."

"It is not at all as one imagined it," Kringelein said. His strong cocktail was making him reflective. "Nowadays even in the provinces one is not out of the world. There are the newspapers. There are the cinemas. There are the pictures in the illustrated papers. But even so the real thing looks quite different. I knew for example that bar stools were high. But they are not so very high, I see. And the nigger behind the bar is the mixer, of course. But there's nothing very wonderful about him at close quarters. As a matter of fact it's the first time I ever saw a nigger in my life. But he doesn't seem at all strange. He even speaks German and you might think he was only blacked."

"No, he's genuine enough. Not much use though. You've got your work cut out to get tight here."

Kringelein listened to the maze of voices, to the clatter and hum and the loud laughter of the women at the bar

in front. "They are not real *demi-mondaines*, are they?"
he asked.

Otternschlag turned the undisfigured side of his face to
him. "You'd like something rather more alluring?" he said.
"No, they're not the real thing. This is a solid respectable
sort of place. No women admitted unless accompanied by
men. They're not *demi-mondaines*, nor real ladies, either.
Do you want to get to know a girl?"

Kringelein gave a little cough. "Thank you, not in the
least. As a matter of fact I could have got to know a girl
this evening. Yes, I assure you. A young lady invited me
to dance with her."

"Indeed? You? Where was that?" asked Dr. Otternschlag, and the half of his mouth showed a wry smile.

"I was in a place, Casino Something-or-other it was
called, not far from the Potsdammer Platz," said Kringelein, trying to copy the staccato speech of the man of the
world as he heard it on Otternschlag's lips. "Fine, fine,
I tell you. The lighting. Positively fairylike." He tried to
find a more expressive word but gave it up. "Fairylike.
Little fountains with variegated lights changing all the
time. Dear, of course. Champagne only. They rook you
twenty-five marks a bottle. Unfortunately I can only
stand a little. Not in the best of health, you see."

"So I see. I know all about that. When a man's collar
is nearly an inch too wide for him, I don't need to be told
any more."

"Are you a doctor?" asked Kringelein in a cold sweat.
Involuntarily he put two fingers inside his collar. Yes, it
had got too large.

"Have been. Been everything one time or another. I
was in the medical service in southwest Africa. Filthy
climate. Taken prisoner in September '14. Prison camp in
Nairrti, British East Africa. Sent home on parole. Went
through the whole rotten business as an army doctor till

the finish. Shell in the face. Diphtheria germs messing
about in the wound till 1920. Two years isolation hospital.
There, that's enough. Full stop. Been everything pretty
well. Who cares?"

Kringelein gazed in horror at this ruin of a man whose
fingers lay cold and lifeless on the table between them.
The bar provided a running accompaniment of assorted
sounds and a Charleston could just be heard from the
yellow pavilion. Kringelein had caught extremely little
of Otternschlag's telegraphic communications; nevertheless tears started to his eyes. His tears came with igno-
minious ease ever since his operation, which had not cured
him.

"And have you no one then who—I mean—are you
quite alone?" he asked in embarrassment, and Otternschlag noticed for the first time what a high-pitched,
charming voice he had, a human, resonant, inquiring,
diffident voice. He put out his cold fingers in front of him
on the table, and withdrew them again immediately. Kringelein looked reflectively at the numerous white stitches
and scars in Otternschlag's face and a sudden resolution
unloosed his lips.

Alone: he knew what that meant—this was more or less
what he said—he too was alone in Berlin, absolutely alone.
He had cut the threads. He had severed various ties—such
were the choice phrases he used—and now he was alone
in Berlin. After spending all his life in Fredersdorf he felt
stupid of course in a great city, but not so stupid that he
could not see his own stupidity. He knew little of life, but
now he wanted to get to know it. He wanted to know life
as it really was. That was why he was here. "But," he
went on, "where is real life? I have not come on it yet.
I have been to a casino, and here I am sitting in the most
expensive hotel, but all the time I know it isn't the real
thing. All the time I have a suspicion that real, genuine.

actual life is going on somewhere else and is something quite different. When you don't belong to it it's not at all so easy to get into it, if you see what I mean?"

"Yes, but what's your notion of life?" replied Dr. Otternschlag. "Does life exist at all as you imagine it? The real thing is always going on somewhere else. When you're young you think it will come later. Later on you think it was earlier. When you are here, you think it is there—in India, in America, on Popocatepetl or somewhere. But when you get there, you find that life has doubled back and is quietly waiting here, here in the very place you ran away from. It is the same with life as it is with the butterfly collector and the swallow tail. As you see it flying away, it is wonderful. But as soon as it is caught, the colors are gone and the wings bashed."

These were the first consecutive remarks that Kringelein had heard Dr. Otternschlag utter, and he was impressed; but he was not convinced. "I don't believe that," he said modestly.

"Take it from me, it is so. It is the bar stool over again," Otternschlag replied; his elbows were propped on his knees and his hands trembled faintly.

"What bar stool?" asked Kringelein.

"The bar stool you spoke of a moment ago. Bar stools are not so very high, you said. You imagined they would be higher, eh? Didn't you say so? Well, then, one imagines everything higher than it is, till one sees it. You come on your travels from your little provincial town with false ideas about life. Grand Hotel, you think. Most expensive hotel, you think. God knows what marvels you expect from an hotel like this. You'll soon know all about it. The whole hotel is only a rotten pub. It is exactly the same with the whole of life. The whole of life is a rotten pub, Herr Kringelein. You arrive, stay for a while, and go on again. Passing through. Isn't that it? For a short stay, what? What do you do in a big hotel? Eat, sleep, lounge about, do business, flirt a little, dance a little, eh? Well, and what do you do in life? A hundred doors in one corridor and nobody knows a thing about his next-door neighbors. When you leave another arrives and takes your bed. *Finito.* Sit for an hour or two in the lounge and keep your eyes open. You'll see that the people there have no individuality. They're dummies, all of 'em. Dead, all the lot, and don't know it. Charming pub, a big hotel like this. Grand Hotel della Vita, eh? Well, the main thing is—have your bags ready packed."

Kringelein took a considerable time for reflection. Then it seemed to him that he had grasped the meaning of Otternschlag's discourse. "Yes, to be sure," he agreed. He put almost too much emphasis on the words.

Otternschlag, who was on the point of dozing off, woke up again.

"Did you want me to do anything for you? Do you want me to introduce you to Life? You've made a fine choice, I must say. I am always at your service, Herr Kringelein."

"I had no wish to be a nuisance to you, sir," Kringelein said with a sad little air of humility. He went on thinking. The polished phrases he had prepared found no utterance. Since he had come to the Grand Hotel he felt that he was in a foreign land. He spoke his native tongue like a foreign language that he had learnt from books and newspapers. "You were so extremely kind," he said. "I was hoping—but, of course, for you everything has another aspect than it has for me. You have it all behind you. You have had your fill. I have it all in front of me. That makes one impatient. Please forgive me."

Otternschlag looked so hard at Kringelein that even the stitched-up eyelid above his glass eye seemed to be focusing on him. He saw Kringelein clearly and completely. He saw his wasted figure in the work-a-day suit of stout gray worsted, rather shiny in places. He saw the sad and yearning expression round the bloodless lips and beneath that absurd mustache. He saw the wasted neck inside the wide, frayed collar, the clerk's hands and untended nails; he even saw the blacked boots, turned slightly in, on the thick carpet under the table. And finally he saw Kringelein's eyes, the blue human eyes behind the pince-nez, eyes in which were so much yearning expectation, wonder, and curiosity. In them was hunger for life, and knowledge of death.

God knows whether some warmth from those eyes penetrated the frigid being of Dr. Otternschlag. Perhaps it was pure boredom that made him say: "True. Quite true. You're right. Right every time. I have it behind me. Yes, I have had my fill. It's all behind me now down to the last unimportant formality. And you say, then, that for you it is all in front. You've the appetite, eh? Of the soul, I mean. Now what's your notion? The usual men's paradise —Champagne? Women? Races? Gambling? Drink? *Tiens!* And so you tumbled for it the very first evening, eh? An acquaintance right off?" Otternschlag said impassively, thankful though he was for the warmth in Kringelein's eyes.

"Yes, quite early on. A lady positively wanted to dance with me. A very pretty girl. Perhaps not quite—I mean, something of a bird of paradise" (he took "bird of paradise" from the *Mickenauer Journal*). "But most elegant. Well educated, too."

"Well educated, too! Well—there! And how did you get on?" Otternschlag murmured.

"Unfortunately I can't dance. One must dance. Apparently it is very important," said Kringelein. His cocktail made him feverishly enterprising and at the same time sad.

"Very important. Very. Important above all things," replied Dr. Otternschlag in a surprisingly alert tone of voice. "One must know how to dance. The mutual embrace in time with the music, the dizzy turning and twirling of two in one, eh? One ought not to give any lady the go-by. One must know how to dance. Oh, how right you are, Herr Kringelein. Learn quickly, as soon as ever you can find time. Then you will never have to say No to a lady again, Herr Kringelein—your name is Kringelein, isn't it?"

Kringelein looked questioningly and uneasily through his glasses into Otternschlag's face. "Why do you ask that?" he asked, and felt that he was being made a fool of.

But Otternschlag went on seriously. "Believe me," he said, "believe me, Kringelein, when I say: He who does not move with the times is a dead man. Waiter, the bill."

Kringelein paid too after this abrupt conclusion and stood up embarrassed. He followed Dr. Otternschlag, whose dinner jacket was stretched tightly over his thin shoulder blades, out of the bar and, stumbling over to the porter, got his key.

"Any letters for me?" Otternschlag asked the night porter. He seemed of a sudden to have forgotten Kringelein utterly.

"No," the porter said, without so much as looking, for one porter is not like another and sensibility of soul is not put on with a porter's cap. "Madame's key was taken upstairs by Mademoiselle," he said in French to a lady immediately after. Kringelein could almost understand it, thanks to his practice in foreign correspondence.

As the lady passed him there was a breath of delicate bitter-sweet scent from her golden evening cloak, open at the neck. Kringelein stared at her, for his manners were lost in boundless amazement. Her hair was black and smooth and she wore a diadem in it. Her drooping eyelids were painted blue black. Her cheeks, temples, and chin were ivory white and the veins were blue. Her mouth was carmine, almost purple, and it was rouged in such long curves that the corners seemed to stretch upwards to her nostrils in a fixed smile. Her hair was drawn down over her cheeks in two smooth black wings, and where cheeks and hair met there was an ochre shadow laid on with extreme art. She looked tall, though she was scarcely of medium height, and this (as even Kringelein could tell) was due to the perfect proportions of her body and to the lightness of her carriage. She was accompanied by a little old gentleman with a top hat in his hand who looked like a musician. "Could you be at the theater at half-past eight, my dear?" the lady asked, just as she passed Kringelein. "I should like half an hour's work before the rehearsal."

Kringelein, who had never seen such a work of art as this lady, showed his amazement and delight in his face. He pulled Otternschlag by the sleeve and whispered in an undertone: "Who can that be?"

"Don't you know, my dear fellow? It's Grusinskaya," Otternschlag said impatiently, and stalked over to the lift. Kringelein stood rooted to the spot. Grusinskaya! Good heavens! Grusinskaya, he thought. For Grusinskaya's fame was such that it had even reached Fredersdorf. So she really exists! That's what she looks like. She's not only to be read of in the newspapers. She's actually on earth. I've stood beside her, brushed against her, and the whole place is scented with her when she goes by. I must write to Kampmann about this.

He set off with speed in order to see her once more and to take a good look at her. At this very moment a little comedy of good manners was proceeding in front of the lift. An exceptionally well set up, elegant, and handsome fellow stepped ostentatiously back two paces from the lift, and made way for Grusinskaya with an easy and at the same time chivalrous gesture as though it were not merely a question of giving her precedence into the lift, but of laying the conquest of an empire at the feet of a queen. Otternschlag, who stood by himself against the wall on the other side of the corridor, muttered, "Sir Walter Raleigh!" Kringelein, on the other hand, now in full career, shot past him and pressed into the lift on the heels of the chivalrous young man. Thus it was that his recently acquired friend remained alone below, since only four could go up at once. They stood somewhat crowded in the little cage of wood and glass. The handsome young man in particular squeezed himself into a corner.

"Ah! So you too are in Berlin, Baron?" Witte, the old conductor, asked, and Baron Gaigern answered:

"Yes, to be sure. I am here too."

Kringelein listened with awe to this talk between fine people. The one-armed man turned the handle, the lift stopped at the first floor, and they all marched off along the raspberry-red carpet to their rooms, Grusinskaya leading, then Witte, then the Baron, then Otto Kringelein. The doors of Nos. 68 and 69 and 70 were opened. It was two o'clock and an old grandfather clock at the turning of the passage struck officiously. The sound of music could be heard faintly from the yellow pavilion, where they were playing the last dance.

Grusinskaya paused a moment between the double doors of her room. "Well, good-night, my dear," she said to Witte. She spoke German to him when she was in a good humor. "Thank you again for this evening. It really went well, don't you think? Eight curtains. Tell me, by the way. Who was that young man? Haven't we seen him before somewhere? At Nice, was it?"

"Yes, at Nice, Lisa. He introduced himself to me one day. We played bridge together once or twice. He appears to have a great admiration for Elisaveta."

"Ah," Grusinskaya replied shortly. She put out her

hand under her cloak and absentmindedly stroked Witte's sleeve. "We are tired out. Good-night, my dear. He's the handsomest man I've ever seen in my life—this baron," she added in Russian. Her voice as she said it sounded as cold as if she spoke of some object displayed for sale in a salesroom.

Kringelein, lingering at his door and thirsting for Life, listened eagerly to the foreign speech. He had a confused notion that the world was vaster and more exciting and quite otherwise than he had ever imagined it in Fredersdorf.

Then the doors closed throughout the hotel. Everyone locked himself in behind double doors and was left alone with himself and his secrets.

THERE is not the faintest sign of fashionable life on the ground floor of a big hotel between eight and ten in the morning. No lights, no music, not a single woman to be seen—unless a charwoman in a blue apron, sweeping out the lounge with damp sawdust, were taken to represent her sex. This, however, did not occur to Count Rohna, who was already at his post, efficient and diligent and calm as ever. He was freshly shaved and a corner of his silk pocket handkerchief made an unobtrusive triangle above the pocket of his coat. It was not at all the right thing in his opinion that the daily cleaning of the hotel should go on under the eyes of the guests. Not done in the best hotels. Unfortunately, however, it was out of his province. It concerned the head housekeeper. In any case the guests paid no attention, for such as are to be seen in a big hotel during the morning are all solid and industrious business men. They sit in the lounge and conduct their business in all languages, selling stocks and shares, cotton, lubricating oil, patents, films, and real estate—and also plans, ideas, energy, and even life itself. They make a heavy breakfast and leave the breakfast room full of cigar smoke in spite of a modest notice on the yellow damask wall paper requesting those who wish to smoke to do so in the gray saloon next door. Newspapers are strewn on every table, every telephone box is not only occupied but beleaguered.

52

The hall porter, Senf, has not the slightest hope of getting news from the hospital before one o'clock. On the fifth floor in the corridor just behind the laundry the page boys are subjected to a kind of parade before going on duty. And the entrance hall of the Grand Hotel is not very different from a bourse.

Take, for example, Herr Generaldirektor Preysing of the Saxonia Cotton Company. Let us take this excellent and thoroughly average business man as a pattern, and then we shall see what men of his class are about between eight and ten in the Grand Hotel.

General Director Preysing, a large heavy man, rather too stout, arrived at the hotel at the impossible hour of 6:20 A. M., and the reason was that express trains do not stop at the unfortunate Fredersdorf. In spite of his utmost endeavors he had not so far succeeded in getting a fast train service for the town, though the factory had been granted a siding for loading its goods. This, however, only by the way. Preysing, then, arrived in a somewhat exhausted and shattered state, and he grumbled to himself when he found that the room engaged for him was one of the most expensive. First floor with sitting room and bath, No. 71, price seventy-five marks. Preysing was a careful man. For example, the real reason why he did not come to Berlin in his car was that he wished to save the expense of putting up his chauffeur. However, as he had an expensive room with a bath to pay for, the first thing he did was to enjoy a long and luxurious immersion in hot water. (In this he closely resembled the other gentleman from Fredersdorf, Herr Kringelein.) After that he lay in bed for a while, but he could not shake off the fatigue and discomfort of a cold night journey. So he got up again and dressed. Then he unpacked his bag with meticulous care and hung his coats over the coat hangers that he had brought with him. Each shoe, each set of underclothing, everything, indeed, was enclosed in a clean linen bag, and on each bag the initials K. P. were neatly marked in red cross-stitch.

While he tied his tie, Preysing looked absentmindedly out on to the street. A morning mist obscured it. It was still early. Street sweepers were brushing the asphalt and yellow buses came like ships through the half light of morning. Preysing looked down, but he saw nothing of all this. He had a heavy day before him. He must collect himself and have everything well thought out. He rang for the valet and gave him his shoes to clean. He had even brought his own polish with him, a brown one and a white. The room was full already of the indefinable smell of a hurried business journey—trunk leather, Odol, eau-de-Cologne, turpentine, cigar smoke. Preysing took out his note case with the deliberate and fastidious movements that were characteristic of him and counted his money. In the inner pocket was a thick wedge of 1,000-mark notes. You could never say in business matters when ready money might not come in useful. Preysing wet his thumb and forefinger as he counted the notes—the sign of a small man who has made his own way. He put the note case back in the inner breast pocket of his gray worsted suit and fastened up the pocket with a safety pin. For a while he strolled to and fro in red-leather bedroom slippers, conducting mute dialogues with the people from the Chemnitz Manufacturing Company. He looked in vain for an ash tray. He disliked having to knock off his cigar ash on the inkstand. Here, too, there was a bronze eagle, like the one that had enchanted Kringelein in No. 70. The general director drummed with his fingers for a moment or two upon its outspread wings. Then the valet brought his shoes, and at ten minutes to eight Preysing was able to leave his room and arrive second at the hotel barber's. In spite of his cares he looked plump and prosperous

enough and in excellent humor, as, freshly shaved, he sat
down to breakfast. And there Herr Rothenburger found
him when he came by appointment at eight-thirty. Herr
Rothenburger was entirely bald. He had not even eyebrows or eyelashes, and this gave him an air of perpetual
astonishment that agreed very ill with his cynical pursuits. He was an intermediary between stockjobbers and
bankers; now and then he took up agencies besides; and he
also sat as director on the board of some small enterprise
or other. He knew everything, repeated everything, and
had a finger in everything. It was he who was the first to
retail the latest stockbrokers' joke and to start those ugly
rumors that bring down the price of shares. Take him all
in all, Herr Rothenburger was a comical, dangerous, and
useful man.

"'Morning, Rothenburger," said Preysing, and stuck
out two fingers with a cigar between them.

"'Morning, Preysing," said Rothenburger, and shoved
his hat back on to his neck. Then he sat down and put his
portfolio on the table. "Back in Berlin again?"

"Yes," said Preysing. "Glad to see you. What'll you
have? Tea, cognac, ham and eggs?"

"Cognac for me. All well at home? Your wife and
daughters? Quite well, I hope?"

"Thanks, quite well. Good of you to send congratulations on our silver wedding."

"Well, of course. And how did the firm signalize the
event?"

"Good heavens! What's the firm got to do with it?
I planted them with my old car and took a new one for
it."

"Yes, of course. *L'état c'est moi.* I am the firm, a Preysing may say. And how is your father-in-law?"

"Thanks, he's fine. Still enjoys his cigar."

"Lord, the years I've known him now. When I think

how he began with six Jacquard looms, in a little bit of a place—and now! Marvelous!"

"Yes, work tells," said Preysing meaningly.

"Everyone talks of it. I hear you've built yourself a magnificent country house, regular castle, park, and all."

"Well, yes. It's come to be quite a nice place. My wife's mad on it. She is a wonderful manager, you know. Quite taken up with her house. Yes, we have a charming place now at Fredersdorf. You must come and see us."

"Thanks. Thanks. Very good of you. Perhaps I may have a business trip to put through—with expenses paid."

After disposing thus of the amiable conventional amiabilities, they got down to the matter in hand.

"A bit unsteady on the Bourse yesterday, wasn't it?" Preysing asked.

"Unsteady? I should say so. Bedlam is nothing in comparison. But since the boom in Bega the whole world has been crazed. Everybody thinks he can do business without security, but yesterday it broke. A thirty-per-cent drop, I tell you—forty per cent. There are lots who are dead and don't know it. Whoever is holding on to Bega—have you any Bega?"

"Had. Sold it out at the right moment," said Preysing —lying of course in the usual and traditional style customary in business; and Rothenburger knew it.

"Well, don't worry. They'll recover again," he said consolingly, exactly as though Preysing's No had been Yes. "What on earth can you rely on when a bank like Küsel in Düsseldorf closes its doors? A house like that! The Saxonia Company is among the sufferers, isn't it?"

"We? Not a penny. What put that into your head?"

"No? I thought it was. One hears all sorts of rumors— but if the Küsel smash hasn't touched you, I can't understand why Saxonia shares have fallen as they have."

"Nor I. I don't understand it either. Twenty-eight per cent is no laughing matter. Other textiles have kept steady that are far worse than ours."

"Yes. Chemnitz Manufacturing Company shares are steady enough," replied Rothenburger to this, without beating about the bush. Preysing looked at him. Eddies of blue smoke curled up between their two faces.

"Let's have it in plain words," said Preysing after a short pause.

"It's for you to put it in plain words. I have no secrets, Preysing. You commissioned me to buy Saxonia Cotton for all I was worth. And so I did—Saxonia shares for the Saxonia Company. Good. We put them up to a very respectable figure—184 was really a very respectable figure. They said you were bringing off a big deal with England. The price went up. They said you were amalgamating with the Chemnitz Manufacturing Company. The price went up. Suddenly the Chemnitz people threw all their Saxonia holding on the market. Naturally the price fell. It fell out of all reason. The Bourse is always irrational. The Bourse is a hysterical woman. I can tell you that, Preysing, after being married to her for forty years. You lost money in the Küsel bankruptcy. *Bon!* The English deal has come to nothing. Good again—but all the same a drop of twenty-eight per cent in one day is too much. There's something more behind it."

"To be sure! But what is behind it?" asked Preysing, and a long ash from his cigar fell into his cold coffee. Preysing was no diplomat. His question was foolish and clumsy.

"You know as well as I do. The Chemnitz people are calling the deal off. You've come here by forced marches to rescue what can still be rescued. But what advice can I possibly give you? You can't force the Chemnitz people to love you. If they chuck all the shares they hold in your concern on the market, it's as good as saying: 'No, thank you. We have no further interest in the Saxonia Company.' The question remains—how to make the best of an unpleasant situation. Do you want to buy up any more of your own shares? You can get 'em cheap enough."

Preysing made no reply for the moment. He tried to think and this was no easy matter for him. General Director Preysing was an excellent fellow, correct, straightforward, of irreproachable character. But he was not a business genius. He lacked imagination, persuasiveness, and push. Whenever he was asked to come to any important decision, he floundered on slippery ice. He could not even tell a lie with any power of conviction in it. He produced only little feeble abortions of business lies. He soon began to stammer and beads of sweat appeared on his upper lip beneath his mustache.

"If the Chemnitz people don't want the amalgamation, it's their business after all. They have more need of us than we of them. But for this new dyeing process they've got hold of, we should take no interest in the matter whatever," he said finally, and thought he had got out of it very cleverly. Rothenburger raised his ten thick fingers in the air and let them fall again on to the table just beside the saucer of honey. "But they *have* got the dyeing process and therefore the Saxonia *has* an interest in the matter," he said amiably.

Preysing had ten answers at once on the tip of his tongue. "We lost nothing in the Küsel affair," he wanted to say, and "the English deal has by no means fallen through," and "the Chemnitz people have brought our shares down precisely because they do want to amalgamate—they'll make a better deal that way." But finally he said none of these things, but only blurted out: "Well, we shall see. I'm having a talk with the Chemnitz people the day after to-morrow."

Rothenburger puffed smoke from his throat. "A talk? Which of them are coming? Schweimann? Gerstenkorn? Smart fellows. You'll need your wits about you. That's a job for your father-in-law if you don't mind my saying so. Well, while there's life there's hope. I must let that be known on the Bourse. If it does no good it can't do any harm. Well, and how do we stand? Do you commission me to go on buying Cotton shares? If there's no one there to-day to hold the market we shall see a regular collapse. You can take that from me. Well?" And Herr Rothenburger snapped open his portfolio and took out an order form.

A flush had appeared between Preysing's eyebrows when Rothenburger made that tactless allusion to his father-in-law. It was just a fleck of red that came and went again over the bridge of his nose. He took his fountain pen from his pocket and after no more than a momentary hesitation he signed the paper. "Up to 40,000 with a limit of 170," he said coolly. To soothe his vanity he made a thick stroke under his signature. He showed thereby that he would stand no nonsense from his father-in-law, or from Herr Rothenburger either.

Preysing stayed behind in the breakfast room and he felt depressed. There was a faint singing in his ears, for his blood pressure was not quite right: and an oppressive sensation in the back of his head often bothered him just when he had important interviews on hand. During the last year he had more than once had reverses and now again things were not looking exactly pleasant. It was not an enviable task to have to bring the Chemnitz people up to scratch if they wanted to drop the amalgamation. And at home the old man would sit in his wheeled chair and feel the sly malicious pleasure of old age whenever his son-in-law was in a tight corner. The negotiations with the State Railways about the express train service had led to nothing. That new dyeing process, by which cheap fabrics could be given tints that hitherto only better qualities would take, had been snapped up under his nose by the Chemnitz Manufacturing Company. That important deal with England had been hanging fire for months. Preysing had been to Manchester twice, and each time the negotiations had gone worse after his return. And now the old man had started interfering in the affair with the Chemnitz Company. He had conducted crafty preliminary negotiations, and old Gerstenkorn had come to Fredersdorf to look into matters and they had argued it all inside out. The famous commercial lawyer, Dr. Zinnowitz, had drawn up a draft contract, which, indeed, had not yet been signed, on the basis that two Chemnitz shares were to be given for one Saxonia. It was good business for the Saxonia—and, when all was said, not bad business for the Chemnitz either. The Bourse knew all about it, so did the whole world (the world of the textile industry). Then of a sudden the Chemnitz people took it into their heads to sing another tune. And now, if you please, when the fat was in the fire the old man sent him, poor old Preysing, to put things right again. Inadvertently he took a sip of his cold coffee with the cigar ash in it and got up with an exclamation of disgust. His back ached after his journey in that slow train; he yawned spasmodically and his eyes watered. He felt weary and in need of comfort; so he went to the telephone room and asked for an urgent call—Fredersdorf 48.

Fredersdorf 48 was not the factory but his home. It was not long before the call came through and Preysing settled his elbows on the ledge for a soothing talk with his wife.

"'Morning, Mulle," he said. "Yes, it's me. Still sleeping, Mulle? Still in bed?"

"What do you think?" the telephone answered in a distant but amiable voice—a voice that was very dear to the faithful and devoted general director.

"It is half-past nine. I have had breakfast and watered my flowers. And you?"

"*Très bien!*" Preysing said a little too brightly. "I'm having a talk with Zinnowitz presently. Is it sunny with you?"

"Yes," said the telephone; it prattled on faintly in an intimate and homely way. "It is a beautiful day. Just think, all the blue crocuses have come out since yesterday."

Preysing could see the crocuses through the telephone, and the breakfast room with its wicker chairs, the bast-covered coffee pot, the table laid, and the knitted cozies over the egg cups. He saw Mulle too. She was wearing her blue dressing gown and her bedroom slippers and in her hand was a watering can with a thin spout for the cactuses.

"You know, Mulle, I don't like it here," he said. "You ought to have come with me. You ought really."

"Oh, nonsense——" the telephone said in flattered tones, and laughed Mulle's kindly laugh.

"I'm so accustomed to you—and another thing, do you know I forgot my razor and now I must go every morning to the barber?"

"So I saw," the telephone replied. "You left it in the bathroom. But I tell you what—buy another. You can get them very cheap at any of the stores. It won't cost more than being shaved every day, and it won't be so tiresome for you."

"Yes. That's true. You're right," Preysing said gratefully. "Where are the children? I'd like to say good-morning to them."

The telephone mumbled unintelligible noises from the background and then it called out in a clear voice: "'Morning, Pops!"

"'Morning, Popsy," Preysing called back joyfully. "How are you?"

"Very well. How are you?"

"I'm very well. Is Babs there too?"

Yes, Babs was there too, and she too asked in her seventeen-year-old voice how he was, and whether it was a fine day, and whether Pops was bringing them anything from Berlin, and the crocuses were out and Mulle would not let them play tennis and it was quite warm and might Schmidt get the lawn ready. And then Mulle joined in, and then Popsy, till at last the telephone shouted and laughed with three voices at once, and the telephone girl intervened and Preysing ended the conversation. He stood for a moment in the box afterwards, and though he could not have put it into words, he felt that he held in his hands the warm sun outside the window and the blue crocuses.

He felt in better spirits when he left the box. There were people who called General Director Preysing a regular family man and they were not altogether mistaken. Next, he got another call put through and spoke with his bank. He spoke rather feverishly, for it was a question of cover for the 40,000, the 40,000 for the reckless and even desperate commission he had given Rothenburger on his own responsibility.

During these unpleasant ten minutes that the general director spent in box No. 4, Kringelein walked down the stairs enjoying at each step the raspberry-red carpet that made his downward progress such a splendid and unusual experience, and finally arrived at the hall porter's desk. Once more he had a flower in his buttonhole. It was the one of the evening before and after spending the night in his bedroom tumbler it was still moderately fresh. A white carnation. Kringelein felt that its spicy perfume put the last indispensable touch to his elegance.

"The gentleman you were asking for yesterday has arrived," the hall porter announced.

"What gentleman?" Kringelein asked in surprise. The

hall porter looked in the book. "Preysing, General Director Preysing of Fredersdorf," he said, and gave Kringelein's peaky, unpretending face a sharp look. Kringelein breathed in so hard that it was almost a gasp.

"Oh, yes, of course. He's come? That's good. Thank you. And where is he?" he asked with blanched lips.

"In the breakfast room probably."

Kringelein walked away and pulled himself forcibly together. He braced himself up till the small of his back was hollowed. Good-day, Herr Preysing, was what he would say. Having a good breakfast? Yes, I am staying in the Grand Hotel too. Certainly. Have you any objections? Is it not allowed perhaps for a man like me? Oh, no. People like us can live as they please, just like others.

Immediately afterwards he was thinking, Why this fear of Preysing? He can do nothing to me. I shall be dead very soon. No one can do anything to me. It was the same not unmixed feeling of freedom that he had felt long ago in Mickenauer Forest among the wild raspberries. Swelled out with courage, he entered the breakfast room. He moved now with a certain confidence in these smart surroundings. He looked for Preysing. It was actually his intention to speak to him. He wanted to be even with him. That was precisely why he had come to the Grand Hotel.

Good-morning, Herr Preysing, he would say. . . .

But Preysing was not in the breakfast room. Kringelein strolled along the corridor. He looked into the reading and writing rooms, and sought him at the paper stall. He even went so far as to ask page boy No. 14 where Herr Preysing was to be found. Nobody knew. All heads were shaken. Kringelein was now warmed up. He chafed at these paltry hindrances and wished to be done with it. Arriving at the threshold of a room he did not know, he asked the telephonist: "Excuse me, do you know Herr Preysing of Fredersdorf?" The man merely nodded. His head was too full of figures to reply. He pointed with his thumb over his shoulder. Kringelein went red, then white. For at that moment Preysing, lost in thought, came out of box No. 4.

At once Kringelein collapsed. His neck broke, as it were, at the nape and his head fell forward. His hollowed back relaxed. His toes turned in. His coat collar went up his neck. His knees gave, and his trousers bagged in wrinkles over his sorry shanks. Within a second the prosperous and distinguished Herr Kringelein turned into the poor insignificant bookkeeper. It was a subordinate who stood there. He had forgotten, apparently, that he had only a few weeks to live and therefore had all the advantage over Herr Preysing, for whom there were still years of tribulation in store. Kringelein, the bookkeeper, stepped to one side and, with his back squeezed against the door of box No. 2, he made his bow and murmured with bent head just as though he were at the factory, "I wish you goodmorning, Herr Generaldirektor."

"'Morning," said Preysing, and passed on without even seeing him. Kringelein stood there for a full minute, flattened against the wall, and tasted the bitterness of his humiliation. He felt his pains, too, suddenly coming back; excruciating pains in that sick and moribund stomach that was secretly of itself preparing the toxins of a lingering death.

Meanwhile, Preysing went on into the lounge, where the well-known commercial lawyer, Dr. Zinnowitz, already awaited him.

For two hours Dr. Zinnowitz and General Director Preysing sat with their heads bent over papers in a quiet corner of the Winter Garden, which till midday was little frequented. Preysing's portfolio had emptied out its entire contents, his ash tray was full of cigar ends, and the backs of his hands were moist with sweat, as they always were under the stress of exacting business discussions. Dr. Zinnowitz, a short elderly gentleman, with the face of a Chinese sorcerer, gave a little cough, as though he were about to make a speech in court, and tapping the bundles of papers in front of him with an authoritative air, spoke as follows:

"My dear Preysing, it comes to this. We enter the conference to-morrow at a substantial disadvantage. Our shares are in a bad way, both on paper and in fact." (Here he tapped the list of quotations in the midday edition of the *Berliner Zeitung*, which a page boy had just brought in. It showed a further fall of seven per cent in Saxonia shares.) "Our shares are in a bad way and the psychological moment, if I may so express myself, for this critical interview has been ill chosen. You know yourself, if the Chemnitz people say No to-morrow, it is all over with the amalgamation. The question can never be raised again. And it is very possible that they will say No, as things are now. I don't say it is certain, but it is possible. It is even probable."

Preysing listened with impatience. He was in a nervous state. The lawyer's studied phrases irritated him. Zinnowitz always spoke as though he were at a board meeting, even if he were quite alone. When he rested his knuckles on the flimsy wicker table of the Winter Garden it became at once the fateful green baize-covered table of a board room.

"Should we cry off?" asked Preysing.

"To cry off is impossible without inviting the worst constructions," observed Zinnowitz. "There is the further question, too, whether even putting it off would be a gain or a loss. There are always chances that might be irretrievably lost by a postponement."

"What chances?" asked Preysing. He could not free

himself of the foolish habit of asking things that he knew
without asking. Hence any discussion in which he took
part always strayed from the point and became something
at once pedantic and confused.

"You know the chances as well as I do," said Dr. Zinnowitz, and his words sounded like a reproof. "It comes back
of course to the situation with regard to the English affair.
Manchester, Burleigh & Son of Manchester—that in my
opinion is the salient point. The Chemnitz Company is
after the English market for their ready-made goods.
Burleigh & Son have this market to a great extent in their
pockets. They have large and constant demands for finished cotton goods, but they themselves produce only the
yarn, and they are eager to export their yarn to Germany
and to import the finished articles in exchange. They have
a great interest in coming to terms with the Chemnitz concern. As to why they do not simply go to them direct, that,
my dear Preysing, you know as well as I do. The Chemnitz
enterprise is not solid enough for these Englishmen. Its
capital is too small. They hang back because they think
the basis is not sound. It would be another matter if the
Saxonia Company amalgamates with the Chemnitz concern. Burleigh & Son would then find the situation a promising one. The idea seems to be that in that case, if you'll
forgive me saying so, your somnolent business would be
freshened up and the somewhat too enterprising Chemnitz
concern sobered down. It comes to this, then, that Burleigh & Son are interested in the Saxonia Company only
if it is amalgamated with the Chemnitz Company, and the
latter will only amalgamate if you have the deal with
Burleigh & Son, and consequently the English market, in
your pocket. Nothing can be done till the agreement between you and the other side is completed. If I may give
you my frank opinion, the negotiations must have been

very incompetently conducted, otherwise we could not have got into such a blind alley. Who has been negotiating with Manchester?"

"My father-in-law," Preysing replied quickly. That was not the fact, and Zinnowitz knew it was not the fact, for he was pretty well informed about the struggle for power in the Saxonia Cotton Company. He swept his hand over the table as though he brushed Preysing's reply on one side.

"I have been," he went on, "in close touch all this while with the enemy's position" (he liked to bring in the military expressions which he had learnt as a captain in the reserve), "and I can tell you exactly how they feel about it. Schweimann has dropped all idea of the amalgamation and Gerstenkorn has begun to waver. Why? The big S.I.R. combine is putting out feelers to ascertain whether the Chemnitz people can be bought out—not amalgamated, but bought right out. Of course, Schweimann and Gerstenkorn would remain as directors and be given salaried posts in addition, whereas now they are saddled with all the risks. On the other hand, if the affair with Burleigh's were in black and white, then—such at least is my humble opinion —they would turn down the offer from the S.I.R. and amalgamate with you. That's their position. But what yours is with Manchester, there I am not quite so clear. I had a somewhat guarded letter from your father-in-law——"

Once again, Preysing interrupted the lawyer's clear exposition with a stupid question. "Is this offer of the S.I.R. definite or only talk? How much have they offered?" he asked.

"That is beside the point," said Zinnowitz, who did not know. Preysing pushed forward his underlip and his cigar with it. It was not at all beside the point, he thought. But he could not quite explain why.

"The affair with Burleigh's isn't exactly in a bad way," he said hesitatingly.

"Not exactly in a good way either, it seems to me," the lawyer replied promptly.

Preysing stretched out a hand towards his portfolio, drew back, and then finally took hold of it. He took his cigar out of his mouth, its end was chewed, and at last, at the third attempt, he pulled out a blue folder in which were filed letters and copies of the replies.

"Here is the correspondence with Manchester up to date," he said quickly, and held out the file of letters. He had no sooner done so than he regretted it. The backs of his hands were once more in a sweat. He began to play with a ring on his finger, a habit of his, but it got him no farther. "In the strictest confidence, please remember," he requested urgently. Zinnowitz replied only by a glance out of the corners of his eyes as he read the letters. Preysing was silent. A gentle rattle could now be heard from the large dining room where the tables were being laid. There was a savory smell in the air as there is in every hotel in the world just before lunch, a smell that makes you hungry before the meal and is intolerable afterwards. Preysing was hungry. He gave a fleeting thought to Mulle at home. She would just be sitting down to lunch with the children.

"Yes——" said Dr. Zinnowitz as he put the letters aside and looked thoughtfully and at the same time absent-mindedly at the bridge of Preysing's nose.

"Yes?" asked Preysing.

"And now," said Dr. Zinnowitz, proceeding after a moment's silence to his pronouncement, "I come back once more to the starting point. The negotiations with Burleigh & Son are still going on. Consequently we still have this trump card to play in our efforts to bring pressure on the Chemnitz people. If we postpone a meeting with them and Burleighs refuse to come to terms, as seems very possible from their last letter of February 27th, then we hold this trump card no longer. Then we shall have no card to play whatever. We shall fall between two stools, instead of sitting on them."

A dark red flush suddenly sprang to Preysing's forehead, the skin beneath its wrinkles was suffused with blood and his veins swelled. He had now and then such crises of anger, of blood pressure and passionate vehemence.

"All this has no sense in it. We simply must have the amalgamation, and there's an end of it," he shouted, and brought his fist down on the table.

Dr. Zinnowitz said nothing for a moment.

"I imagine the Saxonia Company won't be bankrupt even failing the amalgamation," he said.

"No, certainly not. There is no question of bankruptcy," Preysing said heatedly. "But we should have to retrench. We should have to pay off some of the hands in the spinning mills. We should have—but what's the good of talking? I have got to put the amalgamation through. That's what I'm here for. I have got to put it through, and there's an end of it. It's not only—there are other reasons. There is the question of the effect on the management of the business. You understand what I mean. After all, it is I who have made the factory. It is all my organization. That being so, I want to have the credit for it. The old man is getting on. And I don't hit it off with my young brother-in-law. I tell you that quite frankly. You know him, of course—well we don't hit it off. He has brought new-fangled ideas with him from Lyons that don't agree with my notions of business. I am not for bluff. I don't care for sharp practice. I make my decisions on a solid basis. I don't build houses of cards. As long as I am there I intend to be reckoned with, and what I say is——"

Dr. Zinnowitz looked with keen interest at the heated general director, who was beginning to talk irresponsibly.

"You are well known in the trade as a model of business
propriety," he remarked politely, and there was a hint of
patronage in the tone of his voice. Preysing broke off.
He took the blue folder and stuffed it back into his portfolio with trembling hands.

"We agree, then," said Zinnowitz. "The conference will
take place to-morrow and we will do all in our power to
get the draft agreement signed. If only I knew——

"Listen," he continued after a moment's silent reflection. "Will you allow me to take one or two of the letters
away with me? Some of the more promising ones, you
understand me, dating from the earlier stages of the negotiations? I am seeing Schweimann and Gerstenkorn this
afternoon. It would do no harm if—of course, I wouldn't
show them the whole correspondence, only some of it——"

"Impossible," said Preysing. "We have promised Burleigh & Son to regard the matter as strictly confidential."

Zinnowitz smiled at this. "Why it's common knowledge in any case," he said. "However, as you think best.
It is your responsibility. Now is the time to show your
mettle. Everything might turn on a skillful use of the
negotiations with the Manchester people. It is the one
issue on which we stand a chance of straightening out this
somewhat involved affair with the Chemnitz concern.
The thing would be to let one or two of the letters fall into
Schweimann's hands, quite by the way, quite by accident.
A selection, needless to say. A few copies. But—as you
please. It is your responsibility."

Once more Preysing was faced with a responsibility.
The advance of forty thousand for Rothenburger's pur-
chase of shares still lay heavy on him. He positively had a
twinge of heartburn from nervous agitation and his
temples throbbed feverishly.

"I don't like it. It isn't straight," he said. "The negotiations with Chemnitz began long before the affair with

Burleighs, nor was there a word said about it between us
and Gerstenkorn. Now of a sudden everything is made to
turn on it. If the Chemnitz people are willing to accept us
only as a catspaw for the deal with England—and that is
what it looks like—we are not going to the length of letting
them look through our correspondence. I wouldn't hear of
it——"

As stubborn as a mule, thought Dr. Zinnowitz, and
he snapped the lock of his portfolio. "As you please,"
he said, and his lips tightened as he got up to go.

Suddenly Preysing gave in.

"Have you anyone who could make copies of a few of
the letters? I might let you have a few carbon copies.
The original letters must on no account pass out of my
hands," he said in a loud and imperative voice, as though
he had to shout someone down. "It would have to be
somebody whose discretion could be relied upon. I have
some notes to dictate, too, that I shall need for the conference. I don't care to employ the typists supplied by the
hotel. You always have the feeling that they give away
business secrets to the hall porter. It would have to be
soon after lunch."

"No one in my office would have time, I am afraid,"
Zinnowitz said coolly and rather surprised. "We have
several big affairs on hand and they have been working
overtime in the office for weeks past. But wait a bit—you
could have Flämmchen. Flämmchen would do. I'll have
her rung up."

"Who—did you say?" asked Preysing, on whom the
name made an unpleasant impression.

"Flämmchen. Flamm the Second. Sister of Flamm the
First. You know her, don't you? She's been twenty years
with me. Flamm the Second often helps us out when we
have more typing on hand than the office can manage. I
have taken her with me when I have had to go away on

business and Flamm the First could not be spared. She is very quick and intelligent. I should have to have the copies by five o'clock. Then I'll manage it quite unofficially, as I am having dinner with the Chemnitz gentlemen. Flämmchen can bring me the copies direct to the office. I'll telephone at once to Flamm the First to tell her to send her sister here. What time have you engaged the conference room for to-morrow?"

Dr. Zinnowitz and General Director Preysing had quite the right air as they left the Winter Garden with their well-worn portfolios under their arms and crossed the corridor and passed by the hall porter's desk to reach the lounge. Here there were many other men like them, all with the same kind of portfolios and all carrying on the same kind of discussion. But now a few women too had made their appearance, fresh from their baths and scented after their morning toilet. Their lips were neatly painted and they pulled on their gloves with careless ease before passing through the revolving door to the street whose surface was bathed in yellow sunshine.

Just as they were crossing the lounge to the telephone room, Preysing heard his name called. Page boy No. 18 was going along the passage calling out at regular intervals, in his clear, careless, boyish voice: "Herr Direktor Preysing! Herr Direktor Preysing of Fredersdorf! Herr Direktor Preysing!"

"Here," called out Preysing, and put out his hand for a telegram: "Excuse me," he said, and read it as he walked beside Dr. Zinnowitz through the lounge. He went cold to the roots of his hair as he read it.

The telegram ran:

NEGOTIATIONS WITH BURLEIGH & SON FINALLY BROKEN OFF.
BRÖSEMANN.

That's finished it. You need not send for the typist, Herr Doktor. It's finished. Manchester is done with, thought Preysing while he drew nearer all the time to the telephone room. He stuck the telegram into his coat pocket and gripped it there spasmodically between his thumb and forefinger. Finished. There's no need to have any copies made, he thought, and intended to say it aloud. But he did not say it. He cleared his throat which was still husky after his night journey. "It has turned out quite a fine day," was what he said.

"Yes. We're at the end of March now," answered Zinnowitz, who had put off his business manner and become a private person with an eye for the ladies' silk stockings. "Box No. 2 will be free in a moment," said the operator, with his fingers on the red and green stops.

Preysing leant against the padded door of the box and stared mechanically through the glass panel at a broad back. Zinnowitz was saying something, but he paid no attention. He was obsessed by immeasurable fury against Brösemann, this blockhead of a managing clerk who let loose telegrams like this on him just when he needed a stiff back to pull off a troublesome deal. No doubt the old man was behind it with his senile spite. Now you're in the soup and let's see what you make of it, he would be saying with a malicious joy. The poor general director could have cried. His nerves were in a pitiful state after his sleepless night. He was worried to death and his upright principles were no match for all these wretched and baffling complications. He tried to get his thoughts straight, but they twisted and turned in his brain. By his side Dr. Zinnowitz was talking in the tone of a man about town about a new revue all in silver, entirely in silver. Then he felt the door of the telephone box against which he leant for support being gently but firmly pushed open and a large and strikingly handsome fellow in a blue coat forced his way out with a friendly air; indeed, instead of taking it amiss, he politely apologized. Preysing absentmindedly stared him straight in the face. He saw it with a strange distinctness at very close quarters, and he too muttered a conventional apology. Zinnowitz was already in the box. He was engaging the services of Flamm the Second, some competent female who was to make copies of letters, and it was now all utterly pointless. Preysing knew well enough that he ought to put a stop to it, but he could not collect the energy to do it.

"I've fixed it up," said Dr. Zinnowitz as he came out of the box. "Flämmchen will be here at three. There are plenty of typewriters in the hotel. I shall have the letters by five. I'll speak to you on the phone before the conference. We'll bring it off yet. *Au revoir.*"

"*Au revoir,*" said Preysing to the whirling reflections of the revolving door as it ejected the lawyer into the street. Outside the sun was shining. Outside a small destitute man was selling violets. Outside no one was worried by amalgamations and troublesome contracts. Until Dr. Zinnowitz finally disappeared in a taxi, Preysing kept the telegram tightly gripped in his right-hand coat pocket. He now took it out and, holding it in his left hand, went to a table in the lounge. There he carefully smoothed it out and folded it neatly together, and then he put it in the breast pocket of his neat dark gray suit.

At five minutes past three the telephone roused Herr Preysing from his afternoon nap. He jumped up from the couch on which he had lain down after taking off his shoes and collar and coat. He had that comfortless and disagreeable feeling which is the usual result of snatching a few minutes' sleep in an hotel. The heavy yellow curtains were drawn. The room was full of the dry hot air of the central heating. His right cheek was marked with the

impress of his traveling cushion. The telephone rang on
insistently. A lady was waiting for Herr Direktor in the
lounge, the hall porter announced. "Send her up," said
Preysing, and began hastily to make himself tidy. Unexpected difficulties, however, were made in the most
polite manner through the telephone. The hotel had its
rules and regulations. Rohna, the reception clerk, himself
communicated them to Herr Preysing with many apologetic regrets and the smile of a man of the world. It was
not allowed to receive ladies in one's bedroom, and unfortunately no exceptions could be made. "But, good heavens! this is no visit from a lady. It's my secretary, as you
can see for yourself, and I have some work for her,"
Preysing said impatiently. The smile of the reception
clerk became only the more audible. The director was requested to be so good as to take the lady to the room
specially provided for such purposes. Preysing rang off,
replacing the receiver with a violent jerk as he did so.
He felt that he was being submitted to the most shocking
inconvenience. He washed his hands, gargled with a
mouth wash, wrestled with his collar stud and tie, and
hurried down to the lounge.

In the lounge sat Flämmchen, Fräulein Flamm the
Second, the sister of Fräulein Flamm the First. Two sisters
less alike could scarcely be imagined. Preysing had a
vague recollection of Flamm the First as a most reliable
person with colorless hair, a detachable sleeve on her
right arm, and a paper cuff on her left who, with an uncompromising air, barred the way to undesired callers in
Dr. Zinnowitz's outer office. Flamm the Second, Flämmchen, on the other hand, had not a trace of this stolid
demeanor. She was leaning back in an armchair as though
she was quite at home in such surroundings; she swung
one foot in a neat shoe of light blue leather, and looked
as if she was out to have a jolly good time. She was, as her

whole appearance testified, at the utmost twenty years old.

"Dr. Zinnowitz sent me to make the copies. I am Flämmchen whom he said he would send along, I ought to explain," she said without ceremony. She had a dab of red paint in the center of her lips, dabbed on quite casually, merely because it was the fashion. When she stood up she showed that she was taller than the general director. Her legs were long and her figure from head to foot was magnificent. She wore a tight leather belt round her remarkably slender waist. Preysing was furious with Zinnowitz for putting him in such an idiotic situation. The scruples of the reception clerk were now very intelligible. She was scented too. He wanted to send her home. "We had better be quick, hadn't we?" she said in the deep and slightly husky voice that young girls often have. Popsy, his elder daughter, had had a voice like that as a child.

"So you are Fräulein Flamm's sister? I know Fräulein Flamm," he said. There was more rudeness than surprise in his voice. Flamm the Second put out her underlip and blew away a lock of hair that hung over her forehead beneath her small felt hat. The little golden curl rose in the air and fell back slowly on to her forehead again. Preysing did not wish to look; but looked all the same. "Stepsister," said Flämmchen. "I am the daughter of my father's second wife. But we get on quite well."

"I see," said Preysing, and looked at her with troubled eyes. So now she was to make copies of letters from a correspondence that was finished with, that was utterly senseless, utterly unreal. For months he had been counting on the agreement with Burleigh & Son, reckoning on it in all his plans, and he could not readjust himself all at once. It was simply beyond him to wipe out this affair utterly from his mind. Finally broken off. Brösemann. Finally. There was a letter to Brösemann to dictate as well, a stinger. To the old man, too, about the forty thousand. If the Chemnitz affair fell through to-morrow, the forty thousand for steadying the market had been thrown to the winds.

"Right. Come along to the writing room, then," said Preysing, and filled with gloom he preceded her along the corridor. Flämmchen with a smile of amusement kept her eyes on the roll of flesh at the back of his neck as she followed him.

Already the typewriters could be heard in the distance like faint machine-gun fire, with their bells ringing at regular intervals. When Preysing opened the door volumes of cigar smoke came eddying out in huge coils. "Fine room for hearing in," said Flämmchen, and gave a little sniff. Inside the room a man was walking to and fro with his hands behind his back and his hat on the back of his head, dictating in a nasal American voice. He was the manager of a film company. He looked Flämmchen up and down with the rapid glance of a connoisseur and went on dictating.

"This won't do," said Preysing, and slammed the door again. "I must have the room to myself. There's annoyance at every turn in this hotel."

This time he walked behind Flämmchen along the corridor. He was in a rage now, and in the midst of his rage the swaying of Flämmchen's hips warmed and pricked his senses. In the lounge Flämmchen once more attracted all eyes. She was a magnificent example of the female form— of that there seemed no possible doubt. Preysing found it extremely unpleasant to be making his way across the lounge in the company of so striking a creature, and he left her to stand where she was while he arranged with Rohna for the undisturbed possession of the typewriting room. Flämmchen, entirely unmoved by the looks that were fixed upon her from all sides (she was used enough to

them, heaven knows!), carelessly powdered her nose, and
then, without moving from where she stood, took a
cigarette case from the pocket of her coat with a free-and-
easy air and began to smoke. Preysing approached her as if
she were a thicket of nettles.

"We shall have to wait for ten minutes," he said.

"*Bon!*" said Flämmchen. "But after that we must be
quick."

"Are you so punctual as all that?" asked Preysing
unamiably.

"Rather!" answered Flämmchen, and laughed roguishly
in a way that made her nose quite short like a baby's
while her light brown eyes darted a sidelong glance.

"Well, take a seat till then," said Preysing. "And
have something. Waiter, give the lady something," he
said tactlessly, and made his retreat.

Flämmchen ordered a Pêche Melba and nodded her
head quite happily. Also she blew again at her lock of hair,
but without success. She was as beautifully made as a
race horse and as natural in her movements as a puppy.

Baron Gaigern, who had been wandering about the
lounge for a few minutes, looked at her from the distance
with unaffected admiration. After a moment he went up
to her and said in a low voice: "May I take a seat beside
you? But surely you have not forgotten me? Didn't I
dance with you at Baden-Baden?"

"Impossible. I've never been to Baden-Baden," said
Flämmchen, and took a good look at him.

"A thousand apologies. I see now, I must have made
an error and mistaken you for someone else," cried the
Baron hypocritically.

Flämmchen laughed at this. "You don't get over me
with that old story," she said dryly. Gaigern laughed
too.

"Well, let's drop that nonsense. I may sit here, may

I? You are quite right. You could not be mistaken for anyone else. A girl like you is only seen once. Are you staying here? Are you going to dance this evening? Please —I should so much like to dance with you. Will you?"

He put his hands on the table. Flämmchen's were there already. There was a little space in between his fingers and hers and the air in it began to vibrate. They looked at each other and the mutual attraction and sympathy were instantly complete between these two young and charming people. "Good Lord, you've got a way with you," said Flämmchen, enchanted.

And Gaigern answered, equally enchanted, "You promise then? You'll dance this evening?"

"I can't. I've work to do. But I'm free to-night."

"But bother it, I'm not. What about to-morrow? Or the day after to-morrow at five o'clock? Here in the yellow pavilion? That's settled then?"

Flämmchen licked her spoon clean, and said nothing. What was there to say in any case? You picked up an acquaintance as you lit a cigarette. You took a few puffs just as you felt inclined and then you trod it out.

"What is your name?" Gaigern asked meanwhile.

"Flämmchen," said she promptly. Immediately upon this Preysing came up to the table with a proprietary air, and Gaigern politely made way for him by getting up and standing behind his chair.

"We can get along now," said Preysing irritably.

Flämmchen extended a gloved hand to Gaigern while Preysing looked on with displeasure. He recognized Gaigern as the man who had come out of the telephone box and once again he saw his face so distinctly that every pore and every little line in it were revealed.

"Who is that?" he asked as he crossed the lounge at Flämmchen's side.

"Oh, an acquaintance," she replied.

"Indeed. You have a number of acquaintances no doubt?"

"I don't complain. It doesn't do to make yourself too cheap. Besides I haven't always the time."

For some obscure reason this reply was comforting to the general director.

"Have you got a permanent job?" he asked.

"Not at the moment. I am looking out for one. Well, something will turn up. Something always turns up," said Flämmchen philosophically. "I should like best of all to get on to the films, but it isn't easy to make the start. If I could only make a start I should soon get on. But it's so horribly difficult to make a start." She looked with a troubled and comical expression into Preysing's face. She was now like a young cat. All the charm of an animal appeared to meet in the changing expressions of her face.

Preysing, who was far from such perceptions, opened the door of the typewriting room, asking as he did so: "Why the films particularly? You are all film mad." Among the "all" was included his fifteen-year-old daughter, Babs, who adored the films.

"Oh, as to that, I have no illusions about it. But I photograph well. Everybody says so," said Flämmchen, and took off her coat. "Shorthand, or straight on to the typewriter?"

"Type it, please," said Preysing. He was now more lively and in better humor. He had rid his mind of the fact that Manchester had fallen through, and as he took the first and still so very promising letters of this correspondence from his portfolio he felt positively happy. Flammchen was still taken up with her own affairs.

"I am often photographed for the newspapers and so on. Advertisements for soaps are made from me, too. How do I get on to that, you ask? Well, one photographer tells another. I'm very good in the nude, you see. But it's

wretchedly paid. Ten marks a photo. Just imagine that.
No, the best thing would be if someone would take me
traveling as his secretary this spring. Last year I went
with a gentleman to Florence. He was working at a book—
a professor—charming man he was. Oh, well, something
else will turn up this year too," she said, and put the
machine in order. It was evident she had her cares and as
evident that those cares weighed on her as little as the lock
of hair which from time to time she blew into the air off her
forehead.

Preysing, who could not reconcile the casual allusion to
the nude with any scheme of things to which he was accustomed, wished to say something businesslike. Instead of
that he said, gazing meanwhile at Flämmchen's hands as
she adjusted the paper: "How brown your hands are.
Where did you find enough sun for that?"

Flämmchen inspected her hands and then she drew her
sleeve up a little way and looked earnestly at her brown
skin. "That's the snow. I went skiing in Vorarlberg. A
friend of mine took me with him. It was glorious. You
should have seen me when I got back. Shall we make a
start, then?"

Preysing took a turn through the room, which was thick
with cigar smoke, and began to dictate from the farthest
corner.

"Date—you've got the date? Dear Herr Brösemann,
Bröse—got that? Referring to your telegram of this
morning, I have to inform . . ."

Flämmchen carried on with her right hand while with
her left she removed her hat, which she appeared to find
in her way. The room looked on to a dark ventilation shaft
and was lighted by green-shaded electric lights. In the
midst of these business matters Preysing could not help
thinking of a chest of drawers, an old chest of drawers
of birchwood in the entrance hall at Fredersdorf.

It came back to him at night when he woke up after dreaming of Flämmchen. Her hair had the color, the flame-like sheen, of old birchwood, and the lights and shadows of its grain. This hair of hers was clearly before his eyes as he lay in bed at night, breathing the dry air of the hotel bed-room, while the lights of the electric sign flitted across the drawn curtains. The portfolio on the table in the darkness got on his nerves. He got up and put it in his trunk, rinsed his mouth once more with Odol, and once more washed his hands. His suite annoyed him. It was dear and uncom-fortable. It consisted of a minute room with a sofa, a table, and chairs, and a small bedroom with a bathroom beside it. The bath tap dripped and the drip, drip, drip pursued him till he fell asleep. Once again he got out of bed and set an alarm clock. He had forgotten to buy the razor and would have to be early at the barber's. He fell asleep and again dreamed of the typist and her birchwood hair. He awoke once more. The electric sign was still passing to and fro across the curtains, and the hours of night in the strange bed seemed to him disagreeable and confused. He was in a panic at the thought of the meeting with Schwei-mann and Gerstenkorn and his heart thumped in his chest. He had been in a strange confusion of mind ever since he handed over the letters from England and he had a per-sistent feeling that his hands were not clean. Last of all, just as he was falling into a doze, he heard someone come along the carpeted passage, whistling softly. It was the occupant of No. 69, who put a pair of patent-leather shoes outside his door as though life were a matter for enjoy-ment.

Kringelein, too, in No. 70, heard it and woke up. He had been dreaming of Grusinskaya. She had come to him in the counting house and put before him some unpaid ac-counts. He was beginning to feel at home, this Otto Kringelein, this bookkeeper from Fredersdorf, this sufferer from claustrophobia, who wanted to seize one hour of crowded life before he died. His hunger was infinite, but he could not stand very much. His weakness of body many a time got the better of him during these days and forced him to retreat from the scenes of dissipation to his bedroom. Kringelein began to hate his ailments, though without them he would never have made his escape from Fredersdorf. He had bought himself some medicine— Hundt's Elixir. From time to time he took a sip and hoped for the best. It had a bitter taste of cinnamon, and he gulped it down and even felt the better for it.

He held out his cold fingers in the darkness and began on a calculation. His fingers always went dead while he was asleep, as though they were making a beginning, and this was unpleasant. He seemed to see numerals with bent heads prowling round his room, till at last he raised himself and turned on the light. Unfortunately, this life-long habit of the impecunious Kringelein would not desert him now he was a man of wealth. He could not help reckoning up figures. Figures were always pursuing their antics in his head. They formed themselves in columns one below the other and added and subtracted themselves whether he would or no. Kringelein had a little notebook bound in shiny black cloth, which he had brought with him from Fredersdorf, and he sat at it for hours together. He entered his expenses in it, the reckless expenses of a man who was learning to enjoy life and spending a month's salary in two days. Sometimes he was so dizzy that all the four walls with their wall paper of tulips seemed to fall in upon him. Sometimes he was happy, not entirely happy nor as he imagined the rich being happy, but all the same, happy. Sometimes, again, he sat on the edge of his bed and thought of his approaching death. He thought of it hard and with horror, while his ears went cold and he blinked in anguish of heart. In spite of all, he could make nothing of it. He hoped that it would be much the same as going under chloroform, except that you came to again after chloroform and found yourself in a bad way and in agonizing pain—blue pain, Kringelein had called it in his own mind—and also that all those familiar tortures were now to be borne beforehand, not afterwards. When he had thought as far as this, he began to shudder. Yes, Kringelein actually shuddered at the thought of death, although he could form no idea of it.

There were a good many behind the locked double doors of the sleeping hotel who could not sleep. Dr. Otternschlag, indeed, about this time of the night laid a little hypodermic syringe down on his washhand stand and, throwing himself on his bed, floated away on the light clouds of a morphine trance. Witte, the conductor, who had No. 221 in the left wing, could not sleep either. Old people sleep so little. His room was the counterpart of Dr. Otternschlag's. There, too, the water gurgled in the wall and the lift rumbled up and down. It was little better than a servant's room. He was sitting at his window, pressing his forehead against the windowpane and staring at the blank wall opposite. Fragments of a Beethoven symphony were going through his head. He had never conducted it. He heard Bach—the tremendous "Crucify Him" from the Matthew Passion. I have wasted all my life, thought old Witte, and all the never-sung music of his life made a lump in his throat and he gulped it down. There was the rehearsal for the ballet at half-past eight in the morning. He would sit at the piano and play the same old march to the convolutions of the ballet, always the same Spring Waltz and Mazurka and Bacchanal. He ought to have left Elisaveta while there was still time, he thought. Now it was too late. Elisaveta had become an old woman and he could not leave her now. They would have to see it through with her for the few years that remained. . . .

Elisaveta Alexandrovna Grusinskaya could not sleep either. In the depth of night she heard the swift and never-ceasing flight of time. There was a twofold ticking in the dark room—from a bronze clock on the writing table and from her wrist watch on her bedside table. Each told the flight of seconds, and yet one ticked faster than the other. It made her heart beat to listen to them. She turned on the light and got out of bed, put her feet into her trodden-down slippers and went to the looking glass. The passage of time met her there—there most of all. It met her too in her press notices, in the shocking rudeness of the news-papers, in the success of the ugly and clumsy dancers that were now in fashion, in the losses on her tours, in the feeble applause, in the vulgar way her manager, Meyer-heim, talked—everywhere, everywhere, she saw the passage of time. The years she had danced away were in her tired ankles, in the shortness of breath that came over her after thirty-two tours of classical dances, and in her blood, too, that now often pulsed in her neck and flushed her cheeks. It was hot in her room, though the French window on to the balcony was wide open. Outside the motor cars hooted all night long. Grusinskaya took her pearls out of the small suitcase, two handfuls of cool pearls, and put her face down to them. In vain. Her eye-lids were still hot and still smarted from the paint and the footlights; her thoughts still troubled her, and the clock and the watch still raced on. Grusinskaya wore a rubber bandage under her chin, her hands and lips were steeped in ointment. The sight of herself in the looking glass was so hateful that she quickly turned out the light. In the dark-ness she swallowed a veronal tablet and began to weep the hot tears of a lonely and passionate woman; then the drug took hold of her and at last she fell asleep.

Just outside someone got out of the lift. It might be the young man from Nice. Grusinskaya took him with her into her veronal dream. He was in No. 69 and he was the handsomest man she had ever seen. . . .

He whistled softly on his way to his room, not unpleasantly, and merely because he was happy. He was careful in his room to make no noise and when he was in his pajamas and smart blue leather slippers he was more silent than ever. There was something of the wildcat in this handsome young man. Whenever he passed through the lounge it was as if a window of sunshine were opened in a cold room. He was a marvelous dancer, cool and yet passionate. There were always flowers in his room. He loved them and their scent. When he was alone he stroked and even licked their petals—like an animal. He was quick to follow girls in the street. Sometimes he would merely look at them with pleasure, sometimes he would speak to them, and sometimes he would go home with them or take them to a second-rate hotel. Next morning the hall porter would smile, when with a feline and innocent air he made his appearance in the elegant and more or less irreproachable lounge of the Grand Hotel and asked for his key. Sometimes too he got drunk, but in so amiable and high-spirited a fashion that no one could take it amiss. In the mornings it was not very pleasant to have the room beneath his, for then he went through his physical exercises, and soft thuds came at regular intervals through the ceiling. He wore smart bow ties and low-cut waistcoats. His clothes sat as easily on his muscular body as the hide on a pedigree animal. Sometimes he went off in his little four-seater and nothing more was seen of him for a couple of days. For hours together he pottered about in automobile showrooms, sticking his head under the bonnets of motor cars, breathing in gasoline, lubricating oil, and the smell of the warmed-up engine, tapping the chassis, stroking the enamel, the leather, and the upholstery, blue, red, or beige. If he was left alone, perhaps he would lick this too with his tongue. He bought laces from street vendors, cigarette lighters that would not light, little birds of india-rubber, and countless boxes of matches. Suddenly a longing for horses would come over him. He got up at six, went by bus to Tattersall's and inhaled with delight the scent of sawdust, saddlery, stable manure and sweat. Then if an animal took his fancy he rode in the Tiergarten, breathing his fill of the gray early mist of a March morning among the trees, and returned well satisfied to the hotel. He had been found before now in the kitchen courtyard behind the service stairs standing beside a gutter full of slops and refuse and staring up to the top of the five stories where the aërials hung beneath the colorless sky. Possibly he had designs on the one pretty chambermaid in the hotel. Her morals were questionable and she had already been given notice. He made many friends in the hotel, for he was always ready to oblige with a postage stamp, to give advice about long-distance flights, to take an old lady out in his car, or to make a fourth at bridge, and he was well informed as to the resources of the hotel cellar. He wore a signet ring of lapis lazuli on his forefinger with the Gaigern crest, a falcon over wavy lines. At night as he lay in bed he would speak in Bavarian dialect to his pillow. "Good-evening, old friend," he would say. "Yes, you are good. You are my dear old bed. You are fine!" He was never long in falling asleep and never disturbed his neighbors by snoring, gargling, or throwing his boots about. His chauffeur said, down in the servants' quarters, that the Baron was quite a good fellow, but a bit simple. But even a Baron Gaigern sleeps behind double doors and even he, too, has his secrets and hidden motives. . . .

"No other news then?" he asked his chauffeur. He was sitting naked on the carpet in the middle of his room and massaging his legs. He had a magnificent body, and the almost excessively developed chest of a boxer. The skin of his shoulders and legs was a bright tan. The only part of him that was not tanned was the part between his thighs and his trunk which was covered in summer by his shorts. "Is that all you have to say?"

"Quite enough, too," replied the chauffeur. He was reclining on the couch with its imitation Kelim rug, a cigarette hung from his underlip and he was smoking. "Do you suppose they will wait on and on in Amsterdam for the business? Schalhorn has paid out five thousand already. Do you suppose that's going on for ever? Emmy's been lying low at Springe for the last month, ready to take over the goods. In Paris it was a washout. At Nice it was a washout. And if you don't bring it off to-day it will be a washout here too. If Schalhorn is planted with the five thousand, he'll——"

"Is Schalhorn boss?" asked the Baron, sprinkling eau-de-Cologne into the palms of his hands.

"A boss should be able to do the job. That's what I say," grumbled the chauffeur.

"When the time comes, certainly. It doesn't suit me to work the way you and Schalhorn do. The two of you are always messing things up. I've never yet messed a thing up and Schalhorn has never yet been let down. If Emmy is getting nervous at Springe, she's no use to me, and so I told her last time. If she can't keep quiet in her art workshop and let Möhl get on with his copies of antique settings——"

"We don't care a curse for your copies of antiques. Get hold of the pearls first. Then you can get on with your antiques. All that's only one of your notions. It looked all right at first. The pearls are worth five hundred thousand. True enough. And after reckoning two months' expenses there'll still be something left. It may be true that we could get rid of them better in antique settings. Good. Granted. Meanwhile Möhl stays at Springe making copies of your grandmother's jewelry, Emmy's getting mad and Schalhorn's getting mad. Only don't trust to the woman, I tell you. If she loses patience she might play you a dirty trick. So what's to be done? When are you going to leave off amusing yourself and get down to business again?"

"You're getting hungry again, are you? You've forgotten the twenty-two thousand you had from Nice and now you are turning nasty, are you?" said the Baron, still in tolerably good humor; he had now put on black silk socks with white silk sock suspenders and the smart patent-leather shoes which he wore to dance in. Otherwise he was still naked.

There was something about this easy, careless nakedness that irritated the chauffeur. Perhaps it was the loose fall of the shoulders or the supple play of the ribs beneath the skin as they distended in breathing. He spat the end of his cigarette into the middle of the room and stood up.

"I don't mind telling you," he said, leaning over the table, "we're fed up with you. You can't take anything in earnest, I tell you. It isn't in you and no good will ever come out of you. Whether it's cards or betting or relieving an old dame of two and twenty thousand or collaring pearls worth five hundred thousand—it's bloody well all one to you. But there's a difference all the same, and a man who doesn't know when it's time to be in earnest isn't fit to be boss. And if you won't get on with it of your own accord, then you'll be made to. See?"

"Lie down," said Gaigern amiably, and he quietly put the chauffeur's fist aside with a little ju-jitsu grip. "I don't need your help to get on with it. All you have to do is to see to our alibi to-night. Then you can start for Springe at twelve twenty-eight with the pearls. At eight-sixteen to-morrow morning you'll be back again. I'll ring for you

you such competent fellows. It's only I who am good for
nothing, a lily of the field, eh? My chauffeur there yet,
Senf?"

He took an atmosphere of warmth with him through
the revolving door, and in the lounge all eyes followed him
with an indulgent smile. He got into his little four-seater
and went off after his alibi. At half-past ten he even rang
up the hotel from the club.

"Baron Gaigern speaking. Has anybody been to inquire for me? I'm speaking from the West End Club. I
shall not come in before two, or even later. My chauffeur
can go to bed."

At the very moment that this voice on the telephone
was establishing a gentlemanly and unpremeditated alibi
Gaigern himself was clinging to the front façade of the
Grand Hotel between two blocks of imitation sandstone.
His position was not exactly a comfortable one, yet he
enjoyed it. It filled him to overflowing with the joy of
the hunter, the fighter, and the rock climber. He had
light-heartedly kept on his blue pajamas for the undertaking, and on his feet he had light chrome-leather shoes
such as boxers wear. Over these, in case of accidents,
were woollen socks, a pair that he used for winter sports.
They were a precaution against leaving undesired footprints. Gaigern was on his way from his own window to
Grusinskaya's room. He had just short of seven meters
to go in all and he was now halfway. The sham sandstone
of the Grand Hotel was copied from the rough-hewn
blocks of the Palazzo Pitti. It looked magnificent, and as
long as it did not break away, all was well. Gaigern carefully embedded his toes in the recesses between the blocks.
He had gloves on and he was finding them a thorough
nuisance. Nor could he pull them off while he crawled
like a beetle along the wall of the second story. "Damn,"
he said as mortar and molding broke off and fell a floor

lower on to the zinc roof of a balcony. He felt his throat getting dry and he husbanded his breath like a runner on a cinder track. Once more he came to a halt, supported himself for a moment at the risk of his life on the toe of one foot, and then got the rear leg half a meter farther on. He whistled softly. He was wrought up to a high pitch now and so he whistled and kept a cool head. As to the pearls, for the sake of which he was there, no thought of them entered his head. After all he could have got hold of them in several other ways. He could have given Suzette a blow on the head when she left the theater at night with the suitcase. He could have broken into Grusinskaya's room at night. Or finally, four steps along the passage, a skeleton key, and an innocent air if he were discovered in the wrong bedroom. But that was not his way. It was not his way at all. "Everyone must do as his nature bids," as Gaigern had tried to explain to his confederates, that little band of crooks whom for two and a half years he had kept balanced on the verge of mutiny. "I don't catch game in snares. I don't go up mountains by the funicular. What I can't take with my own hands I'll do without."

Obviously talk of this kind opened up whole realms of misunderstanding between him and his accomplices. They made little account of courage, though they all had an adequate share of it. Emmy—with her trim auburn hair—had attempted an explanation. "He makes a sport of it," she said. She knew Gaigern well and probably she was right. Now, at any rate at twenty minutes past ten as he clung to the façade of the Grand Hotel, he was like a rock climber in a difficult chimney or the leader of a raid about to attack a dangerous position.

The chief danger lay in the projecting bay behind which lay Grusinskaya's bathroom. Here the architect's fancy had chosen smooth surfaces. Also there were no window ledges, for the bathroom was tucked away behind and looked out upon the courtyard where the Baron had been observed staring up at the aërials. On the other side, however, of this smooth space two and a half meters in extent was the iron railing of the balcony of room No. 68. Panting slightly and whistling and cursing by turns, Gaigern paused before making the final spring across this even surface that held him up. The muscles of his thighs quivered and his ankles felt the hot vibrating pulse beat of extreme exertion. For the rest, he was very well satisfied with his situation, and the circumstances, gone over a hundred times in his mind, answered to his expectations.

For instance, against observation from the street, which from above looked like a track swarming with ants, Gaigern was completely protected by the powerful lights recently fixed up on the hotel façade. Anyone who looked up would be blinded by the rays of white light. It would be quite impossible to see the small dark blue figure making his way along in the black shadow behind these aggressive rays. Gaigern had picked up this trick by watching a conjurer at a variety show who had in the same fashion dazzled the eyes of the audience while he executed his hocus-pocus against a velvet hanging. He had sawed women in two and made skeletons hover above the stage. Gaigern looked down on the street while he took a rest behind the second arc lamp. At this unusually sharp angle the world had a distorted and flattened appearance. The wall descending sheer from his feet looked perilous and threatening. He leaned his head forward and looked down, without venturing to breathe or wink an eyelid. He had not a trace of dizziness—only in his pulse the sweet and tingling sensation that climbers know well. The round tower of the Gaigern castle at Ried was higher than this. And in the college at Feldkirch when you broke bounds at night you had to descend the whole length of the lightning conductor. The Three Pinnacles in the Dolomites were no joke either. The two and a half meters to the balcony were not easy going, but he had been in worse places. Gaigern ceased looking down and looked upwards over the way. There was an electric sign opposite on the roof. The bubbles of a glass of champagne burst upwards in a spray of electric light. There was no sky. The city ended abruptly just above the roofs and wires and aërials. Gaigern moved his fingers inside his glove. They stuck, and probably they were bleeding. He tried his wind and found it in order again. Collecting his strength and bracing himself for the jump, he took a blind leap into vacancy. The air rushed past his ears and then he found himself hanging on by the railings of the balcony, with the corners of the iron pressing deeply into his fingers. He let himself hang there for a second with his heart thumping, then he drew himself up like an acrobat on a trapeze, got over the railing, and let go. Yes, he lay now on the balcony with the door open into Grusinskaya's room.

"There we are," he said with satisfaction, and for the moment lay where he was on the narrow cement-floored balcony and recovered his breath. Far overhead he heard the engine of an aëroplane and then he saw straight above his eyes the gleam of its lighted cabin moving across the lurid haze that hung over the city. The street below sent up its loud confused roar. For a few minutes Gaigern lay as though on an island of exhaustion and semi-consciousness, while beneath him motor cars hooted impatiently to reach the entrance, for the League of Humanity was giving a banquet in the Little Salon and women in opera cloaks were creeping like colored beetles out of closed motor cars and ascending the three steps into the second entrance of the hotel. Lord, what wouldn't I give for a cigarette, thought Gaigern, but this relief to his exhausted nerves was out of the question. He pulled the glove off his right hand and sucked the cut on his forefinger. A bleeding paw would never do for the job he was on. The thin metallic taste vexed him. He felt the welcome coolness of the cement against his moist back. The return journey would be more difficult, he reflected, and looking through the railing of the balcony he measured the distance with his eye. He had a rope with him. He would have to attach it to the balcony and swing himself across. "Congratulations," he said to himself in the smart officer's voice of his army days. He pulled on his glove again as though he were about to pay a ceremonious call and getting up stepped from the balcony into Grusinskaya's bedroom.

The French window did not stir, only the curtain swayed gently in the air. The parquet floor, too, was pleasingly silent. Two clocks ticked in the dark room, one nearly twice as fast as the other. There was a surprising scent, suggestive of a funeral or a cremation. From the electric sign over the way a triangle of yellow light fell on the floor and extended as far as the edge of the carpet. Gaigern took out his pocket torch, an ordinary cylindrical torch. With this he proceeded cautiously to look round the room. Thanks to his brief dialogue with Suzette on the threshold he had its shape and furniture in his head. He was prepared to counter every artful dodge and to bring the pearls to light wherever they might be concealed, to force trunks, break open cupboards, and to unravel the secret of any lock. But when he had followed the circular light of the torch round the room and encountered his own face three times in the dressing-table mirror, he had an almost comic surprise.

On the dressing table by the mirror lay the suitcase quite peacefully, innocently reflecting the light of the torch from its leather surface. Steady, thought Gaigern, pulling himself together, for the excitement of the chase began to rush to his head. First he put his right hand into his right

pocket for safe custody, for it was still bleeding and there
it would have to remain to prevent it making mischief
and leaving traces behind. He held the torch between his
teeth. With his gloved left hand he carefully laid hold of
the suitcase. Yes, there it was. His fingers rested on the
smooth and polished leather. He turned out the torch
and put it down, and then paused for reflection. There was
an oppressive funereal smell suggestive of the interment of
a deceased grandfather and a funeral oration. Gaigern
began to laugh in the darkness when he hit on the explanation. "Laurels," he remembered, recalling Suzette's voice.
"Madame has had laurels sent her, monsieur. The French
ambassador sent a whole basketful." He knelt down in
front of the dressing table—now the floor creaked ominously as if it were alive—and grasped the case with his left
hand in the darkness. No, no, he thought, and let it go
again. Such things brought bad luck. Pocketbooks, cases,
purses—they were all sinister things. They had a tendency
to refuse to be burnt, to emerge again from the rivers into
which they were thrown, to be discovered in drains by
sewer men, and finally to be laid most disconcertingly on
the table during criminal proceedings. Also, it was not very
pleasant to face two and a half meters across a surface as
smooth as ice with a suitcase weighing about four pounds
between one's teeth. Gaigern drew back his hand and
thought again. He turned on the torch and gazed at the
two locks of the little case in deep absorption. God alone
knows what secret mechanism kept Grusinskaya's treasure
safely shut up there. As an experiment Gaigern took out a
tool and pressed on the round brass disc of the lock.

The lock sprang up.

The case was not locked at all!

Gaigern started at the snap of the spring. It was so
utterly unexpected that his face for the moment looked

perfectly blank. "Well, that's good," he said to himself three or four times. "Well, that's good." He raised the lid and opened the jewel case. Yes, there lay Grusinskaya's pearls.

They were no more after all than a little heap of baubles, very little, if you think of it, compared with all the tales that had been spread abroad about this gift of a murdered grand duke for the adornment of a dancer's neck. An old-fashioned and charming *sautoir* and a rope of medium-sized but perfectly matched pearls, three rings, two earrings with incredibly round and large pearls—there they lay idly in their little bed of velvet while the torch waked their slumbering reflections. Taking every precaution, Gaigern removed them from their case with his gloved left hand and put them in his pocket. It struck him as so ridiculous to have come upon these pearls lying open and unprotected that he felt a reaction almost of sobering disappointment. He was exhausted after tremendous exertions, which after all were superfluous. For a moment he even wondered whether he might not simply regain his room along the passage. Perhaps they have left the bedroom door open as well, he thought, with the incredulity which since his first sight of the pearls had kept his upper teeth exposed in a foolish and childish smile.

The door, however, was locked. In the corridor the lift could be heard ascending at irregular intervals and the gate closing with a click, for No. 68 was very nearly opposite it. Gaigern sat for a few moments in an arm chair in the dark and collected his strength for the return journey. His longing for a cigarette was maddening. But he did not dare smoke in case the smell left a clue. He was as cautious as a savage who guards himself against a taboo. He thought of many things at once and, most clearly of all, of his father's gun cupboard. At the top of the cupboard the tin boxes containing the Balkan tobacco were always kept and in each box the old Baron put every three days a small slice of carrot. Gaigern's thoughts were wafted to his home and this sweet sharp scent; he was running down the worn steps at Ried and he lost count of time while he fancied himself in the nook where as a seventeen-year-old cadet he used to lie hidden and smoke. He came back with a jolt to the job in hand. "Look alive, Flix," he said to himself. "Don't go to sleep, but get on with it." He gave himself nicknames now and then, encouraged himself, treated himself tenderly and praised or scolded his own limbs. "You swine," he said reproachfully to his cut finger, which went on bleeding and sticking to his glove. "You swine, can't you leave me in peace." And he clapped his thighs as if they were horses and praised them. "You're fine fellows. Fine, good beasts. Look alive, Flix."

Leaving the scent of laurel in No. 68 behind, he put his nose out on to the balcony and sniffed. There was that indefinable smell of Berlin in March, gasoline mingled with the dampness of the Tiergarten, and as he pushed past the gently swelling curtain he had already observed that something was not as it should be. It took a few seconds before he realized what it was—his face and body were lighted up in a way they had not been before. He saw the silken reflections on the sleeves of his pajamas and shrank back with the rapidity of instinct into the darkness of the room, like a beast which, after scenting the breeze at the edge of a clearing, glides back into the darkness of the forest. And there he stood, breathing quickly and straining every nerve. The ticking of the two clocks came to him with an extreme clearness and then from some distant part of the great city the hour struck faintly from a church tower—eleven o'clock. The walls of the houses across the street were bright and dark by turns as the electric signs winked on and off again. "Damn the luck,"

Gaigern muttered, and went out on to the balcony. This
time he gave rein to his exasperation as fully and freely
as if No. 68 had been his own room.

The big electric lamps on the front of the hotel had
gone out. The new installation had gone wrong again.
In the little banqueting room the League of Humanity
sat in darkness, and in the cellar electricians were busy
with the switches without avail. Below in the street a
small crowd stood and stared with delight at the hotel
front, where the four arc lights went spasmodically on and
off. Among them was a policeman. Traffic was held up and
motor cars were loudly showing their impatience. The
electric signs opposite were in full play, proclaiming
brands of champagne and doing their utmost to illuminate
the hotel front. Finally two men in blue overalls crept out
of a window of the story below, established themselves on
the glass roof over the main entrance, and began to in-
vestigate the faulty wires. Now that the hotel front was a
center of interest the way back across those seven meters
of it was finally blocked.

Congratulations, thought Gaigern again, and laughed
angrily. Here I am, and if I want to get out I shall have
to break open the door.

He took out his tools and the torch and began, with all
due precaution, to fiddle about with the keyhole; but
without success. A dressing gown hanging near the door
fell to the ground. It touched his face softly as it fell and
the fright it gave him was beyond all bounds. He felt the
arteries of his neck pulsing like machines. The corridor,
too, outside was in a stir. Footsteps went to and fro, people
coughed, the lift gate clicked as the lift went up and
down, a chambermaid called out and ran past and another
one called back. Gaigern gave up the refractory door and
stole out again on to the balcony. Three meters below the
two electricians straddled about on the glass roof with

wires in their mouths. They were being watched with great interest from the street. Gaigern committed one of his characteristic audacities. Leaning over the railings he called out: "What's up with the light?"

"Short circuit," said one of the men.

"How long will it be?" asked Gaigern. A shrug of the shoulders was the only reply. Idiots, thought Gaigern savagely. The pompous self-importance of these two bunglers on the glass roof annoyed him intensely. Anyway, in ten minutes they'll leave off, he thought, and after looking down at them for a short while he retired again into the room. Suddenly the sense of danger came over him, but it lasted only for a second and then died away. And there he stood in the middle of the room in his socks. At least they would leave no footprints to betray him.

Well, at all events, I mustn't go to sleep, he thought. To cheer himself up he felt for the pearls in his pocket. They were warm from his body. He took off his gloves so as to feel their smoothness and to realize how precious they were. The touch of them delighted him. At the same moment, it occurred to him that his chauffeur could not now catch the train for Springe and that a new timetable would have to be made. Nothing went according to plan. The pearls instead of giving any trouble had been left in an unlocked case, and now, in revenge, all was up with his little climb.

A thought that made him laugh interrupted his reflections.

What a woman, he thought. What a very odd sort of woman to leave her pearls lying about like that. He shook his head in astonishment and laughed louder. He knew plenty of women. He found them pleasing enough, but nothing wonderful, and he thought it wonderful that a woman should go out and leave all she possessed in front of a window opening on to a balcony, for anyone to take who chose. She must be a regular happy-go-lucky gipsy, he thought. Or else she must have a great heart, he answered himself. And now in spite of all he felt sleepy. He went in the darkness to the door and picked up the dressing gown which had fallen to the ground a few minutes before and smelt it inquisitively. An unfamiliar bitter-sweet scent came from it, but it did not at all suggest the woman in a muslin ballet costume at whose performances Gaigern had been bored on innumerable occasions. In any case, he wished Grusinskaya nothing but good. He found her quite sympathetic. He hung the dressing gown up carelessly, leaving ten casual fingerprints on the silk, and strolled out on to the balcony again to kill time. The two blue bats were still flapping about over their short circuit. Gaigern wished himself a pleasant time of it and then took up his station between the lace hangings and the door curtain, as erect and alert as a sentry in a sentry box, to await further developments.

KRINGELEIN blinked at the stage through his glasses. A lot of puzzling things were happening over there and it was all going much too fast. He would have liked very much to see one of the girls more clearly, a short dark one in the second row who was always smiling. But there was no chance. There were no pauses in Grusinskaya's ballet. It was a perpetual shimmer as they kept flitting in and out and round one another. Sometimes the girls formed up in lines on either side of the stage, touching the edge of their skirts with downward curving hands, and left room for Grusinskaya herself.

Then she came pirouetting to the front on her toes. Her face and arms were white as wax, and her toes as rigid and steady on the floor of the stage as if they were screwed tightly into it. At last it was impossible to see her face any longer. She became nothing but a whirl of white with silver stripes and Kringelein felt a little seasick before the dance was over. "Marvelous," he said with astonishment. "Splendid. What suppleness of leg. That's first-class. You can only marvel at that." And he marveled gladly, though he felt far from well.

"Do you really enjoy it?" asked Dr. Otternschlag gloomily. He sat in the box and turned the damaged side of his face to the stage. It looked ghastly in the yellow stage lighting which extended far enough to illumine it.

It was difficult for Kringelein to answer this "really."
Actually ever since he had moved into No. 70 nothing was
real to him any longer. Everything was like a fevered
dream. Everything went much too fast. Nothing stayed
long enough to be enjoyed. At his urgent request for in-
struction and companionship, Otternschlag had taken
him round the usual sights—a drive round Berlin, the
Museum, Potsdam, and finally even up the wireless
tower, the Funkturm, where the wind blew a hurricane and
Berlin lay below under a pall of smoke pricked out with
lights. Kringelein would not have been surprised if he had
wakened out of the deep trance of an anæsthetic to find
himself in his hospital bed again. His feet were cold, his
hands cramped, and his jaws clenched. His head was like a
burning cauldron and all the thousand and one things
thrown into it began to sizzle and melt.

"Well, are you content? Are you happy now? Are you
getting to know life?" Otternschlag asked from time to
time. And Kringelein stoutly and obediently answered,
"Yes, rather!"

On this evening, the fifth of Grusinskaya's appearance,
the theater was poorly patronized. It was positively
empty. The stalls were so scantily occupied that they
looked ragged and moth-eaten, and the one or two people
in the front row felt isolated and self-conscious amid so
many empty seats. Kringelein felt the same. Except for
the stage box, which he had taken at Otternschlag's
advice—Kringelein wished from now onwards always to
have the best seats, at the cinema far back, at the theater
well in the front and for the ballet the front row—except
for their box, which had cost him forty marks, only one
other was occupied and this by the impresario, Meyerheim. Meyerheim had dispensed with the *claque* for this
performance. It no longer justified itself and the deficit
was already big enough. There was a slight outburst of

applause before the interval. Pimenov quickly rang up the curtain, and Grusinskaya came to the front of the stage and smiled. She smiled to a silent house, for the feeble applause had forthwith expired and everyone trooped out to the buffet. Something, too, expired in Grusinskaya's face as she stood there to acknowledge an ovation which after all was denied her. Her skin went cold beneath the sweat and the paint. Witte threw down his baton and rushed on to the stage up the iron steps. He was anxious about Elisaveta. He found Pimenov standing there as though at a funeral, while scene shifters dumped down bits of scenery right against his lean old bowed back in its old dress coat. He was always in full dress for every evening performance, as though any evening the Grand Duke Sergei might summon him to his box. Michael, with a leopard skin of spotted plush over his left shoulder and bare powdered legs, was waiting with a despondent air near the stage manager. They were all in trembling anticipation of an outbreak from Grusinskaya. They were trembling actually and literally—knees, hands, shoulders, teeth.

"Forgive me, madame," Michael said in a whisper. "*Pardonnez moi.* It was my fault, I put you out——"

Grusinskaya came with an absent-minded air through the dust and noise made by the shifting of the scenery, trailing her old woollen cloak, and when she stood still and looked at Michael there was a meekness in her face that frightened every one of them.

"You? Oh no, my dear," she said gently, when she had mastered the breaking of her voice and collected her breath, which the last exacting dance had exhausted. "You were very good. You are in very good form to-day. So am I. We were all good——"

She turned abruptly and walked quickly away, taking her unfinished sentence with her into the darkness at the back of the stage. Witte did not venture to follow her. Grusinskaya sat down on a step of gilt wood that lay at the back among a lot more stage lumber and there she sat during the whole time the scene was being changed. At first she clasped her hands round her right calf in the silk fleshings. Mechanically she retied the crossed strings of the ballet shoe. For a few minutes she stroked this tired, silken, and slightly soiled leg as though it were an animal—with unthinking compassion. A little while after she took her hands from there and put them round her bare neck. She missed the pearls keenly. Often and often it had calmed her to let them slip through her fingers like a rosary. What more? What more do you want, she thought deeply within herself. I have never danced so well as now. Not when I was young, not in the Petersburg days, not in Paris, not in America. I was stupid in those days and not very industrious. Now—oh, now I work. Now I know. Now I can dance. What more do you want of me? More still? More I have not got. Must I give the pearls away? Surrender them? Well, I'm ready to. Oh, leave me alone—all of you. I am tired.

"Michael," she whispered. She recognized his shadowy form as it glided past the back of the drop scene.

"Madame," answered Michael with cautious reserve. He had changed his costume and now wore a brown velvet doublet and carried a bow and arrow in his hand, for he was dancing his Archer Dance after the interval.

"Aren't you going to get ready, Gru?" he asked, carefully avoiding a sympathetic tone, when he saw how small and crumpled she looked as she sat huddled up amidst the lumber. The manager's bells rang from eight places at once.

"Michael, I am tired," said Grusinskaya, "I want to go home. Lucille can dance my numbers. It won't matter to anyone. They don't care whether it is I who dance or someone else."

Michael started so violently that he stiffened in every muscle. Grusinskaya, sitting on the step with his knee close to her face, saw the magnificent muscle of his thighs distend, and this involuntary movement in a body she knew so well comforted her a little. Michael had gone pale under his paint. "Nonsense," he said. He was rude from dismay.

Grusinskaya smiled tenderly. She put out a finger and tapped Michael on the leg.

"How often have I to tell you to dance in tights," she said with unusual tenderness in her voice. "You will never really warm up, never be really supple without tights. Believe me when I tell you that, you—revolutionary." She let her hand rest for a few seconds on the warm powdered and youthful skin beneath which his fine muscles stood out. But no, the touch communicated no strength. The bell sounded for the third time. On the other side of the drop scene, with its painting of a little temple, the ballet shoes of the dancers were already scraping over the floor of the stage. Suzette was running up and down the dressing-room passage in an agony like a strayed hen, because Madame sat there instead of changing her costume. Witte, standing at the conductor's desk, took his baton with trembling hand and waited with a set face for the red light which ought before this to have signaled the commencement of the next dance.

"What are you thinking of?" asked Dr. Otternschlag in the box above. Kringelein just at that moment was thinking of Fredersdorf and of the patch of sunlight which on summer afternoons fell on the shabby green wall of the dingy general office. But he came back at once, and very gladly, to Berlin and the Theater des Westens, to the tinsel and glamour of life and his red plush box at forty marks.

"Homesick?" asked Otternschlag.

"No question of that," replied Kringelein with all the callousness of a man of the world.

Witte below raised his baton and the music began.

"Rotten orchestra," said Otternschlag, who was getting heartily sick of his rôle of an amiable mentor and finding the ballet more and more depressing. But this time Kringelein refused to be distracted. The music was just what he wanted. He sank into it as he did into his hot bath at the hotel. He had a chill and heavy feeling in his stomach like a lump of lead. It was a bad symptom, the doctor had said. It did not hurt in the least. It kept to that unpleasant state when a pain is expected but does not come. That was all. That was the only sign death made him. And then came the music to console him a little with its pianissimo on the flutes above the tremolo of the violas. Kringelein's spirits rose, and he floated away on the music, right away into a blue moonlit landscape where a temple was painted on a seacoast, which was painted too.

The program proceeded. Michael as an archer appeared with his snow-white calves and brown velvet doublet. He braced his youthful body and shot with a leap across the stage. He sprang high into the air as though on wires. His gestures made it clear that he wished to shoot a bird, a dove that belonged to the temple. After a prodigal display of leaps and spins he finally vanished into the wings after his arrow.

Applause. *Pizzicato* on the orchestra. Grusinskaya made her appearance on the stage. After all, in breathless haste she had put on the costume of the wounded dove. A large ruby-red drop of blood trembled on her white silk bodice. She is utterly tired out but as light as air, and her arms move in rapid and tremulous wing beats while she gradually glides towards her piteous death. Three times she rallies but she can fly no longer. At last her long delicate neck falls forward, she lays her head on her knees and dies, a poor dove shot through the heart. A shaft of limelight through a disc of blue glass is directed upon her wound.

Curtain and applause. There was even fairly vigorous applause considering how empty the theater was and how few there were to clap. "Encore?" asked Grusinskaya without stirring from her pose. "No," whispered Pimenov in a loud and desperate whisper from the wings. The applause was over. It was over. Grusinskaya still lay where she was for a few minutes like a flake of foam, just as she had died in her dance and with the dust of the stage on her hands and arms and temples. For the first time in her life there was no encore for this dance. I can do no more, she thought. No, I have done enough. I can do no more.

"Clear the stage for the next scene," shouted the stage manager. Grusinskaya had no wish to get up. She wished to lie there in the middle of the stage and to fall asleep— to sleep and forget it all. At last Michael came and raised her to her feet. "*Spassibo*—thank you," she said in Russian, and walked stiffly away to the ladies' dressing rooms. Michael took the nearest way through the wings to the left and made himself ready for the *Pas de deux*.

Grusinskaya stole away to her dressing room and pushed the door open with the toe of her ballet shoe. Sinking into a chair in front of the looking glass, she fixed her eyes on the shoe's dusty and somewhat worn silk. Her feet were weary, unutterably weary. They were heavy and they had had their fill and more than their fill of dancing. In the mirror beneath the glare of the electric light she saw Suzette's old and careworn face. The costume for the *Pas de deux* rustled in her hands.

"Leave me alone," Grusinskaya whispered hoarsely. "I am not well. I can't go on again. Leave me alone, everyone. Give me something to drink," she added, however. She wanted to strike Suzette in her worn and

console her. Suddenly she stopped with a start. What am
I doing, she thought. I have run away from the theater,
I can't have done that. It isn't possible. I must go back.
A church clock struck eleven slowly and clearly close at
hand, though no church tower was to be seen. Grusinskaya
took her hands from the pockets of her cloak and let them
fall in front of her. The gesture recalled the death of the
wounded dove. Too late, the gesture said. The performance
must be just ending. Grusinskaya threw back her head
and looked at the street she was in, and found that she did
not know where she was. She saw a small entrance framed
in blue and yellow electric lights and over it the words:
"Russian Bar." She went across and stood at the door.
She blew her nose like a child while she made up her mind.
Russian Bar, she thought. Suppose I go in? They would
recognize me, and the red-shirted orchestra would play the
Grusinskaya Waltz. What a sensation.

No sensation whatever, she thought wretchedly a
moment later. I can't go in looking as I do. And perhaps
I shouldn't be recognized any longer. Besides, if they did
recognize me—looking as I do now—*tant pis, tant pis.*

She signaled to an old rattletrap of a taxi and, with a
face that was suddenly fixed and cold, had herself driven
to the hotel.

Gaigern stood like a sentry between the curtains and
the lace hangings in room No. 68 and waited for the men
in blue overalls down below to finish their job. But instead
of this they went on crawling to and fro on the window
ledges of the first story. They had been for wire and
pincers and they called out to each other with much zeal,
but still the lights did not go on. Consequently the whole
front of the hotel was all the better illuminated by the arc
lights in the street, by the lighting of its five entrances,
and by the electric signs opposite which advertised now a

brand of champagne, now a variety of chocolate. Moreover Gaigern had not been standing there waiting more
than twenty minutes before the door of No. 68 opened.
The light was turned on and by the very modest illumina-
tion peculiar to hotel bedrooms he saw Grusinskaya enter
the room.

This from Gaigern's point of view was a thoroughly
rotten business. The shock of it went through him like
cold steel. What on earth was the woman doing in the
hotel at twenty minutes past eleven? What could you do
when you could not even count on the length of a theater
performance? His luck was out, he thought with clenched
teeth. Gaigern had a dread of bad luck. And now what but
bad luck could account for these cursed complications in
which he seemed to be trapped? The light from the room
penetrated the lace curtain behind which he stood and
imprinted the shadow of its openwork pattern on the
balcony. There was nothing for it but to calm himself and
keep his heart up. The string of pearls in his pocket had
taken in the warmth of his body. They ran like peas
through his fingers. For a moment it seemed to him
idiotic and absurd that this handful of pearl-colored grains
should be worth a fortune. Four months of lying in wait,
seven meters at the risk of his life, and no sooner was one
risk over than a new one took its place. One danger after
another. His life was nothing but a string of dangers. And
the life of this Grusinskaya was a string of pearls. Gaigern
shook his head and laughed in spite of the fix he was in.
Gaigern was no thinker. Life often made him laugh with
astonished amazement, almost simple-mindedly, for it was
somewhat beyond his comprehension. Now, at any rate,
he pulled himself together and, turning towards the room
behind the lace curtains, he proceeded to wait.

First Grusinskaya stood motionless for nearly a minute
in the middle of the room just below the glass-shaded hang-

ing light and it seemed from her face that she had lost
herself. She stood there till her cloak fell of its own weight
from her drooping arms, and then she stepped over it to
the telephone on the table. It was a minute or so before she
got through to the theater and again a minute or two before she got Pimenov, but she was too utterly weary to be
impatient.·

"Hallo, Pimenov. Yes, it's Grusinskaya. I am in the
hotel. You must forgive me. Yes, I was unwell suddenly.
My heart, you know. I could scarcely breathe. Yes, like
that time in Scheveningen. No, I'm better now. It must
have put you in a fix, I know. How did Lucille get on?
What? Oh, fair. And the audience? What's that? No, I
am not upset. You can tell me if there was a scene. No?
No scene at all? Went off quietly? Not much applause?
A different program, you think? Good. We'll talk it over.
No, I'm going to bed. No, no doctor, please. Nor Witte
either. No, no, no, I want nobody. Not Suzette either. I
only want to be left in peace. You will drive, please, to the
French Embassy and make my excuses. Thank you. Good-
night, my dear. Good-night, Pimenov! Listen, Pimenov, my
greetings to Witte and to Michael too and all the rest as
well. No, don't worry about me. I shall be all right to-
morrow. Good-night."

She replaced the receiver on its hook. "Good-night,
my dear," she said softly after she had done so, standing
alone in the hotel bedroom.

So it was her heart, thought Gaigern. She was unwell.
It had needed all his attention to follow the rapid French
words. So that was why she had turned up at this worst
of all possible moments. She looked wretched certainly.
All to the good, for she would go to sleep and then there
would be a hope of taking his leave of her. The great thing
was to keep calm. He moved cautiously to the edge of the
balcony and looked over. The two idiots in blue were

sitting there in consultation. They had hung up two fine dark lanterns and looked as if they were prepared to put in the entire night on overtime. Gaigern's craving for a cigarette reached the pitch of disease. He opened his mouth wide and took in a gulp of damp gasoline-laden air. Inside the room meanwhile, Grusinskaya had come up to the cheval glass with its two wings. The plundered suitcase lay in front of it. Gaigern's heart suddenly thumped in his chest. However, she pushed the leather case aside without a glance at it, and turning on the light over the center of the mirror she grasped its frame with both hands and pressed her face close up to the glass, as though she meant to plunge right into it. The attention with which she then studied her face had something probing, greedy, and gruesome about it. Odd creatures, women, thought Gaigern behind the curtain. Strange animals. What can she see in the glass to make such a frightful face over?

He himself saw her as a beautiful woman, undeniably beautiful, even though the paint on her cheeks began to run. Her neck, above all, reflected twice over in the side mirrors, was incomparably delicate and flexible. Grusinskaya fixed her eyes on her face as though on the face of an enemy. With horror she saw the tell-tale years, the wrinkles, the flabbiness, the fatigue, the withering; her temples were smooth no longer, the corners of her mouth were disfigured, her eyelids, under the blue paint, were as creased as crumpled tissue paper. Another fit of shuddering, more violent than the previous one in the street, came over her while she looked at herself. She tried to bandage her lips but could not succeed. She hurried across the room and hastily turned out the uncompromising light suspended from the ceiling and turned on the table lamp, but even this did not lend any warmth. With a few impatient movements she tore off her costume and went naked, but for the tights that covered her as far as her hips, to the radiator and leant her breast against the gray-colored pipes. She scarcely thought at all as she did so. She only desired warmth. Enough, she thought, enough. Never again. Finished. Enough. She whispered her irrevocable decision in every language, her teeth chattering all the while. She went into the bathroom and undressed completely. She held her hands under the hot tap and let the warmth flow over her arteries till it began to hurt. She took a friction brush and rubbed her shoulders with it. Then, suddenly, she left off in a fit of disgust and came back naked and shivering and went straight across the room to the telephone. She had to put her lips twice to the telephone before she could speak.

"Tea," she said. "A lot of tea and a lot of sugar."

Then, still naked, she went to the looking glass and looked in it with gloomy intensity. Her body, however, was of unique and faultless beauty. It was the body of a sixteen-year-old ballet pupil, which the severe and disciplined work of a lifetime had preserved unaltered. Suddenly the hatred she felt for herself changed into tenderness. She clasped her shoulders and stroked their smooth sheen. She kissed the hollow of her right arm and hollowed her hands like shells to receive her small and perfect breasts. She stroked the delicate upward curve of her stomach and her slender shadowed hips. She bent her head down and kissed her poor slim sinewy knees as though they were sick children whom she loved. "*Bjednaiaia, malenkaia,*" she murmured to them. It was an endearment of her early days. Poor little one, it meant.

Unconsciously Gaigern, between the curtains, showed pity and admiration in his face. He was embarrassed by what he saw. He knew many women, but he had never seen one whose body was so delicately and perfectly formed. Yet this was really a secondary consideration. It was the helplessness, the lost and tremulous despair of this pitiful Grusinskaya as she stood before the looking glass, that impressed him most. It inspired a sweet and painful sympathy and made him flush to his ears. Though he was a crook, ready to carry off stolen pearls worth 500,000 marks in his pocket, Gaigern was far from being inhuman.

He let go of the pearls and took his hands out of his pockets. He felt in his hands and in his arms a compelling desire to support this poor lonely woman, to take her away and console and warm her—to do anything to put a stop to her terrible shuddering and her whispering of an almost crazed despair.

The waiter knocked at the outer door. Grusinskaya put on her dressing gown—the same one that had startled Gaigern in the darkness—and went to the door in her worn slippers. The tea was discreetly handed in and Grusinskaya locked the door behind the retreating waiter. It had come to this, she thought. She poured out a cup of tea and took a packet of veronal from the bedside table. She swallowed a tablet, drank some tea, and then took a second. She got up and began to walk rapidly to and fro across the room, four paces this way, four paces that.

What is the use of it all? she thought. What is the use of living? What is there to wait for? Why endure the torture? Oh, I am tired. You don't know, any of you, how tired I am. I promised myself to leave off when the time came. *Tiens*, the time has come. Am I to wait till I am hissed off the stage? It is time, *malenkaia*—poor little one. Gru is not going to go to Vienna to-morrow. Gru gives up. Gru is going to sleep. You don't know how cold it is to be famous. Not a soul to care for me, not one. They all live on me. Nobody lives for me. Nobody. Not one. I know no one who is not either vain or anxious. I have always been alone. And who troubles about a Grusinskaya who dances no more? Finished. No, I shall not parade about Monte Carlo, stiff and fat and old like the other famous women who have grown old. "You should have seen me in the days when the Grand Duke Sergei was still alive!" No, that is not for me. And where else am I to go? To Tremezzo to grow orchids, to keep two white peacocks, to have money troubles and to be alone, utterly alone, and to rusticate and die? That is what it comes to at last—to die. Nijinsky is in an asylum waiting to die. Poor Nijinsky! Poor Gru! I am not going to wait. The moment has come—now—now—now—now——

She stood still and listened as though she heard her name called. The veronal was already humming drowsily in her ears and its narcotic influence subdued her to a welcome indifference. Gaston, she thought as she went to the table. Dear Gaston, you were good to me once. How young you were! And how long ago it is! Now you are a minister, fat and bearded and sleek. *Adieu, Gaston. Adieu pour jamais, n'est-ce pas?* There is such an easy way of growing no older. . . .

Grusinskaya poured out another cup of tea. She was now posing a little, playing in sweet sadness a little tragic scene. There was a manner and a grace in her despairing resolve. With a rapid gesture she took the bottle of veronal tablets and emptied them all into her tea and then waited for them to melt. It took too long and she tapped them impatiently with the teaspoon. Then getting up she went once more to the looking glass and began unconsciously powdering her face which was of a sudden beaded with cold sweat. Her lips ceased trembling and assumed the fixed stage smile. She put her hands in front of her face and whispered: "God! God! God!" Now too she noticed the funereal scent which rose from the baskets of faded flowers and hung in the air of the room. She went over unsteadily to the table and tasted the cup of tea with the tip of the spoon. The taste was very bitter. She dropped in one lump of sugar after another with the sugar tongs and

waited for them to melt. This took a minute or perhaps
longer. In the stillness the clock and the watch raced each
other breathlessly.

Grusinskaya got up and went to the door on to the
balcony. Her breath came with difficulty and she had a
longing to look at the sky. She drew back the lace curtain
and collided with a shadowy figure.

"Please do not be alarmed, madame," Gaigern said
with a bow.

Grusinskaya's first movement was not one of alarm,
but—oddly enough—of shame. She drew her kimono more
closely round her and looked mutely at Gaigern as though
deeply puzzled. What is this? she thought dreamily.
Surely I have been through this before? Perhaps she even
felt a certain relief at this postponement of the draught of
veronal. She stood thus gazing at Gaigern for nearly a
minute while her finely penciled arched eyebrows met
above the bridge of her nose. Her lips still trembled, and
her breath was drawn sharply between them in little gasps.

Gaigern, too, felt his teeth beginning to chatter, but
he controlled them perfectly. He had never been in such
extreme danger as at this moment. All his previous enterprises—there had been only three or four of them—
had been carefully prepared and so cautiously executed
that not even the faintest suspicion had fallen on him.
And now there he stood, caught red-handed in another
person's bedroom with pearls worth 500,000 marks in his
pocket, and nothing lay between him and imprisonment
but the little white bell push surmounted by the enameled
tablet requesting you to ring twice for the valet. An access
of sheer fury seized him, but he did not allow it to escape
him. He kept it under, till it turned to strength and calm.
It cost him a tremendous effort not to strike the woman
to the ground. He was like a powerful locomotive under

steam, fueled and charged with atmospheric pressure caus-
ing it to vibrate from the center through every part, and
ready to launch itself with irresistible impetus.

Meanwhile he made his bow. He might have made a wild
dash for the hotel façade. He might have struck Grusinskaya dead or silenced her with threats. It was the prompt-
ing of his good nature that chose a bow, an unpremeditated
but courteous bow, instead of murder and violence. He
did not know that he had gone a bluish white under the
eyes. Remotely he was aware even of danger as an enjoy-
ment, like intoxication or the bottomless abyss of a dream.

"Who are you? How did you come here?" Grusinskaya
asked in German. Her tone was almost polite.

"Pardon me, *gnädige Frau*, I stole into your room. I
am—it is terrible that you should have found me here.
You came in earlier than usual. It is my bad luck. I can
give you no explanation."

Grusinskaya stepped back a pace or two into the room,
without taking her eyes off him, and turned on the cold
light of the chandelier that hung from the ceiling. Very
likely she might have called for help if it had been a rough
and ugly man that she had discovered on her balcony.
But this man, the handsomest man she had ever seen in
her life—as she now brought to mind through a cloud of
veronal—caused her no alarm. Strangely enough it was
Gaigern's charming blue silk pajamas that more than all
filled her with confidence.

"But what did you want here?" she asked, and involuntarily she lapsed into the more familiar French.

"Nothing. Only to sit here. Only to be in your room,"
he said softly. He took a deep breath. There was nothing
for it now but to tell the woman a fairy tale. He could see
that, with a faint gleam of hope. The tell-tale socks over
his shoes worried him; adroitly and surreptitiously he
stepped on each in turn and pulled them off.

Grusinskaya shook her head. "In my room? *Mon Dieu!*
What for?" she asked in her high-pitched bird-like Russian
voice, while a strange look of expectancy shone in her face.

Gaigern, still on the balcony, replied: "I will tell you
the truth, madame. It's not the first time I have been in
your room. Many a time I have sat in your room when you
were at the theater. I have breathed the air you breathe.
I have left flowers for you. Forgive me——"

The tea with the veronal in it was cold. Grusinskaya
smiled faintly, but she was no sooner conscious of doing so
than she recovered herself and asked severely, "And who
let you in? The chambermaid? Suzette? How did you get
in?"

Gaigern resolved on a bold stroke. He pointed behind
him into the night. "From there," he said, "from my
balcony."

Again Grusinskaya had the feeling, as though in a dream,
of having been through this before. Suddenly the memory
came back. One evening at a castle in the south, down in
Abas Tuman, where the Grand Duke Sergei used to take
her, a young officer, a mere boy, had hidden himself in her
room. It was at the risk of his life, and indeed he died later
through a mysterious accident while out shooting. It was
thirty years ago at least. This forgotten incident suddenly
came back to her as she stepped out on to the balcony, and
looked out in the direction in which Gaigern had pointed.
She saw the young officer's face. Pavel Jerylinkov was his
name. She remembered his eyes and one or two kisses too.
The air was cold and she felt at once that the man beside
her on the little balcony radiated warmth. She gave a
fleeting glance to the seven meters of the hotel front that
parted her balcony from the next one.

"But that is very dangerous," she said aimlessly, thinking more of Jerylinkov than of the present moment.

"Not very," replied Gaigern.

the woman to the ground, into a simple, good-natured, big-hearted man who could not see a woman weep without wishing to come to her help. He lost all trace of fear on his own account, and if his heart beat quickly it was simply from pity. He went over to the bed and resting his arms on either side of the little sobbing body he bent over her and mingled his whispered consolations with her sobs. He had nothing particular to say. He would have comforted a crying child or a hurt animal in much the same words. "Poor little woman," he said. "Poor little woman, poor little Grusinskaya, she's crying. It does you good, doesn't it, to cry? Then cry, poor little hurt creature. What have they done to you? Have they ill-treated you? Are you glad I'm here? Shall I stay? Are you afraid of anything? Is that why you cry? Oh, you poor little thing."

He raised one arm from the bed and took the clasped hands from her mouth and kissed them; they were wet with tears and black like the hands of a little girl; her face too was stained with the trickles of black paint from her make-up. This made Gaigern laugh. In spite of her tears Grusinskaya observed the hearty movement of the shoulders that a strong man makes when he laughs. Gaigern left her bed and went into the bathroom. He came back with a sponge and carefully wiped her face. He had fetched a towel too. Now Grusinskaya lay still. She had had her cry out and was content. Gaigern sat on the edge of the bed and smiled at her.

"Well?" he asked.

Grusinskaya whispered something that he did not understand. "Say it again," he begged her.

"You—man," Grusinskaya whispered.

The word went home. It hit on his heart like a tennis ball in fast play. It almost hurt him. The women with whom he usually had to do had no great range of endearments. They called him Schnurzi, Bubi, Darling, or the

"Big Baron." He heard an echo in his soul as though from his childhood, from a world he had left behind. He shut his ears to it. If only I had a cigarette, he thought, feeling that he was getting tender-hearted. Grusinskaya had looked in his eyes for a moment with a strangely melting and almost happy expression. Now she got up and angled with her long toes for the slippers which had fallen from her feet. She recovered her self-possession.

"There, there," said she. "What a sentimental scene. Grusinskaya weeping. That is a sight worth seeing. It is many years since she did such a thing. Monsieur gave me a bad fright. It is he who is responsible for this painful scene."

She spoke in the third person, wishing to put a distance between them, but after what had passed it was not easy to do so. Gaigern had nothing to say in reply.

"It is frightful how the stage frays the nerves," she went on, in German, for she thought that he had perhaps not understood. "Discipline! Oh yes, we have plenty of that. But discipline is horribly exhausting. Discipline means always doing what you don't want to do and take no pleasure in doing. Have you experienced the weariness that comes of discipline?"

"I? Oh, no. I do only what I take pleasure in doing."

Grusinskaya raised a hand to which all its former grace had returned.

"I see, monsieur. You take pleasure in coming into a lady's bedroom, and you come. You take pleasure in a dangerous climb on to a balcony, so you do it. And what is your pleasure now?"

"I should like to smoke," Gaigern said frankly. Grusinskaya had expected something else and the reply struck her as chivalrous and considerate. She went to the writing table and held out her little cigarette box. She stood there in her much worn but genuine Chinese kimono and her trodden-down slippers, and all the charm and glitter and prestige which for twenty years had surrounded her on her travels throughout the Continent surrounded her once more. She had forgotten apparently how tear-stained and utterly wretched she looked.

"We'll smoke the pipe of peace then," she said, and lifting her long and much creased eyelids she looked into Gaigern's face. "And then bid each other adieu."

Gaigern greedily inhaled the smoke of his cigarette. He already felt a great relief, though his situation was still an anxious one. For one thing, he could not possibly leave the room so long as the pearls were in his pocket. If, now that she knew him, he were to keep the pearls he would have to fly that night and in the morning he would have the police on his heels. This would not suit his book at all. Everything now depended on remaining in her room at all costs until the pearls were conjured back into their jewel case.

Grusinskaya had now sat down in front of the looking glass and was intently powdering her face. She removed a line here and a mark there. She was beautiful once more.

Gaigern went up to her and interposed his big body between her and the rifled suitcase. Over her shoulder he launched a sweet and seductive smile.

"Why do you smile?" she asked into the mirror.

"Because, dear, I see something in the mirror that you cannot see," said Gaigern. He said "dear" without ceremony. The cigarette had restored him and now he felt in good form. Now for it, he thought, and spurred himself on. "I see in the mirror what I saw before when I was standing on the balcony," he said, bending over her. "I see in the mirror the most beautiful woman I have ever seen. She is sad and she is naked. She is—no, I cannot say it or I shall go mad. I did not know it was so dangerous to look into a woman's bedroom while she undressed——"

And, indeed, as Gaigern strung together these gallantries in his school-taught French, he actually saw a vision of her in the mirror as she had been, and he felt again the warmth of admiration that he had felt on the balcony. Grusinskaya listened skeptically. How cold I have become, she thought sadly, when no tremor of response greeted these ardent words. She felt the deep shame of a cold woman. She turned to Gaigern with a consciously effective curve of her long neck. Gaigern took her shoulders in his warm and adroit hands and then kissed her deliberately in the beautiful hollow between her shoulder blades.

This kiss, at first cool and remote, lasted long. It penetrated to her spine like a burning needle and her heart began to beat. Her blood became thick and sweet. Her frigid heart began to throb and flutter. Her eyes closed, and a tremor went through her. And Gaigern was trembling, too, when he released her and stood upright. A vein stood out blue on his forehead. Of a sudden his whole being was aware of her, of her skin, of the sharp scent of her body, of her slowly awakening anticipation of delight. The devil, he thought abruptly. He stretched out eager hands.

"I think you had better go now," Grusinskaya said weakly to his reflection in the glass. "The key is in the door."

Yes, the damned key was there now right enough, and now he could go when he chose. But now he didn't choose —for more reasons than one.

"No," he said with a sudden air of command to the woman, who trembled like a still vibrant violin. "I am not going. You know that I'm not going to go. Do you really think I should leave you alone here—I—you?—with a teacup full of veronal? Do you think I don't know the state you are in? I am going to stay with you. *Basta!*"

"*Basta? Basta?* But I wish to be alone."

Gaigern quickly went up to her, took hold of her wrists
and held them to his breast. "No," he said vehemently.
"That is not the truth. You do not want to be alone. You
are horribly afraid of being alone. I know well how afraid
you are. You don't escape me. I know you, you strange
little woman. It's no use play-acting with me. Your
theater is of glass and I see through it. You were desperate
just now. If I go away now you will be more desperate than
ever. Say I'm to stay with you. Say it."

He took her by the shoulders and shook her. He was
wrought up, she knew. Otherwise he would not have hurt
her. Jerylinkov had begged, she remembered. This man
commanded. Weak and relieved, she let her head fall on
the breast of his blue silk pajamas.

"Yes, stay a moment," she whispered. Gaigern looked
away over her head and let out a deep breath through his
teeth. The crisis of fear began to relax while a whirl of
pictures passed quickly before his eyes, as on the films.
Grusinskaya dead in her bed with a fatal dose of veronal
in her veins, and himself flying for his life, and a search of
the house at Springe, and then the prison cell. He had no
idea what it was like in prison, but he saw it distinctly all
the same. He saw his mother too. She died over again, although she had died long ago. When he came back to No.
68 the menace of fear and danger changed to intoxication.
He lifted Grusinskaya up in both arms and held her to his
breast like a child.

"Come, come, come," he murmured in a low voice with
his lips pressed to her temples. Grusinskaya had not been
aware of her body for a long while. She was aware of it
now. For years she had not been a woman. She was a
woman now. A black, singing heaven began to revolve
above her and she rushed up into it. A little birdlike cry
came from her open mouth and drove Gaigern out of his

make-believe into genuine passion and into a depth of joy such as he had never known. The teacup on the table rattled lightly whenever a motor car went by below. At first the white light from the ceiling was reflected in the poisoned liquid, then only the red of the table lamp, and then only the intermittent light from the electric sign shining through the curtains. Two hours raced by. From the passage came the *click-clack* of the lift. The distant church clock struck one amidst the hooting of the night traffic, and ten minutes later the electric lighting was once more in working order on the front of the Grand Hotel.

"Are you asleep?"

"No."

"Are you comfortable?"

"Yes."

"Your eyes are open, I can feel. I feel your eyelashes on my arm when you open and shut your eyes—a big man with eyelashes like a child's. Tell me, are you content?

"I have never been so happy as now."

"What did you say?"

"No woman ever made me so happy."

"Say it again—say it."

"I have never been so happy."

Gaigern murmured into the cool softness of her arm where his head lay. It was the truth. The indescribable appeasement filled him with gratitude. He had never known this in his commonplace love affairs—this intoxication without disillusionment, this thrilling calm after the embrace, this deep intimacy of the body with another's body. His limbs lay relaxed and at peace beside hers, their senses shared a mutual secret. He experienced something that has no name, not even the name of love, a homecoming after long homesickness. He was still young, but in the

arms of the aging Grusinskaya he became still younger
through the spell of her tender, experienced, and thoughtful
caresses.

"What a pity," he murmured into her arm; he pushed
up his head a little higher and made a pillow of her
shoulder, a little warm nest where there was the scent of
a meadow. "I would know you anywhere in the world
blindfold by your scent," he said, sniffing like a puppy.
"Tell me what it is."

"Never mind. Tell me, what is a pity? Never mind the
scent, it has the name of a little flower that grows in the
fields—*Neuwjada*. I don't know what you call it. Thyme?
It is made for me in Paris. Tell me, what is a pity?"

"That one always begins with the wrong woman.
And so one goes on stupidly, night after night, believing
that it must always be like that. What a pity that the
first woman one sleeps with is not like you."

"Oh, you're a spoilt child," whispered Grusinskaya.
She buried her lips in his hair. It was warm and thick
and strongly growing, with a masculine odor of cigarettes
and hairwash. He passed his finger tips down her sides and
felt her breath come and go.

"Do you know, you are so light. As light as anything.
No more than a little foam on a glass of champagne,"
he said in tender admiration.

"Yes. I have to be light," Grusinskaya answered
gravely.

"I should like to look at you. May I turn on the light?"

"No, don't," she cried, and moved her shoulder away.
He felt now that he had alarmed this woman whose real
age nobody knew. And again he was moved to simple pity.
He nestled up to her and they lay still, and thought. The
light of the street was reflected on the ceiling and hovered
to and fro. It was narrow and pointed like a sword, for it
came through a gap between the curtains. Whenever a

motor car went by below a swift passing shadow swept across this shaft of light.

The pearls, thought Gaigern, are for the moment with the devil. If I have the luck and all goes well I can put them back in their case while she's asleep. There'll be an unholy row with my people when I return without them. If only the chauffeur doesn't commit some outrageous folly, if only the beast doesn't get drunk in his fury to-night and send us all to blazes. That business has failed completely. Where we are to get money from now, Lord knows. Perhaps this wealthy old boy from the provinces who groans every night next door in No. 70 might be tapped. Oh well, the devil take it, what's the good of thinking? Perhaps I can simply ask her to give me the pearls. Perhaps I can simply tell her early to-morrow all about it. If I play my cards well, she won't have me locked up in the morning, not she, the little crazy thing, as light as air. She leaves her pearls lying about unlocked! Funny little woman. I know her now. What does she care for pearls? She has done with everything, nothing matters to her. If I hadn't come, all would have been over for her by now. She shall give me the pearls. She is good, yes, as good as a mother, a little tiny mama whom one can sleep with.

Grusinskaya was thinking. The train for Prague leaves at eleven-twenty. If only there's no hitch! I let go of everything to-day and to-morrow there will be a muddle. Pimenov is too weak and the girls twist him round their fingers. But whoever misses the train to-morrow shall get the sack, that's positive. If Pimenov hasn't troubled about the scenery to-night, it won't be packed by to-morrow. The scene shifters ought to be working overtime to-night. If I don't see to everything myself, nothing gets done. Then there's Meyerheim's accounts. Good God, however did I come to run away like that? Witte, he'll leave his own head behind in the hotel if no one looks after him. They all rely on me, and this evening I wasn't there. There will be a regular *débâcle*. Lucille has only been waiting for the chance to make a row. Their names are never in large enough type on the posters. They're never given a proper chance. But they never do a thing for themselves. If I don't hold the whip over them, they go to pieces. They have made me short-tempered and conceited and tired. Heavens, how tired I was yesterday. How little was needed to show them where they would be without Grusinskaya. But now I am not a bit tired. I could get up and dance the whole program, or a new program, or a new dance. I must talk to Pimenov about it. A dance of dread, oh, I could dance that for you now. At first on one spot only and only a tremor, and then three circles on the toes, or no, not on the toes perhaps, perhaps something quite different.

But I live, I live, she thought in a transport. I shall dance new dances and I shall have success. A woman who is loved always has success. You left me starving for ten years nearly now. That's what it was. To think that a foolish boy who comes climbing in over the balcony can give one such strength. A spoilt child who knows nothing of love but the silly talk of girls.

She pulled up the bedclothes and covered Gaigern up like a little child. He murmured gratefully and nestled against her. Their bodies were intimate, but in their thoughts they went their own ways like strangers. All the lovers in the world lie thus—so close together, and so far apart.

It was the woman who first began to grope after the mysteries of the other's soul. She took his head in her hands and held it as though it were a large and heavy fruit, gathered in the sun.

"I don't even know your name, my friend," she whispered in his ear.

"I am called Flix. In full, Felix Amadei Benvenuto Freiherr von Gaigern. But you must christen me too. I want you to give me a name of your own."

Grusinskaya reflected a moment; then she smiled softly.

"Your mother must have thought a lot of you when you came into the world to give you such beautiful names," she said. "The fortunate. The beloved of God. The welcome one. Did you cry when you were christened?"

"I don't remember."

"Do you know, I have a child too. A daughter. How old are you, Benvenuto?"

"To-day I am seventeen, for this is my first love affair. In other respects, thirty" (he made himself out a little older than he was from a touching consideration for the woman who was afraid of her age and who would not have the light turned on). Nevertheless it hurt her. He might be the father of her eight-year-old grandson, Ponpon. She forced herself to think of something else.

"What were you like as a child? Very beautiful? Oh yes, I'm sure you were."

"Quite enchanting. Covered with freckles and bruises and scratches and scrubby and dirty. We had gipsies as grooms and stable boys, like most people on the border where our estate lies. The gipsy children were my friends. I got every sort of vermin and itch from them. When I think of my childhood I always smell stable manure. Then for a few years I was the terror of various schools. Then I was at the war for a bit. The war was fine. I felt at home in it. For all I cared it might have been a lot worse than it was. If there could only be another war I should be all right."

"Aren't you all right now, you fire-eater? What do you do? What kind of a person are you?"

"And you? What kind of a woman are you? I have never known a woman like you. But you make me inquisitive. I have a lot of questions to ask you. You are quite different."

"I am only old-fashioned. I am from another world, another century," Grusinskaya said, and smiled in the darkness as she said it. Tears smarted in her eyes. "We dancers were brought up like little soldiers with iron discipline in the Imperial School of Ballet in Petersburg. We were little regiments of recruits for the beds of the grand dukes. It is said that those who grew too big when they were fifteen had steel rings fixed round their chests to prevent them growing any bigger. I was small and lean, but as hard as a diamond. Ambitious too. I had ambition in my blood like pepper and salt. Duty made a machine of me. There was nothing but work, work, work. No rest, no leisure, never a pause. And then, fame always brings loneliness. Success is as ice cold and as lonely as the north pole. And what it means to keep your grasp on success for three years, for five years, and twenty years, always on and on—but why do I tell you all this? Can you understand me? Listen. Often when you pass by a railway station waiting room or motor in the evening through a small town, you see people sitting motionless in front of the doors with stupid faces and their hands lying heavily on their knees. You, too, are tired and you wish you too could simply sit with your hands before you. Well, try it, when you are famous, disappear from the world and take your rest, let others dance, leave it to those ugly clumsy Germans and negresses, and all the other incompetents, let them dance and take your rest. No. You see, Benvenuto, it can't be done. It's impossible. Work is hateful, you curse it. But you can't exist without it. Three days' rest, and at once you are in a panic. I'm losing my form, I'm getting heavy, my technique is going to the devil. You have to dance. It's an obsession. No drug, no morphine or cocaine, and no vice in the world gets such a hold as work

and success. I can assure you of that. You have to dance,
you have to dance. Besides, it's important. If I give up
dancing, believe me there will not be a single person left in
the world who can really dance at all. All the rest are
dilettanti. But this hectic and hideously practical world of
yours cannot get on without someone who can dance and
who knows what dancing means. I learned from celebrated
dancers of my youth—Kchesinskaya, Trevilova—and
they in their turn had it handed down from the great
dancers of forty and sixty years ago. Often I feel when I
dance that I am dancing to defy the whole world. You all
shout, 'To-day, to-day,' and there you all sit, a theaterful
of money makers, motorists, and war-service men and
shareholders, and there am I—just little Grusinskaya, no
longer young, a thing of yesterday, and all my steps have
been known for two hundred years. And all the same I
carry you away, and then you shout and weep, and laugh
and go crazy for joy. And why? Isn't it just for this old-
fashioned ballet? So, you see, it has its importance.
Certainly, for nothing can be a world success unless it is
important, unless the world needs it. But everything goes
to pieces for it, nothing else remains whole. No man, no
child, no feeling, nothing in life. You are a person no longer.
Do you understand that? You are a woman no longer.
You are nothing but an exhausted sense of responsibility
hunted to and fro over the world. For one of us, life is
over on the day when success comes to an end, on the
day when we no longer believe in our own importance.
Are you listening? Do you understand me?" Grusinskaya
said beseechingly.

"Not all, but most of it. You speak French so fast,"
Gaigern answered. During the months of lying in wait
for the pearls he had often been to Grusinskaya's performances and they had without exception bored him
intensely. He was deeply astonished to find that Gru-

sinskaya seemed to drag this ballet show round with her as a kind of martyrdom. She lay nestling so lightly against him and she had such a pretty and charmingly modulated chirruping voice, and at the same time she spoke such somber words. What was he to say in reply? He sighed and reflected.

"That was good what you said just now about the people at evening with their stiff hands. You ought to dance that," he said at last with some embarrassment.

Grusinskaya only laughed at this.

"That? But one can't dance that, monsieur. Do you think they'd want to see me as an old woman with a shawl over her head and gout in her fingers, sitting like a block of wood and resting——"

She broke off in the middle of her sentence. Even while she spoke her body took hold of the idea and grew tense. She saw the scene and she knew a crazy young painter in Paris who could paint it. She saw the dance, she felt it in her hands and in the bent vertebræ of her neck. She lay silent with open mouth in the darkness. She was so wrought up that she did not breathe. The room was crowded with impersonations she had never danced and still might dance. A hundred true and living figures rose before her eyes. A beggar woman stretched out trembling hands; an old peasant woman danced for the last time at her daughter's wedding; a haggard woman stood in front of a booth at a fair and went through her poor tricks; a prostitute waited for men under a lantern; here stood a servant girl who had broken a dish and was beaten for it, and here was a fifteen-year-old child forced to dance naked before a large, flashy man, and here stood the skinny caricature of a governess; there was one who ran as though pursued though no one followed her, one who wanted to sleep and dared not, one who was afraid of a looking glass, and there was one who drank poison at last and died.

"Keep still, don't speak and don't move," Grusinskaya whispered, and she stared up at the ceiling with its
sword of light. The room had taken on that utterly strange
and enchanted appearance often encountered in hotel
bedrooms. Beneath the window a number of cars whirred
and groaned like wild beasts, for the banquet of the League
of Humanity was over and the departures from entrance
No. II were in full swing. The night had grown cooler.
Grusinskaya came back out of the whirl of her fancies
with a start and a shudder. Pimenov—with his new butterfly ballet—will think I have gone out of my mind. Perhaps I have. The flight of her fancy had only lasted a
minute, yet she returned from it to her bed as though from
a long journey. Gaigern was still there. She was almost
astonished to find this man still there against her shoulder
and to feel his hair and his hands and his breathing.

"What kind of a man are you?" she asked again as she
laid her face to his in the darkness. She was deeply conscious at this moment of her astonishment over such intimate closeness, when in so much they were strangers.
"Yesterday I did not even know you. Tell me who you
are," she asked with her lips close to his. Gaigern was about
to fall asleep. Now he put his arms round her. She felt like
his lean greyhound bitch at home.

"I? There's little to be said of me," he answered obediently, but without opening his eyes. "I am a prodigal
son. I am the black sheep of a good flock. I am a *mauvais
sujet* and I shall end on the gallows."

"Yes?" she asked with a little gurgling laugh deep in
her throat.

"Yes," said Gaigern with conviction. He had begun to
recite the old phrases from the homilies of his schooldays
in fun, but now the warm scent of thyme from the bed
inspired in him a desire to confess and reform.

"I am uncontrolled," he went on into the darkness. "I

am quite without character and unspeakably inquisitive. I can't live an orderly life and I am good for nothing. At home I learned to ride and play the gentleman. At school to say my prayers and lie. In the war to shoot and take cover. And beyond that I can do nothing, I am a gipsy, an outsider, an adventurer."

"Yes, and what else?"

"I am a gambler who is not above cheating. I have stolen too before now. Properly speaking, I ought to be in prison. Meanwhile, I have a jolly good time and do as I please and live on the fat of the land. Now and again, too, I get drunk, and I ought to add that I have been work-shy since birth."

"Go on," whispered Grusinskaya in delight. Her throat quivered with suppressed laughter.

"Further, I am a criminal. A cat burglar," Gaigern said sleepily.

"Nothing more? A murderer, perhaps?"

"Yes, of course. A murderer too. I was within an ace of killing you," Gaigern asserted.

Grusinskaya went on laughing a little at his face which she could feel but could not see. All the same she became suddenly serious. She clasped her fingers behind her neck, and whispered very softly in his ear.

"If you had not come in yesterday I shouldn't be alive now!"

"Yesterday?" thought Gaigern. "Now?" The night in No. 68 lasted an eternity. It was years since he stood on the balcony and watched her. He gave a start. His arms gripped her as tightly as a wrestler's, but her sinewy muscles held out against his pressure, as he felt with a strange joy.

"You must never do anything like that again. You must stay here. I shall never let you go. I need you," he said. He heard himself saying these astounding words in a husky voice that seemed to come directly from the depths of his heart.

"No, now it is different. Now it is all right again. You are with me now," Grusinskaya whispered. He could not understand, for she said it in Russian. But he heard the tone of her voice and this was enough to tune the night once more to rapture. Dream birds started from the branches of the hotel wall paper. He forgot the pearls in the pocket of his pajamas, and she forgot her failure and the deadly dose of veronal in the teacup.

Neither ventured on that fragile word—love. Together they glided into the vortex of their night of love. They went from an embrace to whispered talk, from whisperings to sleep and dreams, from dreams to more embraces. These two had come together from the ends of the world to meet for a few hours in the hotel bed of No. 68 where so many had slept before them. . . .

Love had played no great part in Grusinskaya's life. All the passion of her body and soul went into dancing. She had had one or two lovers, because, like the pearls, and a motor car and clothes from the best dressmakers of Paris and Vienna, they were part of the life of a celebrated dancer. Though she had been besieged, courted, and pursued by numbers of men who had fallen in love with her, she did not in her heart believe in the existence of love. It seemed to her as unreal as the painted drop scenes, the temples of love, and the banks of roses which formed the settings for her dances. But though she was cold and insensitive to love, she was esteemed a wonderful mistress. She herself practised love as a duty imposed by her profession, a part to be played that might sometimes please but always fatigued her and called for a high degree of art. To the nights she spent with her lovers she

gave all the suppleness of her body, its hovering grace, its
subtlety, its tenderness and its sensibility, its impulse and
its *élan*, its appeal and its delicacy, and in short all the
qualities she had brought to perfection in her dancing.
She could intoxicate but she could not be intoxicated.
When she danced she could let herself go in self-oblivion,
and often her partners heard her utter low cries or sing in
low birdlike snatches to herself while she executed the most
difficult and intricate figures. In love, however, she never
lost her self-consciousness. She stood outside and watched
herself. She did not believe in love and she did not need it,
and yet, strange to say, she could not live without it.

For love, she knew, was an ingredient of success. As long
as she was young, as long as flowers and notes poured into
her dressing room, as long as men stood rooted to the
ground wherever she passed, as long as they were ready to
ruin themselves or commit any folly and to sacrifice their
families and fortunes for her sake, she was conscious of
success. It could be estimated in terms of declarations of
love, threats of suicide, pursuits across the world, and
costly presents just as it could in terms of applause, cri-
tiques, and the number of her curtains. She might not know
it, but the lovers whom she bewitched and delighted were
really to her only a public with whom she had a success.
And the first time she realized with a shock of horror that
success was deserting her was when Gaston left her and
married an insignificant woman of good family. The
atmosphere in which she lived began to cool off after being
for so many years in a continual glow. The shadows
lengthened to an inconceivable evening. It was a decline,
though by steps so innumerable and so small that it was
scarcely noticed. And yet the distance she had traversed
was immense. Before the war, she had danced the whole
world into an ecstasy of romantic delight. Now she begged
her little applause from hostile and disillusioned cynics.

And at the end of it all lay utter loneliness and a fatal dose of veronal.

Hence the man on the balcony was much more than just a man to Grusinskaya. He was a miracle. At the eleventh hour he had made his appearance in No. 68 to rescue her. He was success coming to her in a simple shape; the world pressing eagerly to her; the proof that the years of romance when a young Jerylinkov had been shot for her sake were not yet over. She had fallen, and there he had stood to catch her as she fell.

There was a dance in Grusinskaya's repertoire in which love and death danced a *pas de deux*. Youthful poets had occasionally sent her verses harping on the theme that love and death were brother and sister. Grusinskaya this night lived this lyrical commonplace in her own person. The dazed agony of the evening had changed to rapture. It had become an ecstasy of gratitude, a feverish grasping and taking and feeling and holding. The frozen years had thawed. The secret shame of her coldness, concealed all her life within herself, melted away. It was true of her no longer. She had been so wretched and lonely for years past that sometimes she had craved a pittance of warmth from the warm, young body of her partner, Michael. And now to-night, in this ordinary hotel bedroom, in this bed of polished brass, she felt herself glow and pass into new being. Love in whose very existence she had disbelieved had been revealed to her.

Owing to the similarity between No. 68 and No. 69, Gaigern did not at once realize where he was when he awoke. Thinking that he was turning towards the wall in his own room, he encountered the sleeping, breathing form of Grusinskaya. Then he remembered. The deep and wonderful intimacy of their first sleep together weighed sweetly on his limbs. He slipped his cramped arm under her neck and thought with a tender solemnity of the events of the back from her face and exposed the narrow temples with their shadowed hollows. Two deep wrinkles beneath the closed eyes showed the approach of age. Gaigern saw it, but it did not displease him. Her mouth over the delicate though faded chin was wonderful. There was a little powder still on her forehead with its indented line of hair. Gaigern remembered with a smile that she had pulled out a powder box from under the pillow before she allowed him to turn on the bedside lamp. I see you now, anyway, he thought with a primitive feeling of triumph in his conquest. He scrutinized her face, as though it were new country in which he went to seek adventure. He found two mysterious symmetrical lines descending from her temples past her ears to her neck as thin as threads, and lighter in color than the rest of her skin. He passed his finger lightly over them. They were fine scars that framed her face as though they were the edges of a mask. Suddenly Gaigern realized what they were. They were vanity scars, incisions in the skin, with the object of stretching it and preserving its youth. He had read of such things. He shook his head with an incredulous smile. Involuntarily he grasped his own temples. They were smooth and braced by the strong and healthy beat of his pulse.

With an extreme tenderness he laid his face to hers as though he would infuse into her something of his own vitality. The strength, the softness, and the pity that inspired his love for her at this moment filled him with astonishment. He felt clean and upright and a little ridiculous in the emotion he felt over this poor woman whom he had stripped of all her secrets.

He moved away from the bed and stood for a few minutes with contracted brow and open mouth before the looking glass, plunged in reflection. He was wondering whether it was possible to keep the pearls in spite of all. No, it was not possible. For the moment, at least, he was

still Baron von Gaigern, a somewhat easy-going fellow
who kept bad company, in debt, certainly, but otherwise
reputable. If he left the room with the pearls in his possession the police would hear of it within an hour or two,
and his life as a man of leisure was over. He would be
hunted down like any other criminal. And this would not
suit him at all. To become the lover of Grusinskaya was
not in keeping with his program, but this was the fact, and
it altered everything. He weighed the chances as he would
have weighed the chances of a boxing or tennis match.
Enterprises like this were a sport to him, and this time the
game went against him. The change of circumstance
made it impossible to steal the pearls. All he could hope
was to be given them if he was patient. I must wait,
thought Gaigern, and sighed deeply. His calculations so
far were level-headed and perfectly clear. He did not go on
to confess that a great deal more lay behind them. He did
not wish to be ridiculous in his own eyes and he hated
sentiment. He looked into the glass and pulled a face.
The long and short of it is, he thought uneasily, I don't
care to steal pearls from a woman I've slept with. I no
longer even want to. It's against the grain—so that's that.

Neuwjada, he thought, remembering the bed on a wave
of tenderness. Dear Mouna, I'd much rather give you a
present, a big one, something pretty and costly, something
to rejoice your heart, you poor dear. He pulled the pearl
necklace out of his pocket, cautious not to make a sound.
It did not please him now in the least. Perhaps after all
they were false, in spite of all the newspapers' paragraphs.
Perhaps they were not worth half their reputed value.
In any case, it cost him little to say good-bye to them now.

Grusinskaya tried to wake up, but she found her head
swathed in sleep. The veronal, she thought, and closed
her eyes. She had been afraid of waking lately. She dreaded
the shock of facing the hard and naked facts of her life.

an abyss of weakness that cried out not to see, not to understand, not to admit the truth, that cried out for the merciful refuge of a lie. . . .

"*Que faites vous?*" she whispered to the executioner's back. She meant to cry out, but only a whisper came from her stiffened lips. "What are you doing?"

Gaigern gave so violent a start that his head spun right round. His fright spoke as clearly as a confession. Besides, he held in his hands the cube-shaped case of a ring; the suitcase was open, strings of pearls lay on the glass top of the dressing table.

"What are you doing there?" Grusinskaya whispered again. That her blanched and distorted face smiled as she spoke was piteous enough. Gaigern too understood her at once, and again his pity was so intense that he felt it beat in his temples. He held himself in an iron grip.

"Good-morning, Mouna," he said affectionately. "I have come on a wonderful treasure while you were asleep."

"What are you doing with my pearls?" Grusinskaya asked hoarsely. Tell me a lie, tell me a lie, her distraught face implored him. Gaigern went to her and veiled her eyes with his hand. Poor creature, poor little woman.

"It was very rude of me to rummage about among your things," he said. "I was looking for some plaster, or a bandage of some kind, and I thought to myself there would be something of the sort in the little dressing case. But it was your treasures I found. I feel like Aladdin in the cave—— "

Even her eyes had lost their color and become leaden. Now their dark tint came back slowly. Gaigern, to convince her, showed her his right hand which was still bleeding a little. The tension was released and from sheer weakness Grusinskaya let her lips sink on his hand. Gaigern put his other hand on her hair and drew her to his breast. He could be fairly brutal and domineering with the women he usually had to do with. But this one, for some mysterious reason, called forth all his better instincts. She was so fragile, exposed to such dangers, and so much in need of protection—and at the same time so strong. His own existence, always trembling on the edge of a precipice, taught him to understand hers.

"You silly," he said tenderly, "did you think I had an eye on your pearls?"

"No," lied Grusinskaya.

These two untruths formed the bridge which united them again as lovers.

"Besides—I never wear them now," she added with a sigh of relief.

"No—but why not?"

"Well, you would not understand. It is a superstition. First they brought me good luck. Then they brought bad luck. And now as soon as I stop wearing them they bring me luck again."

"Do they?" Gaigern asked thoughtfully. He still had a burden of uneasiness to get rid of. The pearls were safely back in their little bed of velvet. *Adieu. Au revoir,* he thought childishly. To prove it he put his hands in his pockets where he found all his burglarious implements but no booty. This put him in a rollicking good humor. His spirits rose and he felt perfectly happy. He opened his mouth and uttered a shout of joy. Grusinskaya began to laugh, and at this he went over to her and playfully ended his shout on her breast; mouth and eyes and heart were all surrendered to her. She seized hold of his hands and kissed them. There was something genuine as well as playful in this submissive gratitude.

"There, it's bleeding," she said with her mouth on the little wound.

"You have lips like a horse's," Gaigern replied, "as soft as a little foal's, a black one of marvelous pedigree."

He kneeled down and embraced her bare ankles. Just as she was about to look down at him, there came a buzzing sound from the writing table.

"The telephone," said Grusinskaya.

"The telephone?" replied Gaigern.

Grusinskaya sighed deeply. There was no help for it, her expression said, as she took up the receiver as though it weighed a hundredweight. It was Suzette.

"It is seven o'clock," she announced in her hoarse morning voice. "Madame must get up. There's the packing to be done. Will you have your tea now? And if Madame is to have her massage it is high time I began. And Herr Pimenov asks if Madame will please call him on the phone as soon as Madame is up."

Madame considered for a moment.

"In ten minutes, Suzette—no, in a quarter of an hour you can bring in my tea, and then we'll make short work of the massage."

She put back the receiver but held it still in her hand, while she extended the other to Gaigern who stood in the middle of the room, lightly poised on the chrome-leather soles of his boxing shoes. After a moment she took up the receiver again. The hall porter replied with a dutiful promptitude, though he had not closed an eye all night, for his wife in hospital seemed to be in a bad way.

"Number, please?" he asked smartly.

"Wilhelm 7010. Herr Pimenov."

Pimenov was not staying in the hotel. He was in a second-class pension that a family of Russian emigrants had started in the fourth floor of a house in Charlottenburg. Nobody there was awake yet, apparently. While Grusinskaya waited she had a vision of old Pimenov hurrying to the telephone in his old silk dressing gown, with his narrow feet which were always turned out, as though for the fifth position. At last she heard his gentle, nervous old man's voice.

"Oh Pimenov, is that you? Good-morning, *dobroje utro*, my dear. Yes, thanks, I slept very well. No, not too much veronal, only two. Thank you, *tout va bien*—heart, head, and all the rest. What? What is it? Michael has burst a blood vessel in his knee? But, good heavens, why didn't you tell me this last night? This is awful. *That* will go on—well, we know how long that will take. And what have you done? What? Not yet? But you must wire to Tchernov, at once, do you hear? He must come to the rescue. Meyerheim must see to that. Where is Meyerheim? I'll ring him up at once. Too early? Pardon me, my dear, if it is not too early for us, it is not too early for Herr Meyerheim—please. And has the scenery gone to the station? But it must go, please, with the first shift—when does the first shift start work? At six? If it is not there I shall hold you responsible, Pimenov. I can take no excuse. You are the ballet master. It is your business to see to the scenery, not mine. Yes, I shall expect to hear in half an hour at latest. Go to the station yourself. Adieu."

This time she kept the receiver in her hand and merely pressed down the hook with two fingers. She rang up Witte, whose wits were always astray in the mornings, and whose panic over traveling still put him into a fever in spite of all the years of touring and threw everything into confusion. She rang up Michael. He was staying in a small hotel. He was as piteous over his burst blood vessel as a dog that had been trodden on. Grusinskaya shouted her strict injunctions and advice down the telephone. She was always in a rage and most unfair when any of the company fell sick. She rang up three doctors before she found one who was able to visit Michael at once and give him the requisite treatment and apply aseptic bandages. She rang up Meyerheim and entered upon a dispute with him in French, finally commanding him to the hotel at half-past eight to settle their accounts. She sent a telegram by telephone to Tchernov and a second in case of accidents to a young dancer in Paris, who could dance well and was disengaged. After that with the help of Senf, the hall porter, she ascertained the connection with the express from Paris which would enable the young man to reach Prague in time, and then sent a third telegram on the heels of the second.

"Please, *chéri*, turn on the bath," she said hurriedly to Gaigern in the midst of all this, and then drummed out a series of instructions in English to Berkeley on the telephone—for she was not taking the car and meanwhile it was to be thoroughly overhauled. Gaigern went and turned on the bath as he was told. He hung her bath wrap over the radiator to warm. He found the sponge with which the night before he had sponged her tear-stained face and took it into the bathroom—and still she telephoned on and on. He found bath salts and threw in a handful. He would have loved to do something more for her, but there was nothing more to do. Also Grusinskaya appeared to have done with the telephone for the time.

"That's how it is, and every day the same," she said. It was meant to sound like a complaint, but her vitality and the pleasure she took in tackling things were irrepressible. "It has all got to be done. And then Michael says there's too much *chi chi* about Grusinskaya. That is what he calls *chi chi*, as though it were an amusement."

Gaigern stood in front of her, hungry for a little tenderness and intimacy. And indeed she held out both hands to him, but her thoughts were elsewhere. She was thinking of Michael's burst blood vessel. And then she heard the race of the clock and the watch, and quickly seizing the telephone rang up Suzette once more. "Wait another ten

minutes, Suzette," she begged her politely and rather
guiltily. Her eyes fell on the table and last night's teacup.
There it stood washed and clean, looking utterly innocent
and harmless, with the fantastic crest of the hotel in
gleaming gold on its thick porcelain. What a mad night,
she thought. Such things don't happen. And dances such as
I imagined last night cannot be danced. It was my over-
excited nerves. The Viennese would hiss me off the stage if
I appeared in dances like that instead of the wounded
dove and the butterflies. Vienna is different to Berlin.
There they know what ballet is.

Meanwhile she was staring into Gaigern's face, but she
did not see him. This caused him a pain that was new to
him, a vivid and peculiar pain in his chest. "Thyme—
Neuwjada," he said softly, drawing the word from the
deepest rapture of the night. Its scent came with it, the
bitter and also the sweet and the unforgettable. And,
indeed, at this invocation, Grusinskaya turned her eyes to
him again and her face took on a tense look of suffering
although she smiled. "I suppose we must part now——"
she said in a voice loud and inflexible in case it broke.

"Yes——" Gaigern answered. He had forgotten the
pearls. They were actually and utterly erased from his
memory. He was conscious of nothing but the grip and the
stress of his feelings for this woman, and the infinite desire
to be good to her, good, good, good. Helplessly he turned
the signet ring with the Gaigern crest in lapis lazuli round
his finger.

"Here," he said, and held the ring out to her awkwardly
like a schoolboy, "so that you shan't forget me."

But shall I not see you again? thought Grusinskaya, and
at that her eyes became hot and Gaigern's beautiful face
shone through her tears. It was one of those thoughts that
cannot be spoken. She waited.

Let me stay with you. I will be good to you, thought

Gaigern. But he held his mouth fast shut and not a sound escaped him.

"Suzette will be here any moment," Grusinskaya said quickly.

"You are going to Vienna?" he asked.

"First, for three days, to Prague. Then for fourteen days to Vienna. I shall be at the Bristol," she added.

Silence. The ticking of the clock. Motor horns below in front of the hotel. The smell of a funeral. The sound of breathing.

"Can't you come with me? I need you," Grusinskaya said at last.

"I—I can't come to Prague. I haven't any money. I must raise some more first."

"I'll give you some," she said quickly, and as quickly Gaigern answered, "I am not a *gigolo*."

A sudden overmastering impulse flung them into each other's arms and something greater than themselves held them fast bound together at the very moment when they had to part. "Thank you," they both said at once. "Thank you, thank you," in three languages, German, Russian, French, stammering, sobbing, whispering, weeping, jubilant. "Thank you, *merci, bolschoje spàssibo*, thank you."

At this moment Suzette took the tray of tea out of the hands of the injured waiter. It was twenty-eight minutes past seven. The clock on the writing table was racing breathlessly. The watch had given up in exhaustion. On— on—on it ticked reproachfully.

"In Vienna then?" Grusinskaya said with moist eyelids. "In three days? You will follow me. And after that you will come with me to Tremezzo. It will be beautiful, wonderful. I shall give myself a holiday, six weeks or eight. We shall do nothing but live. We shall live. Everything else shall be left behind, all the nonsense, and we'll do nothing but live. We'll be perfectly silly from sheer idleness and happiness—and then you'll go with me to South America. Do you know Rio? I—no, enough. It is time. Go—go, and thank you."

"In three days at the latest," said Gaigern.

Grusinskaya quickly assumed something of the great lady.

"See that you don't compromise me too much in getting back to your room," she said as she shut the double doors behind him.

As Gaigern released his hand without a word from hers he felt it hurt him. It was bleeding again. The passage was deserted. The doors ran together in the long perspective and boots slept lop-eared at their thresholds. The lift was descending and someone in a hurry to catch a train was running along the passage on the third floor. One of the frosted-glass windows on the stairs was open to let out the cigar smoke of the night before. Gaigern stole in his boxing shoes over the pineapple carpet to No. 69 and opened the door with a skeleton key. For the other was still hanging, for the purpose of his alibi, on the board above the hall porter's desk.

Grusinskaya had her bath and then gladly resigned herself to Suzette's hands for massage. She felt strong, elastic, and full of energy. She had a boundless desire to dance and longed for her next appearance. She was sure that a success was in store for her. She was always a success in Vienna. She felt it already in her legs and hands, in her neck as she threw back her head; in her mouth that would not stop smiling. She dressed and went off like a top with the whip behind it. She plunged with irresistible energy into the morning's business, the dispute with Meyerheim, the subterranean battle with the disaffected members of the company and the patient management of Pimenov and Witte.

At ten o'clock, page boy No. 18 brought a bouquet of

roses. "*Au revoir*, beloved lips," was written on a scrap of paper torn from an hotel envelope. Grusinskaya kissed the signet ring with the Gaigern crest. "*Porte bonheur*," she whispered as though to an intimate friend. Now she had something to bring her luck again. Michael was right. I shall give away the pearls for poor children, she thought. Suzette in darned cotton gloves gripped the handle of the suitcase, while the luggage porter carried out the rest. Grusinskaya had no sentimental feelings over the parting from this eventful hotel bedroom with its wall paper that always got on her nerves. Another was reserved for her at the Hotel Imperial in Prague, and also at the Bristol in Vienna, her usual room overlooking the court, No. 184, with bathroom. And one, too, in Rio, Paris, London, Buenos Aires, Rome—an endless perspective of hotel bedrooms with double doors and water laid on and the indefinable odor of restlessness and homelessness. . . .

At ten minutes past nine, a drowsy chambermaid fleetingly swept up the dust in No. 68, threw away the faded floral tributes, took out the tea tray, and finally came back with fresh linen—still damp from the iron—for the next occupant. . . .

WITH the treachery common to alarm clocks, General Director Preysing's failed to rouse him from sleep with the thoroughness and punctuality expected of it. At half-past seven it emitted a brief raucous rattle, and that was all. Preysing, whose mouth was open and parched, moved a little in his sleep and the springs of his bed murmured in response. A gleam of sun showed behind the yellow curtains. Then at eight o'clock the hall porter duly aroused him by telephone, but by that time it was far too late. Preysing held his drowsy head under the shower bath, cursing his forgotten razor. It needed no more to deprive such a slave to routine of all joy in life. In spite of being late he wasted several minutes selecting a suit to put on. And when he had decided on his morning coat, he took it off again in a fit of impatience. He calculated—and perhaps with reason—that a morning coat would put him at a disadvantage. His gray lounge suit, on the other hand, would show the Chemnitz people at once that the whole affair meant very little to him. He made unusual haste, but by the time he had put away all his cases and oddments, searched for, discovered, and pocketed all his keys, looked once more through his papers, and once more counted his money, it was after nine. He shot out of his room and at once collided with a man in the passage.

157

"Sorry," said Preysing, and came to a stop in front of his door, partly to let the other pass and partly to get his second arm into his coat.

"Not at all," the man replied and went along the passage. It seemed to Preysing that he had seen that back before. When Preysing reached the lift, the man was just descending in it. He now presented his front and this too, Preysing thought, he had seen before, though he could not remember where. It was fairly clear, though, that he made a grimace at him as he went off with the lift under his very nose. Preysing, in nervous impatience, ran down the stairs and along the corridor and down into the tiled basement where the hotel barber plied his trade in an odor of damp cellar and *peau d'espagne*. There, enveloped in white sheets like babies, sat several gentlemen waiting hopefully for the manipulations of the white-jacketed barbers. Preysing began to dance with impatience in his thick rubber-soled shoes.

"Shall I have long to wait?" he asked, rubbing his unshaven chin with his hand.

"Ten minutes at the most. There is only this gentleman in front of you," was the reply.

The gentleman who was in front of him was the gentleman of the lift, and Preysing looked at him with disfavor. He was a somewhat insignificant creature, thin and diffident, and he sat squinting into a newspaper with his pince-nez almost falling off his sharp nose. Preysing was distinctly aware that he had come across the man in the course of business, but he could not recall the occasion. He went up to him and, making him a perfunctory bow, said with all the amiability he could command:

"Would you be so very kind as to let me go first? I am in a great hurry."

Kringelein, hunched together behind his paper, collected all his forces. Emerging from behind the leading article and extending his lean neck, he blinked straight into the general director's face and replied, "No."

"Excuse me, but I am in a great hurry," Preysing stammered reproachfully.

"So am I," returned Kringelein.

Preysing turned on his heels in a fury and left the barber's shop. And there sat Kringelein breathing heavily in an atmosphere of shaving soaps, utterly exhausted and done-up after his prodigious effort, but a hero in triumphant possession of the field. . . .

Behind time, unshaven, and with the tip of his tongue scalded by burning coffee, the general director was the last to enter the conference room. The others had had time to emit plentiful clouds of blue cigar smoke into this room, which, with its green tablecloth and imitation damask wall paper and its portrait in oils of the founder of the Grand Hotel, presented an appearance of the highest solidity. Dr. Zinnowitz had his papers all ready to his hand, and old Gerstenkorn presided at the head of the superfluously long table. He acknowledged the new arrival by rising only slightly in his chair, for he belonged to the same close-fisted generation as Preysing's father-in-law. He had known Preysing as a young man and had no great opinion of him.

"Behind time, Preysing," he said. "Quarter of an hour's grace, eh? A late night? Yes, we all know Berlin!"

He laughed with a bronchitic wheeze and pointed to a chair at his side. Preysing sat down opposite Schweimann. He had the objectionable feeling of having got out of bed on the wrong side and his upper lip was moist under his mustache, even before the show began. Schweimann, who had red edges to his eyelids and the large protruding and flexible mouth of an ape, introduced a third gentleman.

"Our colleague, Dr. Waitz," he said.

Dr. Waitz was a young man who looked absent-minded,

but was very far from being so. With his domineering and aggressive trumpet of a voice he could be a very ugly customer in a discussion. So the Chemnitz people had brought *him* along with them, thought Preysing.

"We've met before," he said without enthusiasm.

Schweimann offered the general director a cigar across the table and Dr. Zinnowitz took a fountain pen from his breast pocket and laid it down on the table beside his papers. Further down the table, on the far side of the water bottle and the glasses which quivered on a black tray whenever a motor bus went by, there was still another person, a colorless individual, Flamm the First. She held her shorthand block in her hand. In appearance she was elderly and faded, with a thin white mothlike dust on her cheeks. She was silent and businesslike and by no means easily to be mistaken for Flamm the Second.

"That's a nice fountain pen," said Schweimann to Zinnowitz. "What make is that? Very nice."

"Do you like it? Got it from London. Nice, isn't it," said Zinnowitz as he wrote his flowing signature on a memorandum block. Everybody watched him.

"How much was it? if I may ask," inquired Preysing, and taking his own from his breast pocket, laid it on the table in front of him, whereupon everyone looked at it.

"A little over three pounds without the duty. A friend of mine brought it over," said Zinnowitz. "Rather a jolly thing, isn't it?"

They craned their heads over the table like schoolboys and gazed upon the malachite green fountain pen from London. It was an object well worthy to occupy the attention of these five grown-up business men for three minutes.

"Well, let's get on to business," said old Gerstenkorn at last, in his bronchitic voice, and Zinnowitz resting his white anæmic fingers on the green tablecloth began at once in a fluent and well-prepared speech to launch a statement upon the blue haze of the conference chamber.

Preysing permitted himself a slight release of tension. He was not much of a speaker and he was, therefore, devoutly thankful that Zinnowitz relieved him of this task, and also that his periods flowed off his tongue with the smoothness and precision of a machine. This, however, was no more than a prelude. He said nothing, in fact, but what had long since been gone over again and again in preliminary negotiations. He was merely reviewing the state of affairs once more, and, in doing so, he fished one document after another out of his portfolio, holding the long columns of figures close to his short-sighted eyes in order to read them off without hesitation.

Now this, to repeat, was the state of affairs: the Saxonia Cotton Company, which dealt chiefly in cotton stuffs, bed covers, and, as a means of utilizing waste products, in a very popular make of house flannel, was a medium-sized undertaking with plenty of capital. Its assets in land, buildings, and machinery, in raw material and finished goods, in patents, etc., and particularly in debts outstanding, reached a very respectable figure. The annual turnover and the net profits maintained a sound average level. The dividend for the previous year was nine and a half per cent.

Zinnowitz read out these, after all, very satisfactory figures, and Preysing listened to them with pleasure. Everything in the business was aboveboard and in order, and the output from waste products, which alone brought in marks 300,000 gross, had been organized by himself. He glanced at Gerstenkorn. Gerstenkorn, in the meditative and rather simple fashion of the old and sly, was swaying his gray scrub of a head to and fro. Schweimann was fussing with his cigar and did not appear to listen. Waitz checked every figure that was quoted by some notes which he had in a small book bound in leather. Flamm the

First, a model of a private secretary, strove to efface herself by staring at the reflections in the water bottle, while she held her pencil like a small sharp fixed bayonet. Zinnowitz drew forth another lot of papers from the pile before him and passed on to consider the position of the Chemnitz Manufacturing Company. His long thin Chinese beard bobbed up and down as he spoke.

The Chemnitz Manufacturing Company—as the figures showed—was an appreciably smaller undertaking. It had scarcely half the assets and its balance sheet revealed an extremely shaky state of affairs. The least possible had been written off, but nevertheless an astonishing high dividend was shown. The annual turnover was high. The net receipts, however, were scarcely in proportion. For all that, the Chemnitz Company showed a surprisingly large balance. Zinnowitz's voice as he read the last figures implied that he begged leave to query them, and he looked at old Gerstenkorn.

"Rather more," said Gerstenkorn. "Rather more. You can put it at 250,000 marks in round figures if you like."

"You can't reckon in that fashion," said Preysing, who had got nervous. "You have to make allowance for the depreciation of the new machinery for the new process. You cannot simply write off the old machinery."

"Yes, we can. Yes, we can," said Gerstenkorn obstinately.

Dr. Waitz trumpeted: "Our figures are underestimated, rather than overestimated."

Dr. Zinnowitz handed a paper across to the general director, who proceeded to study the figures on it with close attention. He was familiar already with the upshot. The Chemnitz Manufacturing Company was not by any means a sound enterprise. Floated at the outset with insufficient capital, its credit was stretched to the utmost. Nevertheless it had a big turnover; it paid; it obviously throve; and it had the market on its side. Saxonia Cotton, on the other hand, hung fire. Sound and well capitalized as it was, it was all the same a somnolent concern. Cottons, bed coverings, and house flannel. The world for the moment was not requiring bed coverings and house flannel. And the old man at Fredersdorf knew what he was about when he wanted to come in on the top of the market for knitted goods and turn it to the advantage of his own business.

"It doesn't matter. Let's get on," he said with the tolerant air of a man in the weaker position. Gerstenkorn took the balance sheet from Preysing's hand and tapped the paper. He laughed huskily.

Zinnowitz had meanwhile turned his eloquence to the state of shares, and here there was plainly a snag. Saxonia in actual fact issued twice as much stock as Chemnitz did. Accepting this as the basis, all the preliminary negotiations for the fusion of the two concerns had reckoned two shares of Chemnitz as the equivalent of one Saxonia. Now, however, the Chemnitz shares had gone up and the Saxonia shares had gone down. Hence the center of balance had shifted and—as Dr. Zinnowitz admitted with a conciliatory movement of the hand—the basis of exchange, owing to the astonishing boom in the shares of the Chemnitz Manufacturing Company, was no longer the same. Preysing listened with irritation to the smooth legal voice as with pedantic exactitude it brought forward nothing but those unpleasant facts which he knew only too well. His cigar ceased to afford him any pleasure and after a few strenuous pulls he put it down. At a certain moment in Zinnowitz's exposition of the case, Dr. Waitz leapt forward like an actor at his cue. He made objections with rapid gesticulations of his hands over the green table; he read figures from his notebook without so much as glancing at it; new figures, different figures. Preysing contracted the muscles of his forehead till his eyes started from his head, so intense was his effort to retain it all and to see through it all and to keep a clear view of the whole question. He took one or two hotel envelopes that were lying on the table and scribbled down notes on them secretly and agitatedly like a schoolboy in a fix.

Dr. Zinnowitz, for his part, threw the merest glance towards the trusty Flamm the First, and she duly took down the aggressive remarks in shorthand on her blue-lined block. Dr. Waitz summed up in his bellowing voice. No, it was not to be imagined that the shareholders in the Chemnitz Manufacturing Company were going to submit to an amalgamation that halved the value of their stock. There was no occasion whatever, in his opinion, to give the Saxonia priority over the Chemnitz Company, supposing an eventual (he mouthed the word "eventual" like a strolling player) fusion between the two. Why should this flourishing concern be brought into submission, as it were, and shoved into a corner?

Zinnowitz looked at Preysing, and Preysing obediently began to speak. It was his habit to give utterance to matters of importance in a low and nasal voice and with a dreary lack of emphasis. He employed this method of showing an outward calm and superiority because inwardly he had no confidence in himself. The backs of his hands were moist as he threw himself into the battle. Schweimann's eyes crept like little gray mice out of the red cavities where they lived, and Gerstenkorn stuck his thumbs in his waistcoat with the air of a man who was enjoying himself. Such conferences took place every day in the Grand Hotel—here in this "great pub" many a job was rigged which afterwards the shareholders had to make the best of. Sugar went dearer, silk stockings cheaper, coal short—these and a thousand other contingencies depended on the issue of battles fought out in the conference chamber of the Grand Hotel.

So Preysing spoke, and the longer he spoke in that voice of his that sounded as if it had been kept on ice, and the closer he came to grips with the business, the more ground he lost. Gerstenkorn's telling little interjections whistled in the air like bullets. There were moments when Preysing would gladly have turned tail and fled from the field, dropped the whole rotten business of the amalgamation and gone home to Fredersdorf to Mulle and Popsy and Babs. But as he was the managing director, and as life was not all a bed of roses, and as this amalgamation meant a lot to the business and everything to his own personal standing, he stuck bravely to his post. He produced once more the statements of his assets and clung fast to this thoroughly sound demonstration of a thoroughly sound business. He wearied the Chemnitz people by falling into rambling details, and Zinnowitz had several times to get him afloat again like an unwieldy boat gone aground. He tied nooses and hanged himself in them. He made obstinate stands on mere side issues with the pigheadedness of sheer stupidity. He devastated them with the exact figures of the manufacture of house flannel from cotton waste, for this was his pet subject, and forgot to make the important points which he had scribbled on his envelopes. And at last he stuck in the middle of a sentence which had begun like a flourish of trumpets and ended like a blind alley. He took out his handkerchief and wiped his mustache and lit a cigar that tasted like hay. And suddenly it occurred to him that he was sitting at the table with hustlers, men of no principle; he felt the deep embitterment of a self-respecting man who is thought a fool for his pains.

Now, however, Gerstenkorn removed his fat common

thumbs from the armholes of his waistcoat and began to state his opinion. This Gerstenkorn, with his scrubby square head and bronchitic voice, was a clear and ready speaker. He made use of every available dialect in order to say what he wished in the fewest words. His business talk was spiced with expressions from the dialects of Saxony, Berlin, Mecklenburg and from Yiddish.

"And now stop a bit and let the grown-ups talk," he said without taking his cigar from his mouth, and this had the desired effect of making his slovenly speech even more slovenly. "You've told us now what the Saxonia is good for and that we knew already. It don't go down, all the same. We've gone into all that with our principal shareholders and the upshot was to think twice and twice again before we went in for the amalgamation. They don't see the fun of pulling the hot chestnuts out of the fire for your cotton business. So now you have it straight. Our position has improved appreciably since you first approached us. Yours has remained stationary, if I am not to be rude and say it has deteriorated. Under the circumstances—to speak plainly, my dear Preysing—the amalgamation has lost its attraction for us. We have come here this morning with instructions in our pockets under these circumstances to let the negotiations drop. At the time when you approached us, it was another story."

"We didn't approach you," Preysing said quickly.

"How can you say that, man? You did approach us. Dr. Waitz, please give me the correspondence. Here we are —on September 14th you approached us by letter."

"That's not correct," Preysing persisted obstinately, and he made a grab for the file of papers in front of Zinnowitz. "We did not approach you. Our letter of September 14th followed upon a personal exchange of views instigated by yourselves."

"If you talk of instigating, why, your old man sounded

me in strict confidence as between old friends a good
month before that."

"We did not approach you," said Preysing. He clung
to this fact which was a mere side issue as though it were
of vital importance. Zinnowitz sounded a warning note
with his narrow feet under the table. Abruptly Gerstenkorn
let the matter drop. He smoothed the green tablecloth
with his square-shaped hands. "Right," he said. "*Bon!*
Then you did not approach us if that pleases you better.
And whether you did or not, the circumstances were not
the same as now. You will not deny that, Herr Generaldirektor?" (The change from the familiar to the official
style sounded threatening.) "At that time we had reasons
for wishing a close connection with the Saxonia Cotton
Company. What reasons have we to-day?"

"You need more capital," said Preysing, quite rightly.
Gerstenkorn swept this aside with two of his fingers.

"Capital! Capital! We have only to issue shares to have
all the money we want chucked at us. Capital! There's
one thing you forget. You had your time in the war. You
were able to make a good thing then out of army cloth
and blankets. Now it's our turn, eh? We don't need capital.
We need cheap raw material so that we can profit to the
full by our new process, and we need new outlets for export
abroad. I'll tell you the views of the company quite frankly
Herr Generaldirektor. If the amalgamation were of any
help to us in these directions, then we're for it. Otherwise
not. Now, please, if you have anything to say?"

Poor Preysing! If he had anything to say! Now had
come the point he had been afraid of ever since getting into
the slow train at Fredersdorf. He threw a timid glance
across at Zinnowitz, but Zinnowitz was examining his
well-tended bloodless fingernails and made no reply.

"It is no secret that we have excellent connections
abroad. To the Balkans alone we export house flannel to

the annual value of 65,000 marks," he said. "It stands to reason that in the event of an amalgamation we should do everything in our power to open up a bigger foreign market for your products too."

"Are there any circumstances that would enable you to give this assurance a more definite form?" asked Dr. Waitz from lower down the table. He even rose halfway from his seat as he said it. This was a habit contracted in his former activities as counsel for the defense in criminal proceedings. Wherever he might be he always looked as though he wore a barrister's gown and he had not lost the tone with which he used to browbeat nervous witnesses. The general director allowed himself to be browbeaten.

"Can you tell me what circumstances you mean?" he answered with his pitiful habit of asking what he knew already.

Schweimann who sat opposite him had not so far opened his large flexible ape's mouth. He opened it now.

"The reference is to the proposed understanding with Burleigh & Son," he said without more ado. Gerstenkorn held a long cigar ash trembling on the end of his cigar in the keenest suspense.

"Unfortunately I am not in a position to make any statement on that question," Preysing answered at once. He had prepared this reply long beforehand and learnt it by heart.

"Pity," said old Gerstenkorn. Whereupon there was a general silence lasting several minutes.

The bottle of water rattled on the tray because a bus was going by outside, and the surface of the water catching a ray of sun threw trembling rings of light on to the frame of the portrait in oils of the founder of the Grand Hotel. Preysing's brain worked feverishly during these seconds. He did not know whether Zinnowitz had shown those ominous copies of the letters—now so entirely meaningless and unjustifiable—to the Chemnitz people. Once again he had that unclean and uncomfortable feeling in his hands. His unshaven chin began to itch in a ridiculous way. From the corners of his eyes he threw his legal adviser a questioning and imploring glance. Zinnowitz, as though to soothe him, closed the lids of his oblique and sagacious Chinese eyes. This was an extremely obscure gesture. It might mean Yes. It might mean No. It might mean nothing whatever. Preysing pulled himself together. I must see it through, he thought—though it was more a sensation than a thought.

"Gentlemen," he said, standing up—for the velvet upholstered chair made him hot and uncomfortable behind. "But, gentlemen, we must after all stick to the main point. The basis of all negotiations between us so far was our credit balance and the standing of the Fredersdorf manufactory. You have had every opportunity to look into that matter. Herr Kommerzienrat Gerstenkorn has satisfied himself personally as to the state of our concerns, and I must draw the line at vague and incalculable elements being brought into the discussion to-day. We are not speculators. I certainly am not a speculator. I deal with facts, not with rumors. It is no more than a stock-exchange rumor that we meditated a business arrangement with Burleigh & Son. I have had to contradict it once already and I cannot admit that——"

"You can't take in an old stager like me with a tale like that. We all know what such contradictions are worth," Gerstenkorn threw in. Schweimann perked up. He sniffed with dilated nostrils and ape's mouth as though he already scented export possibilities with England. Preysing began to lose his temper.

"I refuse," he shouted, "I refuse to have this affair with England mixed up with the business before us. I am not going to reckon with castles in the air. I have never done manly. But it gets us no further. So you will pardon me if I take these gentlemen into our confidence in this matter."

Zinnowitz floundered on with his conciliatory discourse, interspersing a number of "thoughs" and "seeing thats," and "notwithstandings" and "on the other hands." Preysing had gone pale; he could tell from the prickling sensation as the blood flowed from his temples that he must be as white as a sheet. So, thought he, Zinnowitz has shown them the letters. Good God, but that's swindling. It is not far from actual fraud. "Negotiations finally broken off. Brösemann," he thought, and he saw the blue-black and blurred writing of the telegram. He put his hand into the breast pocket of his gray office suit, where he had stowed the telegram away, and pulled his hand out again as though from a hot oven. If I don't get up at once and say what's happened, there'll be no end of a muddle, he thought, and he stood up. And if I do say it, they will break off, there will be no more talk of the amalgamation, and I can go back to Fredersdorf as the scapegoat, and he sat down again. In the vain hope of accounting for this aimless and undecided movement, he poured out some more of the nauseating water and swallowed it down like medicine.

Schweimann and Gerstenkorn in the meanwhile had cheered up considerably. They were a couple of extremely *rusé* business men. Their attention was caught by the vehemence with which Preysing negatived the English affair and did his utmost to exclude it. Their keen noses scented something behind this—export, profits, competition perhaps. Gerstenkorn whispered what he thought into Schweimann's large right ear: "In the case of anyone else a contradiction like that would be as good as saying Yes. But in the case of this blockhead Preysing it is even possible that he is simply telling the truth——"

Gerstenkorn broke in roughly: "There's no object in our legal friend talking himself hoarse," he said, leaning over the table. "Before we say any more, I must ask Herr Preysing to tell us plainly how far the negotiations with Burleigh & Son have gone."

"I refuse," said Preysing.

"I must insist on it, if I am to continue the discussion," said Gerstenkorn.

"Then," said Preysing, "I beg you in any further discussion to regard that matter as non-existent."

"Am I to conclude then that all prospects of an agreement with Burleigh & Son are over?" asked Gerstenkorn.

"Conclude what you like," said Preysing.

At this they were all silent for nearly a minute. Flamm the First discreetly turned the leaves of her block and the slight rustle of the paper broke the stillness of the conference chamber. Preysing looked like a sickly infant. It sometimes happened that from behind his managing director's face there peeped out the perplexed and obstinate look of a small boy. Zinnowitz, feeling that everything was over, was drawing little triangles on the cover of a file of papers with his malachite fountain pen.

"Then I suppose there's nothing further to be said for the present," Gerstenkorn said finally. "I suppose we may as well conclude our little discussion. We can always continue it in writing."

He got up, and his chair made grooves in the thick pile carpet of this very handsome conference chamber. Preysing, however, kept his seat. He took out a cigar with elaborate care, and with elaborate care cut off its end; then he lit it, took a pull, and began to smoke with an abstracted and deeply meditative expression on his face. His cheeks were speckled with tiny red veins.

There is no doubt that General Director Preysing was a thoroughly respectable man, a man of principle, a good husband and father, a man who stood for organization and order and the strongholds of convention. His life went by

"Is he leaving then?" asked little Georgi.

"Why should he be leaving? No, he's staying on."

"I only meant because he's never been called in the morning before."

"Well, you see to it, anyway," said the hall porter. And hence the telephone buzzed punctually at nine in Dr. Otternschlag's small and inexpensive room.

Otternschlag roused himself from his dreams as strenuously as any much occupied man, and then he lay where he was and wondered at himself. "What's up?" he asked himself and the telephone. "What's up now?" Then for a minute or two he lay still and thought hard, with the disfigured side of his face pressed into the rough linen of the hotel pillow. Wait a bit, he thought—it's that Kringelein, poor fellow. We have to show him a bit of life. He's waiting for us. He's sitting waiting for us in the breakfast room.

"Shall we get up and dress?" he asked himself. "Yes, so we will," he replied after an effort, for he had a good sleeping draught of morphine in his veins. Nevertheless, there was a certain alacrity about him as he hurried here and there over his dressing. Somebody was waiting for him. Somebody was grateful to him. With one sock in his hand, he sat on the edge of his bed and fell to considering plans. He made a program for the day. He was as preoccupied as if he had a party of tourists to conduct. He was important and sought after. The chambermaid as she took a broom and pail out of a closet next door to No. 218 was astonished to hear Dr. Otternschlag humming a song after a fashion while he brushed his teeth. . . .

Meanwhile, Kringelein was already seated in the breakfast room, still exhausted, excited, and exultant after his exacting victory over General Director Preysing in the barber's saloon. Also, ten minutes before, he had made the acquaintance of the engaging and delightful Baron von

Gaigern. Gaigern had been busy. After emerging minus
the pearls from his night with Grusinskaya he had shot
straight into an explanatory scene with the chauffeur,
conducted in whispers, but none the less vehement. Immediately after that, when he had had his bath, done his
exercises, and rubbed himself over with toilet vinegar,
he had run into the provincial gentleman of No. 70, from
whom in one way or another he hoped to raise the few
thousand marks of which he now stood in immediate need.
Inwardly he was filled with a radiantly blissful and devour-
ing eagerness and impatience. Though it was only an
hour since his parting with Grusinskaya, he felt already
an uncontrollable, yet tender, desire for her. Through his
whole being he felt the longing to be with her again with
all possible speed. Gaigern reveled in this hitherto unknown feeling with all the *joie de vivre* and all the alertness
with which every fresh experience inspired him. He started
upon his enterprise with Kringelein with enormous gusto.
He went off like a rocket and in a quarter of an hour he
had gone an immense way towards winning his confidence.
Kringelein was captivated at once. He exposed his timid
employee's soul with all its eagerness for life and all its
acceptance of death, and what he did not say or could not
express Gaigern guessed for himself. When at fourteen
minutes past nine Kringelein had wiped the last traces of
his egg from his vigorous mustache with the hotel napkin
they were already friends.

"You must understand, Baron," said Kringelein, "that
I have come into a little money after living always in very
restricted circumstances—oh yes, in very restricted circumstances. A man like you can have no idea of what that
means. To be afraid of the coal bill, you know, to be un-
able to go to the dentist, until, after putting it off year
after year, you find yourself minus most of your teeth—
you don't know how. But I won't talk about it. The day

before yesterday I ate caviare for the first time. You may well laugh, you eat caviare and so on every day, of course. When our general director entertains people he has caviare sent by the pound from Dresden. Well, caviare, champagne, and all the rest of it are not life, you may say. But what is life, Herr Baron? You see, Baron, I am no longer young, and besides I am not in good health, and then you suddenly feel afraid—so afraid—of missing life altogether. I don't want to miss life, if you understand?"

"You can't very well miss that. It's always there. You live—and that's all about it," said Gaigern.

Kringelein looked at him. He saw his good looks and his good spirits, and possibly, as he did so, his eyelids reddened a little behind his glasses.

"Yes, of course, for a man like you life is always there. But for a man like me——" he said in a low voice.

"Funny. You talk of life as though it were a train you have to catch. How long have you been after it, three days? And not got a glimpse of it yet in spite of caviare and champagne? What did you do yesterday for example? Kaiser Friedrich Museum, Potsdam, and at night the theater. Well, and what pleased you most? Which picture? You don't know? Of course not. And the theater? Grusinskaya? Yes, Grusinskaya," said Gaigern, and at the name his heart gave a bound like a silly boy's. "What do you say? It made you sad; it was so poetical. But all that has nothing to do with life, Herr Direktor" (he said "Herr Direktor" from pure goodness of heart, because he was shocked by the plain plebeian name of Kringelein; and Kringelein blushed with pleasure). "Life is—look here, you know when you see those cauldrons of pitch boiling, bubbling, and smoking in the street and making a stink for miles around. Well, now go and put your nose over those tar fumes. It's beautiful. It's hot, and it has such a strong and pungent smell that it bowls you over, and the thick black drops glisten, and there's strength in it, nothing sweet and insipid. Caviare! You want to catch hold of life, and if I ask you what color the trams are in Berlin you can't say because you haven't troubled to look. Now listen, Herr Direktor, with a tie like yours you'll never get even with life, and you'll never feel happy in a suit like that. I'm telling you this quite frankly, for there's no object in paying compliments. If you'll put yourself in my hands I promise you that we'll soon put some go into the business, and the first thing is to go to a tailor. Have you any money on you? A check book? No. Well, put some ready money in your pocket. Meanwhile I'll get my car out of the garage. I've given my chauffeur a few days off —to see his girl at Springe—so I drive myself."

Kringelein felt as if there was an east wind about his ears. The remark about his tie (bought in the Arcade for two marks fifty) and his good suit made a thoroughly painful impression on him. His hand went timidly to his over-big collar. "Quite so," said Gaigern, "it doesn't sit right and the stud shows all the time. Of course, you can't see life like that."

"I thought—I didn't want to lay out money on clothes," Kringelein murmured, and he saw figures capering giddily in his account book. "I'll gladly spend money on other things but not on clothes——"

"Why not for clothes? Clothes are half the battle."

"Because it isn't worth while now," Kringelein said in a low voice, and the soft, silly tears smarted in the corners of his eyes. He couldn't, confound it, think of his approaching end without emotion. Gaigern looked vexed. "It really is not worth while. I mean—I have not many more opportunities left for wearing new clothes. I thought—the old ones would be good enough to last me out," Kringelein whispered guiltily.

Good Lord, has everyone got a teacupful of veronal

ready to his hand? thought Gaigern, whose sensibilities had been quickened by the tender scenes of the past night. "Don't reckon things up, Herr Kringelein. One's apt to reckon all wrong. You should not go on wearing old clothes. You should meet each moment as the moment requires. I am a man of the moment in this sense, and I'm all the better for it. Come along now, and put a few thousand marks in your pocket and then we'll see whether there isn't some fun in life. And now, let's be off."

Kringelein got up obediently, and as he did so he felt that danger compassed him on every side. A few thousand marks, he thought, with his mind in a fog. A good day. One day at a few thousand marks. As he followed Gaigern he was still putting up a resistance, and the walls of the breakfast room danced before his eyes. He felt uprooted. His will was gone. His feet in their blacking-leather boots took their own way with him along the hotel passages. He was afraid. He was uncontrollably afraid of Gaigern, of the threatened expenditure, of the smart tailor; he was afraid of the gray-blue motor car as he got into the front seat; he was afraid of life, although he was afraid of missing it, too. He clenched his dilapidated teeth together, pulled on his cotton gloves, and began his good day.

As Dr. Otternschlag at ten minutes to ten coasted round the walls of the lounge searching for Kringelein, he was handed a letter by the hall porter.

"My Dear Doctor," it ran, "I regret that I am unexpectedly prevented from keeping my engagement with you to-day. With respectful greetings, yours truly, "Otto Kringelein."

It was Kringelein's style but no longer altogether his handwriting. Hard, jagged strokes had crept into the smooth copperplate hand, and the dots of the i's had a tendency to fly away, like balloons cut adrift, to burst somewhere in the sky with a lonely and tragic little report that no one hears. . . .

Dr. Otternschlag held the letter out in front of him. The lounge was a dreary waste of endless vacant hours. He pottered along past the newspaper stand, past the flower stall, past the lifts, and past the pillars to his customary seat. Frightful, he thought. Ghastly. Hideous! His leaden cigarette-stained fingers hung down, and he stared with his blind eye at the charwoman who, contrary to all orders, was beginning in broad daylight to sweep out the Lounge with moist sawdust.

Kringelein's embarrassment as he stood in the fitting room of the large tailor's shop was terrible. Three elegant gentlemen were busily occupied with him. Twelve very shabby Kringeleins were reflected in the mirrors set at acute angles to each other. One elegant gentleman brought in coats and suits, one elegant gentleman knelt on the floor and pulled down the bottoms of his trousers, one elegant gentleman merely stood by and surveyed Kringelein with a half-closed professional eye and murmured unintelligible words. On a sofa, beneath pictures of impossibly beautiful film actresses, sat Baron Gaigern, flapping his stitched gloves on the palm of his hand and looking away from Kringelein as though he were ashamed of him.

Pitiful matters came to light, dread secrets of the bookkeeper, Otto Kringelein, of Fredersdorf. His braces had given way and been mended, and then when they had given way again, they had been clumsily held together with string. His waistcoat, which had got much too big for him, Anna had taken in by stitching two thick tucks in the lining at the back. He wore his father's shirts, and they were too large for him. He wore india-rubber bands round the sleeves above his elbows to prevent their superfluous length overwhelming him. He possessed cuff links

approached him with an air of embarrassment, a person
who at the same time was appallingly familiar to him as
the real Kringelein of Fredersdorf, and then the vision
passed. A second later the sight was no longer new. The
miracle of transformation was past.

Kringelein was now breathing deeply and with effort,
for he was being menaced by an attack of acute pain.

"I think it suits me very well," he said like a child to
Gaigern.

The Baron did the handsome thing. With his own large
warm hands he smoothed the new coat down over Kringelein's shoulders.

"Yes, I think we'll have this suit," Kringelein said to
the three gentlemen. He secretly felt the cloth between his
finger and thumb, for he knew something about cloth. It
was in the very air at Fredersdorf, even though you were
employed only in the counting house.

"Good material. I'm in the trade," he said with respect.

"Genuine English cloth. We get it direct from London,
Parker Bros. & Co.," replied the one with the pinched-up
eyes. Preysing does not wear cloth like this, thought Kringelein. Preysing's suits were usually of that solid gray
worsted which the factory had had in stock for years, and
sold off cheap to its employees annually just before Christmas. Kringelein took possession of his suit as he dug his
hands into its clean new pockets.

His fears were changed abruptly into the joy of buying
and possessing, and for the first time he experienced the
giddy exhilaration that comes of spending money. He
broke down the walls behind which he had lived for a
lifetime. He bought and bought. He did not ask the price,
but simply bought. He stroked stuffs and silks, felt the
brim of hats, sampled waistcoats and belts, matched one
color against another, and appreciated their harmonies
with the relish of a connoisseur.

"The gentleman has wonderfully good taste," said one. "Most distinguished," said another. "Most appropriate and correct."

Gaigern stood by, impatient to be off, and added his praises. From sheer boredom he looked at his hands. There was a cut on the right and the left looked naked after giving away his signet ring. Surreptitiously he passed them in front of his face to see whether any scent from the night clung to them, a bitter-sweet scent of danger and calm, *neuwjada*, the little flower that grows among the fields.

Kringelein bought a brown lounge suit of rough English tweed, a pair of dark gray trousers with a fine white stripe to go with an elegant morning coat; he bought a dinner jacket and trousers, which only needed the position of a button or two altered; he bought underclothing, shirts, collars, socks, ties, a coat such as Gaigern wore, a soft and astonishingly light hat, bearing the trade mark in gold of a Florence firm, and finally, carrying in his hands a pair of wash-leather gloves just like Gaigern's, he repaired to the pay desk. There things went very smoothly. Kringelein was quickly at home when he encountered the familiar jargon of ledgers and the atmosphere of the counting house. He paid a thousand marks down, the rest to follow in three instalments. "There we are then," said Gaigern with relief. An array of politely supple backs escorted the transformed and enchanted Kringelein to the mirrored door of the establishment. Outside, it was sunny but cold. The air was like iced wine, Kringelein observed in passing. Hitherto he had always crept about. Now he stepped out. He had three steps to go from the entrance of this fashionable emporium to the gray-blue four-seater, and three times he raised his new-shod feet from the pavement with a vigourous and elastic step.

"Pleased?" asked Gaigern, laughing and with his hand

already on the starter. "What does it feel like? More yourself?"

"Splendid. Tip-top. First class," Kringelein replied as he sat down beside him with a nonchalant air. He took off his pince-nez and rubbed his eyes with his finger and thumb. It was a habit of his when fatigued.

It had just occurred to him that he would no longer be there when the last instalment was due.

Gaigern's fingers were all impatience. At the street crossings there were red and green and yellow lights to direct the traffic and policemen stood there and laughingly held out warning arms. The car shot along past houses, trees, advertisement kiosks, blocks of pedestrians at street crossings, past fruit barrows, hoardings, and timid old ladies who went tripping across the street at the wrong moment with long black skirts in the middle of March. The sun threw a moist yellow gleam on the asphalt. Whenever a great clumsy bus was in the way the little four-seater gave two hoots. It sounded like the barking of excited dogs.

There were many people in Fredersdorf who had never been in a motor car. Anna, for example, had never been in a motor car. But Kringelein was in one now. His lips were tightly compressed, his elbows and shoulder joints were rigid, and the rush of air made his eyes water. Taking the corners made a severe demand on his nerves and his heart went up and down beneath his new silk shirt. It was the same fearful joy as when in his childhood the merry-go-round was erected on Mickenau Heath and you could have three rides for a penny.

Kringelein stared at Berlin as it flew past in streaks. He began to feel fairly familiar now with the great city. For example, he recognized the Brandenburg Gate from afar and also the Gedächtniskirche, which he greeted with a respectful glance.

"Where are we going?" he shouted into Gaigern's right ear, for the noise of the engine seemed deafening and he felt he was in the midst of an uproar of the elements.

"A little way out, to have lunch, along the Avus," Gaigern answered unconcernedly.

The street raced to meet the car with ever increasing swiftness. They drew near the wireless tower, the Funkturm. Kringelein had been there the evening before with Dr. Otternschlag when night was closing in. He had been tired out by then and incapable of grasping anything. The remarkably smooth surfaces of the new and only half-finished pavilions out in this neighborhood had pursued him in his dreams and now reality and dream lay imposed one on the other, half menacing and half incomprehensible.

"Are they going to finish building that?" Kringelein shouted, and pointed to the exhibition buildings.

"It is finished," was the answer. Kringelein marveled. It was all bare like a manufactory, but it did not look ugly like the factory at Fredersdorf.

"An odd city," he said, shaking his head, and blinked the harder. He felt a shock that contracted the skin of his scalp, but it portended nothing. Gaigern had merely stopped at the north gate of the Avus and now he was already off again.

"Now, we can let it rip," he said, and, before Kringelein understood what he meant, he had done so.

At first the wind grew colder and colder, and blew harder and harder, until at last it beat like a fist against his face. The engine sang on a rising note and at the same time something ghastly occurred to Kringelein's legs. They were filled with air. Bubbles rose in his joints as if they would burst. For several seconds, that seemed to last an incredible time, he could not breathe, and moment after moment he thought, Now I'm dying. This is what it's like then. I am dying.

His chest caved in and he gasped for breath. The car swallowed up one object after another before it could be recognized, streaks of red, green, and blue. A patch of red just became a car before it vanished into nothingness behind, and all the while Kringelein could not breathe. He felt now an unimagined sensation in his diaphragm. He tried to turn his head towards Gaigern. Strange to say, he succeeded without finding it torn from his shoulders. Gaigern sat a little forward over the wheel and he was wearing his wash-leather gloves though they were not buttoned up. This for some reason was reassuring. Just as what was left of Kringelein's stomach strove to escape at his throat, Gaigern's closed lips began to smile. Without taking his eyes off the Avus road whirling past like an unwinding spool, he pointed somewhere with his chin, and Kringelein obediently followed the direction with his eyes. Having some intelligence, he realized after a guess or two that the speedometer was before his eyes. The little pointer trembled slightly as it pointed to 110. Good Lord, thought Kringelein, and swallowing down his fears he bent forward and gave himself up to the rush of speed. Suddenly the new and appalling joy of danger overcame him. Faster! cried a frenzied Kringelein within him whom he had never known before. The car complied with 115. For a few moments it kept to 118, and Kringelein finally gave up all thought of breathing. He would have liked now to whirl on and on into darkness, on and on in the shock of explosion, and to get right beyond and out of time. No hospital bed, he thought, better a broken skull. Hoardings still whirled past the car, but the spaces between began to alter. Then the gray ragged streaks beside the road became pine woods. Kringelein saw trees eddying more slowly to meet the car and stepping back into the wood like people as the car went by. It was just as it was on the roundabout at Mickenau when it slowed down. Now he could read the names of oils, tires, and makes of cars on the placards. The rush of air relaxed and streamed in his throat. The speedometer sank to 60, trembled a little then 50—45— and then they left the Avus by the south gate and drove along soberly between the villas of the Wannsee.

"There—now I feel better," said Gaigern, and laughed all over his face. Kringelein took his hands from the leather cushion in which till now he had dug his fingers and carefully relaxed his jaws and shoulders and knees. He felt completely tired and completely happy.

"So do I," he answered truthfully. He spoke very little while they sat after this on the empty glass-roofed terrace of a restaurant looking over the Wannsee and watched the sailing boats rock at their moorings. He had to think out the experience he had been through. What is speed? he thought. It can't be seen or taken hold of, and, if it can be measured, that too is probably only a trick. How is it then that it goes through and through you, and is even more beautiful than music? Everything was still revolving in circles around him, but this was just what pleased him. He had the bottle of Hundt's Elixir on him, but he did not take any of it.

"I must offer you my heartiest thanks for this wonderful drive," he said studiously, expressing himself in a manner he considered fitting to the circles in which he now moved. Gaigern—who had chosen very plain fare, an egg on spinach—made light of the obligation. "It amused me," he said. "It was your first experience and it's so seldom you find anyone who experiences something for the first time."

"But you do not give one the impression of being blasé yourself, if I may say so," Kringelein replied very aptly. He was quite at home in his new clothes and in his silk shirt. He sat and he ate in a different manner, and his thin hands emerging from the cuffs of his shirt gave him par-

ticular satisfaction. They had been manicured that morning by a pretty girl in the hotel basement.

"Good Lord! I, blasé!" Gaigern said delightedly. "No,
certainly not. Only, a man like me has a full life." He had
to smile. "Though you're right. There are things that even
a man like me experiences for the first time—funny
things," he added to himself. He clenched his fine teeth
softly together and thought of Grusinskaya. He was devoured by impatience for the moment when he should
have her in his arms again with all her tender need of him
and hear again the sad twittering notes of her birdlike
voice. The hours till then were a desert. He gave himself
three days, inwardly fretting with impatience, in which to
raise the few thousand marks that would keep his associ-
ates quiet and enable him to set off for Vienna. In the
meanwhile he paid every attention to Kringelein and hoped
that things would take a favorable turn.

"What is the next item on the program?" asked Kringelein, and blinked at him with a sincere and grateful look
from his blue eyes. Gaigern took to this quiet fellow from
the provinces, who sat like a child at a Christmas party.
A human kindliness and warmth were so implicit in his
nature that his victims always benefited by their due share
of them.

"Now we are going to fly," he said in the soothing tone
of a children's nurse. "It's very jolly and not dangerous,
not half so dangerous as a motor car on a fixed track."

"Was that very dangerous?" asked Kringelein with
surprise. Now that he had overcome it he was conscious of
his alarm only as a pleasure.

"Can't be otherwise," said Gaigern. "One hundred and
eighteen kilometers is no trifle, and the road was wet.
You never know when you may strike a slippery patch,
and any moment the car may skid. Bill, please," he said
amiably to the waiter, and he paid for his modest dish of

spinach and poached eggs. There were still twenty-four
marks left in his pocketbook. Kringelein paid too. He had
only had a few spoonfuls of soup, for he suspected his
stomach of rebellious and mischievous designs. As he put
back his pocketbook—it was the old shabby one of his
Fredersdorf days—he had a fleeting and now meaningless
vision of his account book in black waxed cloth. Till that
morning since his ninth year he had entered every penny
he spent in such a little book. It was not worth while doing
it now. The time for it was past. A thousand marks in one
morning was altogether beyond entering. A part of Kringelein's world had fallen in noiselessly and without a sign.
Kringelein, as he followed Gaigern down from the empty
restaurant terrace to the car, moved his shoulders luxur-
iously in his new coat, new suit, and new shirt. Now
everyone stood with a bow to let him pass. I wish you
good-morning, Herr Generaldirektor, he thought, and saw
himself flattened to the greenish-gray wall of the second
floor of the counting house at Fredersdorf. He put away his
pince-nez when he had taken his seat beside Gaigern and
exposed his naked eyes to the bright March sunshine. It
was with a pleasant excitement and confidence that he felt
the engine starting up.

"The road or the Avus again?"

"Oh, the Avus," replied Kringelein, "and at the same
pace," he added lightly.

"Ah, you have pluck then?" said Gaigern, and accelerated.

"Yes, I have," said Kringelein, leaning forward with
taut muscles, ready with parted lips to enjoy life to the full.

Kringelein stood leaning against the white and red rails
of the aërodrome, trying to get the hang of this astounding
world which had come round him since the morning. Yesterday—it seemed a hundred years ago—yesterday he had

ascended in the lift, stupidly as though in a dream, to the restaurant of the Funkturm; there had been no pleasure in it and Dr. Otternschlag's pessimistic comments made it all even more unreal and ghastly. The day before yesterday—and that seemed a thousand years ago—he was junior clerk in the counting house of the Saxonia Cotton Company at Fredersdorf, a little miserable employee among three hundred other miserable employees, in a gray worsted suit, who had been given sick leave on a mere pittance. To-day, now and here, he was waiting for a pilot to take him up on a long special flight at a price correspondingly high. It was one of those thoughts that you could not see to the end of, though Kringelein's mind was alert and collected as it had never been before.

It was quite untrue that he had pluck. The pleasure that confronted him threw him into a perfect panic. He did not want to fly. He did not want to in the least. He would have liked to go home, home—not to Fredersdorf, but home all the same to his room, No. 70, with the mahogany furniture and the down quilt of silk. He wanted to lie in bed and not to have to fly.

When Kringelein set out to seek life, something misty and formless hovered before his eyes, something at the same time well upholstered and filled out, with plenty of draperies and fringes and a profusion of ornaments, soft beds, heaped plates, voluptuous women, both in painted effigy and real life. Now that he was really seeing life, now that he began, as it seemed, to be in the middle of it, it had quite another aspect. It made demands upon him and a keen wind whistled about his ears, and he had to break through walls of anguish and danger before one small drop of its sweet and intoxicating experiences could reach his lips.

Flying, thought Kringelein. He knew it already in his dreams. His dream of flying was like this: Kringelein stood on the platform of Zickenmeyer's Hall with the members of the musical club round him, and he sang a solo. He heard his own fine tenor voice rising higher and higher and higher. It cost him not the least effort. It was a pure spontaneous pleasure that came of itself. Finally he ascended himself on the highest note and flew away upon it, accompanied by music of the clouds while the members of the club looked up at him. At first he hovered beneath the roof of Zickenmeyer's Hall, and then he flew quite alone and there was nothing whatever all around him. At last he realized that it was all a dream and that he must return to the bed where Anna was sleeping the frowsy sleep of slovenly and bad-tempered middle age. The anti-climax was frightful, and he cried out in horror as he woke to the dark stuffy room, the small window, the cupboards smelling of moth powder, and the little iron stove with a saucepan on the top.

Kringelein blinked. Flying, he thought, and shrank into himself as he stood on the Tempelhof aërodrome. Here, too, as outside round the Funkturm and along the Avus were the same glaring colors—yellow and blue and red and green. Mysterious towers rose into the air. Everything was attenuated and spare. The wind blew silvery clouds of dust fitfully over the expanse of asphalt beyond the rails and cloud shadows raced across the aërodrome. The little machine in which the ascent was to be made was already there. Three men were busy with it. The engine raced and the propeller revolved idly. Blocks were in position in front of the small wheels, and the ribbed silver wings vibrated to the throb of the engine. Others were landing, greeted by the hoarse note of a siren (like the one that was sounded at the Fredersdorf factory at seven in the morning, so perhaps all this was only a dream), others were taking off, heavily on the ground, lightly once they were in the air; silver ones with metal wings, golden ones with

rigid wings of wood, and great white ones with four planes
and three whirling propellers. The aërodrome was so very
large and so wonderfully still, and all the men there were
slim and bronzed, happy and silent, and they wore white
flying costumes with close-fitting caps. Only the machines
had voices as they trundled over the ground barking
hoarsely like great dogs.

Gaigern approached with the pilot, a decent fellow with
the bow legs of an ex-cavalry officer. Gaigern appeared to be
in his element out here. He was hail-fellow-well-met with
everybody.

"We're getting off at once," Gaigern announced.

Kringelein, who had had some experience of what Gaigern meant by "getting off," was horribly alarmed. Help,
he thought. Help! I'm not going to fly—but he would not
for the world have said it aloud. "Oh, are we pushing off?"
he asked, like a man of the world. He was proud of the
expression "pushing off," which he used for the first time
in his life.

The next thing was that Otto Kringelein sat strapped
in the little cockpit in a comfortable leather seat and
"pushed off" into the gray blue of the March sky. Next
him sat Gaigern whistling softly, and that was some conso-
lation in a moment of utter prostration.

At first it was no more than a bumpy ride in a car and
then the machine began to make a furious and appalling
racket. Suddenly it shook off the earth beneath it and
climbed. It did not by any means soar. It was not such a
simple business as Kringelein's dream flights on his tenor
notes. It sprang up into the air by jumps as though up
steps—sprang and sank, sprang and sank. This time the
sense of uneasiness was not in his legs as during the motor
run at 120 kilometers an hour, but in his head. Kringelein's
skull hummed. It became thin. It became quite glassy,
and he had to shut his eyes for a moment.

"Air-sick?" asked Gaigern, shouting in his ear, and he wondered whether he could then and there prevail with Kringelein to give him 5,000 marks—or only 3,000—or even a miserable 1,500, with which to pay his hotel bill and buy a ticket for Vienna. "Do you feel bad? Have you had enough?" he added kindly.

Kringelein pulled himself together manfully and courageously and replied with a cheery "No." He opened his eyes in his humming glassy head and fixed them first on the floor of the machine, which at least had its relative stability, and then raised them to the little oval of glass in front. Through this he saw again the figures and the trembling pointer. The pilot turned his keen profile and gave Kringelein a friendly smile. Kringelein was much relieved and highly honored by this glance.

"Three hundred meters up at a hundred and eighty an hour," Gaigern shouted in his humming and deafened ears. Then all at once everything became gentle, light, and smooth. The machine climbed no higher. It banked to the tune of its metallic engine voice and swept on above the city lying dwarfed beneath. Kringelein ventured to look out.

The first thing he saw was the sunlit, ribbed metal sheets of the wings, and they seemed to quiver with life; then—far below—Berlin checkered in tiny squares, with green cupolas and a ridiculous toy railway station. A patch of green was the Tiergarten, a patch of blue gray with four white specks of sails was the Wannsee. The edge of the little planet lay far beyond, arched in a gentle curve. Over there were mountains and forests and brown plough land. Kringelein relaxed his cramped lips and smiled like a child. He was flying. He had stuck it out. He felt fine. He had a new and vigorous sense of his own being. For the third time that day his fear left him and gave place to happiness.

He tapped Gaigern on the shoulder and in response to a

questioning look said something that was swallowed up unheard in the noise of the engine.

"It is not so bad after all," Kringelein said. "There's nothing to be afraid of. It isn't so bad."

And with this Kringelein included not only the monstrous tailor's bill and not only the run on the Avus, and not only the flight in the aëroplane, but everything else as well and in particular the fact that he had soon to die, to die right out of this little world, leaving all its terrors behind and climbing perhaps even higher than aëroplanes can fly. . . .

The streets behind the Tempelhof aërodrome went to Kringelein's heart as they drove back. They were so like the dreary streets of Fredersdorf. Chimneys rose up behind railway embankments, and his distended nostrils were on the alert for the smell of size that in Fredersdorf always issued from the finishing shops. As he passed these poor streets, he was more than ever conscious that he wore a new suit and drove in a car. He tried to find a word for this curious mixture of feelings, but he failed. He did not recover his spirits till they reached the Hallescher Gate. There they were held up for half a minute. The flight still ran in his veins like a calm but powerful intoxication, and full of eagerness he asked with a politeness that came from his heart: "And what has the Baron in store for me now?"

"Now—speaking for myself I have to go back to the hotel. I have an engagement at five. But why not come too? I am only going to dance," he added, when he saw the forlorn and dejected look in Kringelein's eloquent eyes.

"Thank you very much, I'll come with pleasure. I can't dance though, unfortunately."

"Oh, rot. Everyone can dance," said Gaigern.

Kringelein reflected upon this remark until they were well into the Friedrichstrasse.

"And after that? What could we do after that?" he asked with importunate insatiability. Gaigern made no reply. He drove on fast till he had to pull up in front of the red traffic signal on the Leipsigerstrasse.

"Tell me, Herr Direktor," he asked while they were at a standstill, "are you married?"

Kringelein made so long a pause for reflection that the traffic signals turned to yellow and green and allowed them to proceed again before he replied.

"Have been. I have been married, Herr Baron. I have separated from my wife. Yes, I have taken my freedom, if I may put it so. There are marriages, Herr Baron, which are so irksome and sickening to both parties that one of the two can't see the other without getting into a rage. The husband can't see his wife's comb in the morning with the combed-out hair in it without the whole day being spoiled for him. It's quite wrong, certainly, for how can a woman help it if her hair comes out? Or again when you want to read at night your wife keeps on talking, talking, talking, and if she doesn't talk, she sings in the kitchen. If a man is musical, singing of that kind makes him ill. And every evening when you are tired and want to sit down with a book, it is always, 'Come, chop up the firewood for to-morrow morning.' It costs a penny more to have the bundle of firewood chopped up and that comes to a farthing a day, but no, that wouldn't do. 'You're a spendthrift,' your wife tells you, 'for all you care we shall end in the workhouse.' And then, you see, there's my father-in-law's shop and she'll inherit it in time. She'll be all right. So I took my freedom. My wife never suited me, to tell you the truth, for I was always above the sordid cares of life, and that she never could forgive me. When my friend Kampmann gave me the old numbers of *Kosmos* for five years back, my wife went and sold them as waste paper; she got twopence for them. There you have the whole woman, Herr Baron. Now—we are separated. In any case she'll have to get on without me very soon, and a week or two sooner or later makes no odds. She'll go back to the shop and sell the unmarried employees pickled herrings and sausage for their suppers. That's how I got to know her myself, so perhaps she'll get hold of another fool. And a fool I was, I can tell you, when I married, not a notion of life nor of women either. Since I've seen all these pretty girls in Berlin it begins to dawn on me by degrees. But there, it's too late for all that."

This speech, which Kringelein brought up out of his inmost soul, lasted from Leipsigerstrasse to Unter den Linden.

"Oh, things aren't so bad as all that," Gaigern replied absent-mindedly, for he had the trying crossing near the Brandenburger Tor to negotiate and there was an incompetent owner driver in front of him. The fumes of a sordid little kitchen rose from Kringelein's words. Those fumes depressed him and robbed him of the impulse he had had to demand a loan of 3,000 marks.

And Kringelein, with his silk shirt, driving in a motor car, would also have been glad now to take back some of his unpremeditated confessions.

"So we are going to dance," he said, all the more glibly. "I am most extremely obliged to the Herr Baron for taking me under his protection. And what could we do to-night?"

Secretly Kringelein expected a reply that would give expression to unexpressed wishes of his own. He had a hankering after something that was suggested by many pictures in the Museum, but a little more tangible, something that the newspapers he read described as an "orgy." He supposed that men about town had the key to such things. The evening before Dr. Otternschlag had acceded to his obscurely expressed inclination for the fair sex by taking him to see the ballet and Grusinskaya. Well, that, so Kringelein thought, had been a mistake. Very pretty to look at, but too poetical. Very stirring and magnificent, but it sent you off in a doze and finally it brought on pains in the stomach. To-day, however. . . .

"The best thing you could go to to-night is the great boxing match in the Sporthalle," said Gaigern. "We'll see if the hall porter has a ticket left."

"Boxing does not interest me in the least," said Kringelein, with the superior air of a reader of *Kosmos*.

"Doesn't interest you? Have you ever seen a fight? Well, just go and see one and you'll be interested quick enough," Gaigern promised him.

"Will you come too, Herr Baron?" Kringelein asked quickly. He felt in splendid form after the drive and the flight, alert and vigorous and ready for anything, but he knew he would collapse like a blown-up india-rubber doll the moment the Baron deserted him.

"I'd go like a shot," Gaigern answered, "but unfortunately I can't. I haven't any money."

Meanwhile they had passed the budding trees of the Tiergarten and the hotel front was already in view further down the street. Gaigern slowed down to twelve kilometers to give Herr Kringelein time to express himself. Kringelein was utterly taken back by Gaigern's laughing remark. They had stopped at entrance No. V. They had already got out. And still Kringelein had not digested his surprise.

"I'll take the car to the garage," Gaigern called out when Kringelein was once more on his rather stiff and tingling legs, and he disappeared round the corner. Kringelein walked thoughtfully on and passed through the revolving door whose mechanism had no longer any terrors for him. No money, he thought. He has no money. Something must be done about it.

Rohna and the hall porter and all the page boys and even the one-armed lift attendant observed the transformation in Kringelein's appearance and then discreetly looked the other way. The lounge was full of the odor of coffee and of people and talk. It was ten minutes to five. In his usual armchair sat Dr. Otternschlag with newspapers lying all round him. He surveyed Kringelein with an indefinable expression of scorn and sadness. Kringelein went up to him without any apparent concern and held out his hand.

"The new Adam," said Otternschlag, without taking the hand, for his own was cold and moist and this embarrassed him. "The butterfly has emerged. And where have you been flitting about? if I may be allowed to ask."

"I've been shopping. Then a motor drive along the Avus: lunch on the Wannsee; and then I went up in an aëroplane." His tone towards Otternschlag had altered without his knowing it.

"Splendid," said Otternschlag. "And what now?"

"I have an engagement at five. I am going to dance."

"Ah—and after that?"

"After that I mean to go to a big boxing match in the Sporthalle."

"Indeed," said Otternschlag. That was all. He took up his paper and holding it in front of his face began to read with a feeling of mortification. In China there were earthquakes, but the paltry matter of 40,000 dead did not suffice to alleviate his boredom. . . .

When Gaigern reached the second floor with the intention of changing his clothes he found Kringelein waiting at his door.

"Well?" he asked with impatience. It began by degrees to get on his nerves to have this odd little man tied round his neck.

"Was the Herr Baron playing a joke on me or is it true that the Herr Baron is embarrassed for money?" Kringelein asked hurriedly. It was one of the most difficult things he had ever had to say and he made a mess of it in spite of all his careful preparation.

"The absolute truth, Herr Direktor. I am down and out. The luck's against me. I have only twenty-two marks thirty in my pocket and to-morrow I shall have to hang myself in the Tiergarten," said Gaigern, and laughed all over his handsome face. "But the worst is that within three days I have to be in Vienna. I have fallen in love, I may tell you. I am gone on a woman to a degree that no words can describe and it is an imperative necessity to follow her. And not a penny to bless myself with. If only somebody would tip me up enough to gamble with to-night——"

"I want to gamble too," said Kringelein quickly and from the bottom of his heart. The 120-kilometers-an-hour feeling and the flying feeling came over him again.

"*Tiens!* Then I'll pick you up at the Sporthalle and we'll go to a nice club I know of. You stake a thousand and I'll stake twenty-two," said Gaigern, and with that he shut his door and left Kringelein standing outside. For the moment he had had enough of him. He threw himself on his bed in his clothes and shut his eyes. He had a listless and bored feeling. He tried to recall the girl with the lock of blond hair on her forehead, but without success. Something else always came between. Either it was Grusinskaya's bedside lamp, or the balcony railing, or a bit of the Avus, a bit of the aërodrome, or Kringelein's torn braces. Too little sleep last night, he thought, chafing and fretting. He fell into a three-minute sleep, an abyss of healing darkness, as he had learnt to do in the war. He was awakened by a chambermaid knocking at the door. She had a note for him, and it was from Kringelein.

"MY DEAR BARON," wrote Kringelein. "Would you permit the undersigned to regard you as his guest, and at the same time accept the small sum enclosed as a loan? You would be doing him a favor by allowing him to be of any service to you and in his situation money is no longer of importance. With most respectful greetings,

"Yours very truly,
"OTTO KRINGELEIN.
"Enclosures: Entrance ticket. Two hundred marks."

The stamped hotel envelope contained an orange-colored ticket for the boxing match and two crisp hundred-mark notes, numbered in ink on the sides. The dots of the i's in Kringelein's signature were missing. He had finally said good-bye to them in the reckless exhilaration of this memorable day. . . .

Preysing's joints felt hollow as he stood alone in the lounge after the close of the conference, when the provisional agreement had been signed and Dr. Zinnowitz had taken his leave with all sorts of complimentary remarks. The feeling of a great success, the consciousness of having successfully bluffed the Chemnitz crowd, and the strain of talking and of triumphing under false pretenses were all entirely new to the general director and left him in a strange and not unpleasant tumult. He looked at the hotel clock—past three—and went mechanically to the telephone room to get a call put through to the works. Then he pottered about for a longish while in the gentlemen's lavatory and let hot water run over his hands while he stared at himself in the glass with an idiotic smile. Next he wandered into the dining room, which was half empty, and ordered the lunch on the menu without a glance at it. He became impatient before the soup arrived and began to smoke a cigar. He had no idea it would taste so good. While he scanned the wine list he hummed a tune which he had picked up somewhere in Berlin. He felt a distinct desire for a sweet wine that would be warm to the tongue and he found a Wachenheimer Mandelgarten 1921 which seemed to promise well. Later he detected himself sipping his soup noisily—it sometimes happened in moments of distraction that his table manners betrayed his humble

origin. The situation he was in appeared to him fortunate
but extremely obscure. The swindle—so he forcibly described it to himself and the word, very surprisingly, inspired him with a new kind of pride—the swindle he had
perpetrated during the negotiations could be maintained
at best only for three days. During these days something
would have to happen if ruin was not to overwhelm him.
The provisional agreement could be canceled within fourteen days. Preysing had poured the first two glasses of
the cold, heady, and sun-sweet wine too fast down his
parched throat. His brain became slightly foggy and
through the fog he saw the main chimney of the works
break in three pieces and explode. That meant nothing.
It was merely a reminiscence of a dream that came to him
at regular intervals. He had just reached the fish when a
page boy crowed his "trunk call for Herr Preysing" across
the subdued murmur of the dining room. He drank one
more good mouthful of wine and marched off to box No. 4.
He forgot to turn on the switch. He stood in the darkness
and, with the receiver to his ear, he put on that iron mask
of the employer so notorious at Fredersdorf. Through a
shrill buzzing caused by a disturbance on the wires he
heard Fredersdorf speaking.

"I want Herr Brösemann," said the general director
with the unemphatic tone of command due to his position.
Half a minute passed before the head clerk came to the
telephone. Preysing resented the delay and drummed on
the ground with his heels. "There you are at last," he said
when Brösemann called through. Brösemann's respectful
demeanor could be guessed through the telephone and was
received as a fitting tribute. "Anything fresh, Brösemann,
beyond your most unnecessary telegram of yesterday?
No—not on the phone; we'll talk of that later. For the
moment, I request that that business be regarded as not
having happened, do you understand? I want to speak to

the old gentleman now, Brösemann, do you hear? Asleep?
I'm afraid he will have to be wakened. No. I am sorry.
Yes, yes, at once, Brösemann. No, all further instructions
by letter. I'm waiting, then——"

Preysing waited. He scratched the ledge with his fingernails. He took out his fountain pen and tapped with it on
the walls. He cleared his throat, and his heart beat with a
distinct triumphant insistence. The transmitter in front of
his mouth smelt of a disinfectant. A chip was broken off its
rim, as he noticed while he impatiently handled it in the
darkness. Then he heard the old man at Fredersdorf.

"Hallo. Good-afternoon, Papa. Forgive me, please, for
disturbing you. The conference is only just over. Thought
it would interest you to hear the result at once. The provisional agreement is signed. No. Signed, signed." (He had
to shout now, for the old man had a pig-headed way of
making himself out deafer than he was.) "Hard work,
you say? Well, we brought it off. Thanks, thanks, no ova-
tions, please. But listen, Papa. I must go to Manchester at
once. Yes, it is imperative absolutely, absolutely imperative. Right. Right. I'll tell you in detail by letter. What's
that? You are glad? So am I. (Yes, Fräulein, I've finished.)
Au revoir."

Preysing remained standing in the unlighted box and
it was only now that he thought of switching on the small
light. What's this? he thought in astonishment. What's
this about going to Manchester? What put that into my
head? But it's true enough—I must go to Manchester.
I've fixed the matter here, and I'll fix it there too. Quite
simple, he thought, and a new self-confidence entered into
him and blew him up like a balloon. This one little successful excursion into deceit had changed a solid, conscientious
business man into an intoxicated gambler and speculator,
whose jerry-built foundations threatened every moment
to collapse.

"Nine marks twenty for the call," said the operator.

"Put it on the bill," replied Preysing. He was again lost in thought. "I ought to ring up Mulle," he said to himself; but he did nothing of the sort. He felt a strange disinclination to talk to Mulle. It was a little too warm there in the dining room at home. Mulle liked overheated rooms; it seemed to Preysing that he could smell the cauliflower in the dining room at Fredersdorf; it seemed to him that he could see the folds of her cushion, printed in red on Mulle's round plump cheeks, as she woke from her afternoon nap to take hold of the telephone. He let it go. He did not ring her up. He left the telephone box and went back to the dining room, where a well-trained waiter had, meanwhile, put his wine in fresh ice and now set freshly warmed plates before him.

Preysing ate, drank his bottle of wine, lit his cigar, and then went with hot head and cold feet up to his room. He felt surprised at himself in a pleasant and nebulous way, but he was, at the same time, quite done up by the morning's transactions. The thought of a hot bath was tempting and he turned on the water. Just as he began to undress, it occurred to him that a hot bath was unwise on a full stomach. For a painful moment, he positively felt the heart attack that threatened him in the enameled bath; and he let the comforting and steaming water run out again. The fatigue and discomfort he felt became concentrated in an itching of his face and when he scratched it he felt his unshaven cheeks. Taking up his hat and coat as though for an enterprise of great importance and avoiding the hotel barber, with whom he was still annoyed after the experience of the morning, he went to look for a reliable hairdresser in the neighboring streets.

And now a strange thing happened to General Director Preysing, a man of principles, but without a razor, a man of sound views, who, none the less, had done something

questionable, an unlucky man whose head was turned by
success for the first time—it may seem a coincidence, and
yet, for all that, it may have been the irrevocable decree
of fate. This, in any case, is what happened.

The small barber's shop that Preysing entered was clean
and inviting. There were four chairs and two of them were
occupied. One customer was being attended by a young
curly-headed and amiable assistant, and the other by the
proprietor himself, an elderly gentleman with the look and
the demeanor of an official of the royal household. Preysing
was ushered into the third chair and enveloped in sheet
and bib. A moment's patience was politely requested—
the senior assistant had just gone out to lunch—and then
a bundle of illustrated papers was put into his hands to
appease him. Preysing, too jaded to make any objection,
leant his head back on the head rest and, soothed by the
perfume-laden air and the busy chatter of the scissors,
turned over the pages of the papers.

He did this with indifference at first, and almost with
distaste, for he thoroughly disliked this frivolous manner
of passing the time. His choice was for sound and substantial reading. But after a while he smiled all the same over
this joke and that, emitting, as he did so, short puffs
through his nose. Once, too, he turned the pages back to
look more closely at a *décolleté* drawing, and it was then
that he opened a page which remained open during the
whole time that he sat in the barber's chair. Yes, he became
so deeply absorbed in the contemplation of this photograph in a magazine that it quite upset him when the
senior assistant returned from his meal and made ready
to shave him.

Nevertheless, the photograph which so captivated him
was nothing out of the common. Photographs of this description were to be found by the hundred in periodicals
that were not in Preysing's line. The picture was of a naked

girl standing on her toes and endeavoring to look over a
screen that was too high for her to see over. Her arms were
raised and, in this attitude, her extremely pretty breasts
were shown to particular advantage. The muscles of her
long and slender back were also visible. Her waist was incredibly slender and this slenderness was carried on in her
hips until, widening, they swept in two long soft curves
to her thighs. Here the body was given a slight turn to
the front, so that you could just see her shadowy bosom,
her thighs and knees as she stood straining upwards in
eager curiosity. This exceptionally well-favored and charming girl also had a face and—here lay the extreme provoca-
tion of this particular picture—this face was known to the
general director. It was Flämmchen's short-nosed, gay, and
innocent kitten face, and the smile, too, was the confiding
smile of Flamm the Second. It was the same lock of hair,
with a high light cunningly thrown on it by the clever
photographer, and above all it was her complete spon-
taneity and her matter-of-course unconcern, as she displayed her figure, stark naked before all the world, the
figure that—as Preysing now remembered—she had accu-
rately and modestly described as "good." Preysing went
red as he held this picture before his eyes; a sudden hot
flush sprang to his forehead and clouded his mind, as often
occurred in those fits of rage at which the whole factory
trembled. Then every vein in his body began to throb
singly. He felt it; he felt his blood surge, and he had not
felt this for years.

Preysing was fifty-four. Not an old man, but a man who
had gone to sleep, the passive husband of a Mulle who had
gone to seed, the amiable Pops of grown-up daughters. He
had walked unmoved behind Flamm the Second along the
hotel corridor and the soft tingling in his blood had sub-
sided again of itself. Now as he sat and gazed at this photograph of the nude, it rose up again and took his breath

away. "If you please——" said the barber, and, with a graceful flourish, he laid the razor to Preysing's cheek. Preysing kept hold of the magazine, lay back and closed his eyes. At first there was only red; then he saw Flämmchen. Not Flämmchen in her clothes at the typewriter and not the unclothed Flämmchen of the photograph in black and white, but a violently exciting mixture of both. A Flämmchen of golden brown flesh and red pulsing blood, naked, however, and on tiptoe, looking inquisitively over a screen.

General Director Preysing was not accustomed to the workings of his fancy. Now, however, it was at work. It had been in gear ever since he laid the telegram on the table that morning and gone on to lie, without shame and without discrimination. And it ran away with him entirely, and in a manner that was at once alarming and intoxicating. While the razor glided over his face with the lightness of a practised hand, Preysing passed through unexampled, incredible experiences with the naked Flämmchen and with himself too, experiences of which he would never have thought himself capable.

"Shall I trim the mustache?" asked the barber.

"No," said Preysing in a flurry. "Whatever for?"

"The tips are a little gray. That adds to your age. If I may advise—the gentleman would look ten years younger without a mustache," the barber whispered into the mirror with that cajoling smile common to all barbers.

But I can't go back to Mulle without a mustache, looking like a fool, thought Preysing as he looked at himself in the glass. True, his mustache was gray, and there was always perspiration beneath it on his upper lip. Oh, bother Mulle! he thought. That settled it. His marriage vow was already broken.

"Yes, take it off. A mustache like that can always be grown again."

"Certainly, with no trouble at all," the barber agreed, and he made a fresh lather for the great undertaking. Preysing held up the photograph again—but now it satisfied him no longer. He was done with looking. He wanted to grasp and feel. He wanted to feel Flämmchen burn. . . .

In the hotel, the absence of the mustache was spotted at once, without the least notice being taken of it. They were well accustomed enough, heaven knows, to the most strange transformations in provincial personages after a brief stay in a big hotel. Preysing, breathing hard, made a hasty inquiry for letters. One from Mulle was thrust into his hand. He put it, unread and unregarded, in his pocket and went straight across to the telephone boxes. I must ring up Mulle, he thought. But that will do later. He went into the local-calls box, and ringing up the office of Justizrat Zinnowitz, had a brief conversation with Flamm the First.

He asked whether her sister happened to be at the office.

No, she had gone.

Where could she be found?

Flamm the First, after a moment's pause, said that perhaps she had got delayed. But she would certainly be at the hotel any moment now.

Preysing gaped like a fool into the telephone. At the hotel? Here? In the Grand Hotel? How was that?

Yes, said Flamm the First, discreetly choosing her words. So at least she had understood. Flämmchen was going to the hotel, and, as far as she knew, it was to take down some letters. But possibly, it may have been an engagement of another description. You could never be sure with Flämmchen. She had her ways and they were by no means the ways of Flamm the First, she implied. But punctual she certainly was; when she undertook anything, she went through with it, and it was positive that she was going to the hotel.

Preysing thanked her and rang off in confusion. He dashed back with a harassed air, straight across the lounge to the porter's desk. The beat of the music could be heard clearly from the Yellow Pavilion.

"Has my secretary inquired for me?" he asked Herr Senf. The hall porter looked up at him. His care-worn face showed that he was at a loss.

"Who, please?"

"My secretary. The young lady to whom I was dictating letters yesterday," Preysing said irritably.

Little Georgi intervened.

"She did not inquire for you, but she was in the lounge not ten minutes ago. The slim fair lady, you mean? I believe she is in the tea room now—in the Yellow Pavilion straight through the lounge, second turn behind the lift, if you'll be so good—you will hear the music."

Can it possibly be any business of a general director, in a gray worsted suit, to follow in the wake of the highly seasoned strains of a jazz band, along unfamiliar corridors, in search of a frivolous young typist, with whom he has, properly, not the slightest concern? But Preysing did it. He had left the rails. The crash was to follow. But he did not know it. He only knew that his blood circulated as it had not done for fifteen or twenty years, and that he must at any price keep hold of this sensation and follow it out to the end. His mustache was gone. He was not going to telephone to Mulle; and, as he opened the door into the Yellow Pavilion and stepped into its unfamiliar atmosphere, he had almost forgotten Chemnitz and Manchester as well, with all the efforts they had cost him and the complications that still had to be cleared up.

At this hour, twenty minutes past five, the Yellow Pavilion is crowded with people, day after day. The yellow silk curtains are drawn. Yellow lights line the walls, and on every one of the small tables there is a light with a yellow shade. It is hot. Two electric fans are whirring. The air is a buzz of voices. People sit elbow to elbow, for the small tables have been crowded up together in order to leave the middle of the room free for dancing. The vaulted ceiling is painted with dancing figures in lilac and gray; sometimes it looks like a false mirror above the dancing crowd below. All that goes on here has a remarkably angular and jerky appearance. The dancers do not circle round, but zig-zag to and fro, and Preysing who had come here on the tide of his tumultuous blood in search of a particular person found himself at a loss. He saw no one at full length, for everyone was always cutting across everyone else, so that only a head or an arm or a leg was visible at one time—as in a certain kind of modern painting which Preysing detested for its perversity. But the chief and most remarkable feature of the Yellow Pavilion was the music. It was produced with incredible gusto by seven gentlemen in white shirts and short trousers, the famous Eastman Jazz Band, and its vivacity was frantic. It drummed on the soles of the feet and tickled the muscles of the hips. There were two saxophones that could weep, and two others derisively mocking their tears. The music sawed, snapped, stood on its head, laid eggs of melody, cackled, and proudly jumped on them—and whoever got within range of this music fell into the zig-zag rhythm of the room as if bewitched. Preysing, in any case, who—pushed to and fro by waiters with trays of ices—remained standing by the door, observed a certain springiness in his knee joints while at the same time he kept an impatient look-out for Flamm the Second. His shorn and rejuvenated upper lip was once more beaded with perspiration. He took out his handkerchief and wiped his face, and then put back his handker-

chief in his outside breast pocket, usually reserved exclu-
sively for his fountain pen. He even, with an embarrassed
side glance, pulled up a corner of it to make a neat little
white triangle in the approved style, as though he thereby
established his right to be present in these gay regions of
the Grand Hotel. In any case, no one bothered about him.
He was at liberty to stand there as long as he liked, while
he sought among the dancers for one slender young girl in
particular, among the two hundred other slender young
girls.

"When you weren't there at ten minutes past five, I
thought, He's let you down. You'll see he's let you down,
I thought to myself," said Flämmchen, who was dancing
with Gaigern an indolent variation of the Charleston,
something new, with a syncopating jerk of the knees. Their
two bodies moved like one.

"Out of the question. I've been thinking of you all
day," said Gaigern. He said it as lightly and indolently
and casually as he danced. He was only an inch or so taller
than Flämmchen and he looked down into her kittenish
eyes with a smile. She wore a thin blue silk dress, a cheap
necklace of cut glass, and a neat little close-fitting hat
bought at a sale for one mark ninety. She looked enchanting in this finery of a girl with her own way to make in the
world.

"Is it true that you thought of me?" she asked.

"Half truth, half fib," answered Gaigern candidly. "I've
had a frightfully boring day," he added with a sigh. "I've
been taking an old fellow around. Enough to make you
weep."

"Why do you do it, then?"

"I want something out of him."

"Oh, I see," said Flämmchen, quickly understanding.

"You must dance with him later on," said Gaigern,
drawing her a little closer.

"There's no 'must' about it."

"No. But I'm going to beg you to as nicely as I know how. He can't dance, you know, but he wants to so much. Just walk him about a bit along the wall—to please me."

"Well—I'll see," Flämmchen agreed.

They went on dancing in silence. A moment later he drew her body a little closer to his own. He felt her back yield to his hand. But instead of being pleased, he was vexed.

"Well. What's up?" asked Flämmchen, who was quick to notice it.

"Oh, nothing," answered Gaigern, who was annoyed now with himself.

"What do you want then?" Flämmchen asked, only eager to please. He was so handsome with that mouth of his and with the scar above his chin and his slightly oblique eyes. She was a little in love with him.

"I want to do something a bit mad. That's all. I want to bite you or play the fool with you or pull you about— well, I am going to see some boxing to-night. There'll be something doing there at least."

"I see," said Flämmchen. "You're going to see boxing this evening. I see."

"With the old fellow," said Gaigern.

"If you—— Oh, that's the end," said Flämmchen, for music had stopped, and she began at once to clap loudly and without stirring from the spot. Gaigern tried to get her away from the middle of the room to the table where he had left Kringelein. But the music began again as they were halfway through the crowd. "Tango," Flämmchen cried in an ecstasy, and she simply took possession of him. The way she stretched out her hands for his both beseeched and implied his consent. Without a pause they fell into the slow languishing tango step and room was made for them on all sides when it was seen how beautifully they danced.

"You dance very well," Flämmchen whispered. It was almost a declaration of love. Gaigern had nothing to say in reply.

"You were quite different yesterday," Flämmchen said a little later.

"Yes—yesterday," Gaigern answered. It sounded as though he said "a hundred years ago." "Something has happened to me between yesterday and to-day," he added. There was a sympathy between Flämmchen and him of the easiest and most spontaneous kind, and suddenly he obeyed his impulse to tell her all about it.

"I fell in love last night, really and utterly, I mean," he said in a low voice in the midst of the tango as it sobbed and sawed and sung and filled the whole room. "That makes everything different. It goes through and through you. It is like——"

"But there is nothing extraordinary in that," said Flämmchen mockingly to conceal a stab of disappointment.

"Yes, yes, it *is* something extraordinary. You want to get out of your skin and become another person, you see. You find of a sudden that there's only one woman in the world and everything else is nothing. You find you can never sleep again except with this woman. You're carried off in a whirlwind—as though you had been rammed into a great gun and shot off up to the moon or somewhere where nothing is the same."

"What does she look like?" asked Flämmchen, and every other woman in the world would have asked the same question.

"Ah—what does she look like? That's just it. She is very old, and so thin, and so light that I could lift her up with one finger. She has wrinkles—here and there—and eyes tired with weeping, and she talks in a jargon like a clown till you have to laugh and weep—and this is so utterly delightful that I cannot resist her. It is simply real love."

"Real love? There isn't such a thing," said Flämmchen. Her face stared with that astonished and capricious expression that you sometimes see in pansies.

"Yes, yes, there is such a thing," said Gaigern. This impressed Flämmchen so much that for a second she stood still in the middle of the tango and looked at Gaigern and shook her head. "How he talks——" she muttered at the same time.

This however was the moment when Preysing's searching eyes picked her up at last in the languorous maze of the tango. With reproachful and keen impatience he waited till the long dance came to an end, and then he proceeded to fight his way to the table where Flämmchen had taken a seat between two men both of whom Preysing already knew by sight. These unacknowledged acquaintanceships are always happening in hotel life. You brush against someone in the lift; you meet again in the dining room and in the cloak room and in the bar; or you go in front of him or behind him through the revolving door—that door that never stops shoveling people in and shoveling them out.

"Good-evening, Fräulein Flamm," said the general director in his dry voice which embarrassment made even more unamiable; and then he planted himself beside her chair and hollowed his back to let the waiters get past. Flamm the Second screwed up her eyes in the effort to focus this unexpected apparition.

"Oh—the Herr Direktor," she said amiably when she had done so. "Are you dancing too?"

She gazed from one to the other of the three icy faces. She was used to this expression in her male companions. "Do you know each other?" she asked with an elegant wave of the hand which she had picked up from a film star. She could not proceed to introductions for she did not know her cavaliers' names. Preysing and Gaigern muttered something, and Preysing rested one hand on the table with the air of taking possession, just as a tray of orangeade swept dangerously past his head.

"Good-afternoon, Herr Preysing," said Kringelein, all of a sudden, without stirring from his seat. Each single one of his vertebræ ached from the fearful exertion it cost him not to tremble and collapse into the pitiful Kringelein of the counting house. He held his shoulders rigid, his lips and teeth too, and even his nostrils, and these in consequence dilated with a malicious and equine expression. But he sustained himself on the height of this great moment; his will power tapped undreamt sources of strength in his well-cut black jacket, his linen, his tie, and his manicured fingernails. What certainly went very near to throwing him off his balance was the fact that Preysing too was altered. He still wore his well-known Fredersdorf suit, but he had no longer a mustache.

"I am not sure—pardon me—have we met before?" Preysing asked as politely as his intense preoccupation over Flämmchen allowed.

"To be sure. I'm Kringelein," said Kringelein. "I am in the works."

"I see," said Preysing more coolly. "Kringelein, Kringelein. One of our representatives, are you?" he added with a glance at Kringelein's smart attire.

"No. Bookkeeper. Junior bookkeeper in the counting house. Room 23, Block C. Third floor," said Kringelein, conscientiously but without enthusiasm.

"I see," said Preysing again, and sank into reflection. He preferred to say no more for the present about the undesired and incomprehensible presence of a junior clerk from Fredersdorf in the Yellow Pavilion of the Grand Hotel. "I want to speak to you, Fräulein Flamm," he said, withdrawing his hand from the back of her chair. "It is about a new job of typing," he explained in his office tone, and this was particularly aimed at this fellow from Fredersdorf.

"Right," said Flämmchen. "What time would suit you, then? Seven, half-past seven?"

"No. Immediately," Preysing said peremptorily, as he wiped his face. This personage from Fredersdorf also had a handkerchief in his breast pocket, a silk flag of mutiny and impertinence.

"I am sorry, I can't immediately," said Flämmchen amiably. "I am engaged—as you see. I cannot very well desert these gentlemen. I have promised Herr Kringelein a dance."

"Herr Kringelein will be so good as to forgo it," said Preysing stiffly. It was a command. Kringelein could feel his rigid lips expanding to the obsequious smile of twenty-five years of subordination. He forced it back. He appealed for help and strength to Gaigern. The Baron had a cigarette in the corner of his mouth. The smoke ascended past the eyelashes of his left eye and he screwed up this eye with a roguish and knowing wink.

"I have no intention of forgoing it," said Kringelein. No sooner had he got it out than he stiffened like a hare squatting in a furrow. Suddenly this obstinate demeanor on Kringelein's part brought his case to Preysing's recollection. He had had it before him only a few days before.

"That is remarkable, indeed," he said with the dreaded nasal tone of the factory. "Very remarkable. Now I know where I am. You reported sick, isn't that so? Herr Kringelein, eh? Your wife is in receipt of support from the sick fund on account of your serious illness. We gave you six weeks' sick leave on full pay, and here you are amusing yourself in Berlin. You are indulging in a style of living quite out of keeping with your position and your income.

Remarkable. Very remarkable, Herr Kringelein. Your
books shall be very carefully examined. You may depend
upon that. Your pay shall be stopped, since you are so
well off, Herr Kringelein. You shall——"

"Now, children, don't quarrel here. Keep that for your
office," said Flämmchen with disarming good humor.
"We are here to amuse ourselves. Come along, Herr
Kringelein. We're going to dance now."

Kringelein got on to his feet. His knees felt like india-
rubber, but they became noticeably firmer when Flämmchen laid her hand on his shoulder. The music was rattling
off something pretty fast—something akin to the 115-
kilometers-an-hour motor run and the aëroplane propeller.
It inspired him with the strength to utter the remarks,
for which twenty-five years of a subordinate's existence
had prepared him. As Flämmchen dragged him away
towards the middle of the room, he turned his head and
exclaimed loudly: "Do you imagine you own the world,
Herr Preysing? Are you different from me? Has a man like
me no right to live?"

"Now, now, now," said Flämmchen. "This is not the
place to squabble in. You're here to dance. And don't look
at your feet, but at my face, and just walk, just walk
straight ahead, and I'll guide you."

"If that's not a case of peculation——" Preysing
blurted out, trembling with rage.

Gaigern continued to smoke. The word aroused in him
an odd feeling of professional sympathy, and with it a
strong and contemptuous dislike of the corpulent and
perspiring director. You need a few leeches applied to you,
my friend, he thought to himself.

"Let the poor devil have his fun," he said half aloud.
"You can see he's not long for this world."

I didn't ask for your advice, thought Preysing, but
he did not venture to say it; for he suspected that he would

meet more than his match in the Baron. "Would you be so good as to inform Fräulein Flamm that I am waiting for her in the lounge on a matter of urgent importance. If she does not come by six o'clock, I shall not require her services," he said, bowed stiffly, and retired.

Alarmed by this ultimatum, Flämmchen appeared in the lounge at three minutes to six. Preysing, who had been sitting on hot bricks, got up with a smile of heart-felt relief. He smiled so seldom that it came as an engaging surprise.

"There you are," he said foolishly.

For hours he had been possessed and tormented by one single thought—was Flämmchen to be had? His experiences with women had been few and long since closed. He had only the vaguest notions about the girls of the younger generation, though at bachelor parties and in the course of comfortable talks on his business journeys he had often heard it said that they made very little of entering on temporary liaisons. He looked Flämmchen up and down from her crossed legs in silk stockings to her cut-glass beads and her painted mouth (she was pursing her lips and touching them up at that moment), and he was at a loss to know where in her whole unconcerned person the answer to his thoughts was to be found.

Flämmchen snapped her powder box and asked: "Well, what is it about?"

Preysing kept on with his cigar and said it all in a breath.

"It is that I have to go to England and I want to take a secretary with me. In the first place for my correspondence, but also for the sake of a little company. I am very nervous, very nervous (he said this by way of an unconscious bid for her sympathy), and need someone on the journey who will take care of me. I don't know if you understand me. I offer you a confidential post in which it —in which you—in which——"

"I understand perfectly," Flämmchen said quietly, when he got tied up.

"I think we could put up with each other very well on the journey," said Preysing. The curious surging and throbbing in his veins had been banished by the difficulty of this conversation, but as he looked at Flämmchen he had the consoling impression that she could very quickly conjure it all up again if she only would. "You told me that you had traveled last year, too, with somebody and that made me think—I think it might be very fine if you only would. Will you?"

Flämmchen thought it over for five long minutes.

"I must think it over first," she said, and then she sat lost in reflection and puffed at her indispensable cigarette.

"To England?" she said at last. The golden brown of her skin had become rather lighter, and this perhaps showed that she had grown paler. "I have never been to England yet. And for how long?"

"For—I can't say exactly at the moment. It depends. If the business I have there goes off well I would possibly take a fortnight's holiday afterwards. We could stay in London or go to Paris."

"It will go off all right, I'm sure. I could tell that from the letters," said Flämmchen with assurance. Optimism was the element she lived in. Preysing was cheered by the fact that she knew about the affair he had on hand and that she prophesied success.

"You must tell me, too, what salary you ask," he said in a flattering tone.

This time it took Flämmchen even longer to reply. She had to draw up a comprehensive balance sheet. The renunciation of the incipient affair with the handsome Baron figured on it, also Preysing's ponderous fifty years, his fat, and his heavy breathing. Then there were one or two little bills, requirements in the way of new underclothing, pretty shoes—the blue ones were nearly done. The small capital that would be necessary to launch her on a career in the films, in revue, or elsewhere. Flämmchen made a clear and unsentimental survey of the chances the job offered her. "A thousand marks," she said. It sounded a princely amount, and she was under no illusion as to the sums that were nowadays laid at the feet of pretty girls.

"Perhaps a little extra for clothes to travel in," she added, a little more timidly than was usual with her. "You want me to look my best, naturally."

"You need no clothes for that. On the contrary," Preysing said with warmth. He considered this a most apt rejoinder. Flämmchen greeted it with a melancholy smile which showed up strangely on her blooming pansy-like face.

"That's settled, then?" said Preysing. "There are one or two things to be seen to here to-morrow. We must have our passports in order. Then we could set off the day after. Are you glad to go to England?"

"Very," answered Flämmchen. "Then I'll bring my little portable here to-morrow and I could take down any letters right away."

"And to-night—if you'd like it, I thought we might go to the theater. We must at any rate have a glass of wine to seal our contract."

"To-night, too," said Flämmchen. "Very well, to-night, too." She blew her lock of hair aloft and dropped her extinguished cigarette end in the ash tray. She could hear the music from the Yellow Pavilion distinctly. One can't have everything, she thought. A thousand marks. New clothes. London, too, was not to be despised. "I must telephone to my sister," she said as she got up. Preysing felt a hot impassioned wave of gratitude rise and overwhelm him. He went behind her and carefully took hold of her elbows. They were lightly pressed to her sides.

"Will you be kind to me?" he asked softly. And as softly

with her eyes cast down to the raspberry-colored carpet,
Flämmchen answered: "If it's not forced on me——"

Kringelein, Motorist, Flier, and Conqueror, went furiously on with the day on which he had begun to live.
Perhaps he felt very like those stunt fliers who pass within
an ace of death as they loop the loop. He had begun to
throw himself head over and now he was whirled on in
obedience to forces he could not control. To turn about
would mean a crash, and so he had to go through with it—
forwards, downwards, upwards, he could not tell whither,
for his sense of direction was lost. He was a tiny hurtling
comet that soon must burst into atoms.

Once more the car hummed along the Kaiserdamm, once
more they were at the nucleus of modern Berlin. The
Funkturm with traversing beams cut illuminated sections
out of the city. In front of the Sporthalle there was a black
and compact throng, like bees clotted about the entrance
to a hive, motionless and busily humming. Kringelein had
never seen anything so immense as the interior of the hall
and never such a mass of people in one spot. He made his
way to his seat through an elbowing crowd, following
Gaigern who went on before like a tower. It was well to
the front, close to the bare and brilliantly illuminated
square patch on which the eyes of fourteen thousand
people were concentrated. Gaigern went into many ex-
planations, but Kringelein did not understand a word.
He was afraid this time, too; for he could not endure the
sight of blood and fighting and barbarity. He was tortured
at the moment by the memories of his duties as a ward
orderly, which the war had imposed on him, since he had
been unfit for anything else. He looked with alarmed
amazement at the men of muscle as they stepped into the
ring and took off their dressing gowns and exposed their
hard flesh. He heard the stentorian voice of the announcer

and clapped whenever everybody else clapped. If it gets
too bad, I shall look away, he thought in secret when the
first round began. But, at first, it looked to him as if the
two fine sinewy fellows up there with their broken noses
were only going to fool about. "They are playing like
kittens," he said to himself, and smiled with relief. Gaigern, on the other hand, was now so intense and excited
that Kringelein wondered. The hall was still and so were
the boxers. Sometimes they could be heard drawing in
careful breaths through their nostrils and their quick feet
in their boxing shoes were almost silent. Then, in the midst
of the stillness, came the dull rounded thud of leather—
and a thrill went through the hall from end to end and
right up to the gallery, below the roof, where a thousand
faces loomed through the haze. More, thought Kringelein,
for the sound of the blow filled him with a sweet and
feverish satisfaction that quickly turned to hunger. The
gong went in no time, and men sprang over the ropes
with jugs, chairs, sponges, and towels. The boxers lay in
their corners breathing hard. Their tongues hung out like
the tongues of hunted animals. Water was sprinkled over
them, but they were not allowed to drink even a mouthful.
Some of the splashes even fell on Kringelein below, and he
wiped the drops from his coat with awe and a wonderful
sense of fellowship with the man in the corner nearest him.
Gong. Immediately the square of light was cleared again
for the fight.

The murmur of the spectators abruptly ceased and
turned to rapt attention. Hit followed hit. Shouts from the
gallery—then silence. Another hit. The first blood trickled
down over the eyes of one of the two—and he laughed.
Hit, hit, and now and then a pant. Kringelein came upon
his clenched fists in his coat pockets. They seemed to him
like two hard inanimate objects he had found there. Gong.
Again the corners of the ring were a turmoil of flapping

handkerchiefs and tapping and massaging hands. The bodies of the two now shone with sweat. Below, every face showed cold and green in the hard light and men were standing up and engaging in excited debate.

"Now we're getting to work at last," said Gaigern just after the third round began. Kringelein shuddered slightly at this typically Gaigernian anticipation of stirring events.

The boxers above—he could not distinguish one from the other, for both had broken noses and it was only between the rounds that he sided with the man in the corner nearest him—now went for each other wildly. When they clinched it sometimes looked like an enraged and misplaced tenderness. "Break away," shouted fourteen thousand throats. Kringelein shouted too. They ought to fight—those two up there—not reel locked together against the ropes. He wanted above all to hear once more the round full thud of the leather glove on flesh.

"Blynx is groggy. He can't hold out much longer," Gaigern muttered, and he showed his strong teeth under his upper lip. Again and again the referee in his white silk shirt jumped in to part the two bleeding muscular bodies. Kringelein thought it very good-natured of them to let him. He fixed his eyes on the one who was "groggy," a technical term which appeared to mean that though he did not know it he was coming to the end of his tether. This man Blynx now had a blue swelling that hung like a fruit over his right eye. His back and shoulders were smeared with blood, and sometimes too he spat out blood at the referee's feet. He held his head sunk low; this might be correct but it made an impression of great cowardice on the inexperienced Kringelein. Whenever this Blynx received a blow Kringelein felt a vivid and bestial joy rise from the depths of his being. He could not see enough of it. He greeted every hit that went home with a little cry of relief and then with mouth open and head extended he waited for the next. Gong. Interval. Round. Gong. Interval. Round. Interval. Round . . .

In the seventh round Blynx was knocked out. He reeled, head first, fell to the ground, turned on his back, and lay there. The twenty-eight thousand hands thundered applause. Kringelein heard himself yelling hoarsely and saw his hands clapping like mad. He was not very clear about what was going on in the ring above. The man in the silk shirt was standing over the prostrate Blynx and making hammer-like counts with one arm. Once Blynx made a movement as horses do when they have fallen on the ice, but he did not get up. There was a fresh outburst of applause from the hall. People climbed over the ropes. There were embracings, kissings, roarings through the megaphone, and frenzy in the gallery. When Blynx had been carried out, Kringelein collapsed in utter exhaustion on his hard chair. He had overtaxed himself and his shoulders and arms hurt him.

"There, you are quite played out with enthusiasm," Gaigern said to him. "You get carried away with it, eh?"

Kringelein remembered an evening he had spent a thousand years before.

"It's something different to yesterday evening at Grusinskaya's ballet," he answered, and he thought with pity and distaste of the empty theater, of the ghostly and sadly circling nymphs, of the wounded dove in the moonlight, and of the feeble applause accompanied by Otternschlag's comments.

"Grusinskaya!" said Gaigern. "Well, yes, that's quite another affair." He began smiling to himself. "There's too much *chi chi* with Grusinskaya," he went on. He could see her at that moment. He could actually see her in her dressing room at Prague, resting and thinking how tired the night before had made her, how tired, but how young, how full of courage. . . .

"This fight was not up to much. The real event comes on now," he said to Kringelein. Kringelein was glad to hear it. He thought himself that there must be more to come—the thud of heavier blows, louder panting, and even more frenzied participation. More, he thought. More. More. On with it! On with it!

Two gigantic forms stepped into the ring, a white man and a nigger. The nigger was tall and slim with a velvety skin from which the light was reflected in gleams of silver. The white man was thick-set. The muscles stood out in his shoulders and he had a square brutish face. Kringelein loved the nigger at once. The whole hall loved the nigger. The megaphone announced the fight and an incredible silence followed. And then it all began again as before. There were the same initial play and the nimble foot work, the jumps, the stealthy approach with lowered head, and the elastic jump back. When they fought at close quarters the white body and the black were enlaced with the grim ardor of passion. Blow upon blow and nothing between but the gong for breathing space. Three minutes' fighting, one minute's breathing space, three minutes alternating with one minute fifteen times for an hour long. But this time the whole fight went faster and more furiously, with sudden onsets of the black man and wild outbreaks of the white blazing up like a stubborn fire.

Kringelein melted like wax. Kringelein was cooped up no longer in his dilapidated body. Kringelein was one among fourteen thousand, one green distorted face among countless others, and his voice was indistinguishable in the one great roar that issued from every throat at once. He drew his breath when every breath was drawn, and he held it back when the whole hall gasped in sympathy with the boxers. His ears burned, his fists were clenched, his lips were dry, his stomach chilled, and he swallowed the sweet spittle of excitement down his parched throat. On, on. . . .

In the last two rounds the nigger, Kringelein's nigger, seemed to be having the best of it. Again and again repeated blows from his fist drummed in succession on the body of the white man, who twice was forced to lean on the ropes with outstretched arms. Each face wore a tranced smile. The breath was pumped from their bodies as though from machines. The last round was accompanied by an unbroken uproar and thunderous stamping throughout the hall. Kringelein roared and stamped too. Then the gong went, and it was over. Kringelein lay back in his chair covered with sweat. The megaphone made itself heard. The megaphone made an announcement. It announced that the white man had won.

"What? What's that? Outrageous!" roared Kringelein through fourteen thousand throats. He climbed on to his seat. All climbed on to their seats and roared against the decision. The hall went raving mad. Kringelein went raving mad. On with it, get on with it, fight it out! The gallery was in an uproar, whistling, screeching. The wooden tiers seemed likely to collapse in the dust and haze and tumult of a serried mass of indignant and outraged humanity. The boxers stood in the brilliant light between the ropes and shook hands awkwardly with their gloves on and smiled as though they were being photographed. The hall began to rain down boxes, cigarette packets, oranges, and finally glasses and bottles. The clean floor of the ring was covered with trampled wreckage. A continuous shrill whistling echoed round the roof. Towards the rear some were stamping and striking each other, and the confused tumult of the fourteen thousand presented a scene of panic. Kringelein got something very hard and heavy on the head, but he did not even feel it. Kringelein's fists were clenched. Kringelein wanted to be in the thick of the fray and to chastise the referee for his decision. He looked round for Gaigern. Gaigern was in front near the ring. He stood out alone above the rest, and he was laughing as one laughs when caught in a spring shower. Kringelein in his unbounded excitement was seized by a sudden and powerful attraction to this man who stood there laughing and looking like Life itself. Gaigern grabbed hold of him and led him out of the hall—now filled by a frantic mob. Kringelein walked out behind him as though protected by a warm and impenetrable shield.

On they went. Past the Gedächtniskirche, whose walls were white in the light of the thousand lights all round, and where the cars threw gleaming reflections on the oily asphalt. Everybody looked black in the brilliance of the illuminated shop windows of the Tauentzienstrasse. Then abruptly came the silence and darkness under the trees of the Bavarian quarter. Little squares started out of the darkness, with gravel and hedges and lamps, and still they went on, until finally they reached the gambling club.

It occupied the large rooms of an old-fashioned Berlin house which had been refitted as a club. Men in dinner jackets moved noiselessly about. There were many coats in the tiled cloakroom. Kringelein recognized a pale, lean figure, smartly clothed in black, who was smoothing his thin hair off his forehead, as himself. It came as a surprise to encounter himself in the glass. I can really stand a good deal, he thought. For the space of a second he thought of his friend Kampmann, the solicitor. It seemed as though he had known him in a dream. They made a short stay in a room with standard lamps and an open fire, where everyone talked and had drinks. In the next room there were a few tables of bridge. It was no better than nap, thought Kringelein, who was hungering for new sensations.

"We are going to the back," said Gaigern to a gentleman who was there. "Come with me, Herr Direktor, we'll go to the back."

The back was at the end of a narrow ugly corridor with

many doors opening on to it. Through the last brown folding door they entered a smallish room, which was so completely veiled in a brown gloom that the walls were scarcely visible. All the light was concentrated on a table in the middle as it was on the ring in the Sporthalle. A few people were sitting and standing round the table, twelve or fourteen only. They had an intent and business-like air and exchanged brief remarks that were quite unintelligible to Kringelein.

"How much do you want to stake?" asked Gaigern, who had gone aside to a desk where a lady in black, with the air of a governess, was sitting as though at a cash desk. "What did you think?"

Kringelein had thought of ten marks. "I don't exactly know, Herr Baron," he said dubiously.

"Let's say five hundred marks for a start," Gaigern proposed. Kringelein, incapable of protest, took out his old pocketbook and produced five M.100 notes. A handful of brightly colored counters was thrust into his hand, green, blue, and red. He heard others like them falling on to the table with little raps beneath the square green-shaded lamp. He waited impatiently for what was to follow.

"Now stake where you like," said Gaigern. "It's no use my explaining. Stake what and where you like. Those who play for the first time usually win."

How many times that day had Kringelein put himself in peril? He knew now that this was the only way with life. He knew now that fear and pleasure go together like the nut and the shell. He had an inkling that he might lose in an hour or two as much as he had earned in the forty-seven years of his dead-and-alive Fredersdorf existence. He knew that in this obscure room with the laconic men and the green table he could only let himself be whirled on as before and so gamble away the three or

four weeks of vagabond life that remained. And Kringelein in this new form of looping the loop was almost curious to know what would happen next. On, then—on!

His ears and his lips had gone white as he stepped up
to the table and began to play. His hands felt as though
they were full of sand. He staked. A little shovel appeared
and took up his green counter with the rest. Someone said
something that he did not understand. He put down
another, this time somewhere else. He lost. Another. He
lost again. Gaigern across the table staked something,
won once, then lost again. Kringelein threw a quick imploring glance across, but it was not observed. Here everyone was concerned with himself alone. Every eye was
riveted on the green surface of the table. Each man bent
all his force and will to draw the winnings to himself.
"No luck," someone said somewhere. It was an ominous
word to hear in this brown back room beneath the green
billiard-room lamp. Kringelein, utterly preoccupied with
himself alone, went to the lady in black and drew counters
for another five hundred marks. He returned to the
table. Another man was now shoveling up the counters.
They made a gentle rattling sound. Restless fingers arranged them meticulously in little piles. Kringelein took
his store in his left hand and staked with his right hand
at random and almost unconsciously. He staked and lost.
Staked and won. What a surprise when his green counter
returned to him, accompanied by a red one! He staked
and won. He put a few counters in his pocket because he
did not know what else to do with them. He staked and
lost thrice in succession. He left off for a few minutes.
Gaigern, too, had ceased to play. He stood with his hands
in his pockets and smoked. "Finished for to-day," he said.
"My money's gone." "Allow me, Herr Baron," Kringelein
whispered, and thrust one of the two red counters he still
possessed into Gaigern's hand, which trembled as he took

it out of his pocket. "I'm too flat for play to-night," Gaigern muttered. He had a keen nose for luck. This was part of his questionable way of life, and at present the luck was against him, unless his love affair with Grusinskaya was to be called luck. Kringelein returned to the table and carried on.

A clock rasped out one o'clock as Kringelein with a little propeller whirling behind his forehead ceased to play and cashed his counters at the desk. He had won three thousand four hundred marks. He felt his wrists go limp and begin to quiver, but he controlled them bravely. Nobody troubled about him or his winnings. Kringelein had won all he would have earned in a year at Fredersdorf. He pushed it all into his torn leather pocketbook.

Gaigern stood by yawning and looked on. "I'm broke, Herr Direktor. You must take care of me. I haven't a farthing," he said in a tone of indifference. Kringelein with his pocketbook in his hands stood there not knowing what to do or what was expected of him.

"I shall have to come down on you for something substantial to-morrow," said Gaigern.

"Yes, please do," replied Kringelein with an air. "And now what happens next?"

"Good Lord. You're persevering. There's nothing now but drink or women," Gaigern replied. Kringelein turned a white and dissipated face from the mirror after putting on his hat to go. He put fifty pfennigs into the open palm of an undersized club servant who opened the street door for them. Again he put his hand in his pocket and this time it was a hundred-mark note he came upon and he shoved the tightly folded piece of paper into the page boy's hand as they stepped out into the dark and silent street. He had quite lost his senses. He no longer knew what money was. In a world where in the morning you spent a thousand marks and won three thousand at night, Kringe-

lein the Fredersdorf bookkeeper wandered as though in a
labyrinth, an enchanted forest where no path, no light
directed his steps. The little four-seater was waiting under
a lamp, dumb but alive. There was something of the
patient devotion of a dog in its trusty vigil that stirred
Kringelein to gratitude.

On and on. It was raining now. The screen wiper made
its half-circular sweeps, and Kringelein watched it going
to and fro, to and fro. The smell of the gasoline now made
him feel at home in a warm little home of his own. Long
streaks of red and blue and yellow were reflected in the
wet surface of the street. A glaring jet of flame burning on
persistently in the dead of night threw up in black relief
a gang of workmen soldering a rail. The car went much
too slowly to please Kringelein. He gave Gaigern a side
glance. Gaigern was smoking, his eyes on the road, his
thoughts heaven knew where. The town at half-past one
at night looked as though some accident had occurred.
It was completely alert and crowded with people, almost
more crowded than by day. At the crossings where now no
police were on duty, there was a continuous warning hoot
of cars. Above, a red and fiery sky rested like a portent of
disaster, traversed at regular intervals by jerking shafts of
light from the searchlights of the Funkturm. On they
went.

A staircase filled with the noise of music from three
floors. Flags and paper snakes below, halfway up blind
mirrors in gilt stucco frames, a medley of people, some
drunk, some melancholy, cadaverous girls dark under the
eyes. Kringelein forced his way upstairs past their powdered backs. The whole place was full of cigarette smoke.
It hung in thick blue clouds round the paper shades that
gave an up-to-date air to the electric light fittings on the
staircase. Below the noise was loud and uproarious. On the
first floor a less disorderly music issued from folding doors

234   GRAND HOTEL

within which dancing was in progress. One floor up again
and there was silence. A girl in virulent green stockings
was sitting on the stairs with a glass in her hand and
pretending to be asleep as they passed by. Her bare
shoulders brushed Kringelein's new clothes and awoke
him to expectancy. They entered a long, almost dark
room. Only on the floor a few lanterns with paper shades
that shone opaquely. There was music here too, but you
could not see where it came from. Girls' legs were to be
seen dancing in the light of the lanterns, distinctly seen as
far as the knee but beyond all was swallowed in darkness.
Kringelein wanted to keep tight hold of Gaigern's hand
like a little boy. Everything here was obscured and in-
distinct. What went on beyond the painted partitions
which separated the ottomans and low tables was left to
the imagination. Kringelein observed that he was drinking
iced champagne. He had visions of many forms. They
crowded upon him with a strange and eerie sweetness.
Kringelein sang a soft accompaniment in his high tenor
to the melody of two invisible violins. Kringelein rocked
to and fro. His head lay pressed in the cool hollow of a
girl's arm.

"Another bottle?" a waiter asked him severely. Kringelein ordered another bottle. Kringelein was sorry for the
waiter, who looked like a consumptive when he bent down
to the light of the lantern to write down the order. Kringelein was in a soft-hearted condition. He was absurdly
sorry for the waiter and for the girls who were so jolly and
were all legs and had to dance so late, and he was absurdly
sorry for himself. He drew the limp, warm, deathly strange
body of a girl across his knees which began to tremble as
he sought her face. A drunken rapture of sadness came
over him with the scent of powder from this unknown
woman. He could be heard singing. Gaigern, lost in his
reflections, was sitting bolt upright on a wicker chair near

by. He heard the high tremulous voice singing, "Rejoice in life while the l-a-amp still burns." Fathead, thought Gaigern with malevolence. On the way back I'll get hold of his pocketbook and then for Vienna, he thought frowning, as he clung to the verge of his perilous existence. . . .

Kringelein was standing in a little stuffy cloakroom washing his face on which a chill sweat kept breaking out. He pulled out the little bottle of Hundt's Elixir and drank three mouthfuls and hoped for the best. I'm not tired, he said to himself, not a bit. Not a trace of tiredness. There was still a lot to be done that night. He savored the cinnamon taste on his tongue and went back to the girl in the gloom among the ottomans. On—still on!

Kringelein alighted upon a mouth, as though upon some inconceivable island of adventure. With his lips there, he lay stranded a while. Little waves of drunkenness washed him away. "Be nice, Bubi," a voice was saying, meaning him. He became motionless listening intently to himself. For one dreaming moment's space he had his hands full of ripe red juicy raspberries from Mickcnau Forest—and then something came swiftly nearer, something frightful, like a sword and a flash of lightning and a wing of flame. . . .

Suddenly Gaigern heard him groan. It was a piercing and incredible sound, full of dread and tortured humanity.

"What's the matter?" Gaigern asked in the utmost alarm.

"Oh—pains," came the answer, wrung from the darkness near Kringelein's face. Gaigern picked up one of the lanterns and put it on the table. There sat Kringelein rigid and upright on the upholstered seat with his two hands clasped like the links of a chain. The lamp was blue and it made Kringelein's face blue, with a great round black mouth from which groans issued. Gaigern knew this mask of pain from severely wounded cases in the war. He quickly put an arm under Kringelein's head and, like a good comrade, supported his heaving shoulders.

"Dead drunk?" asked the girl. She was very young still and very common in her dress of black sequins.

"Be quiet," Gaigern answered.

Kringelein raised his eyes to him, tortured and torn with pain. He forced himself to a piteous and heroic attempt at good form. "Now it's I who am 'groggy,'" he said with his blue lips, and he meant his dazed, almost unconscious, fought-out, and collapsing condition. It was a lame but courageous joke that broke in the middle and ended in groans.

"But what's up with you?" asked Gaigern in alarm.

And Kringelein replied almost inaudibly: "I think— I've got—to die——"

It is quite a mistake to suppose that hotel chambermaids spy through keyholes. Hotel chambermaids feel no interest whatever in the people behind the keyholes. Hotel chambermaids have a lot to do and are tired out, and they are all a little disillusioned, and besides they are entirely occupied with their own concerns. Nobody bothers about anyone else in a big hotel. Everybody is alone with himself in this great pub that Dr. Otternschlag not inaptly compared with life in general. Everyone lives behind double doors and has no confidant but his reflection in the looking glass or his shadow on the wall. People brush past one another in the passages, say good-morning or good-evening in the lounge, sometimes even enter into a brief conversation painfully raked together out of the barren topics of the day. A glance that travels up does not reach the eyes. It stops at your clothes. Perhaps it happens that a dance in the Yellow Pavilion brings two bodies into contact. Perhaps someone steals out of his room into another's. That is all. Behind is an abyss of loneliness. Each in his own room is alone with his own ego and is little concerned with another's. Even the honeymoon couple in room No. 134 are parted as they lie in bed by a vacancy of unspoken words. Many wedded couples of boots and shoes that stand outside the doors at night wear a distinct expression of mutual hatred on their leather visages, and many have a jaunty air though they

237

are hopeless and lop-eared. The valet who collects them suffers terribly from chronic indigestion, but who cares? The chambermaid on the second floor has started an affair with Baron Gaigern's good-looking chauffeur, and now he has gone off without a word, and she is in no end of a way over it, there is no question of her looking through keyholes. At night she tries to think, but she is too sleepy, and she cannot sleep because the chambermaid in the other bed is a consumptive and sits up and turns on the light and coughs. Everyone between his four walls has his secrets; even the lady with the expressionless face in No. 28, who is always humming, and the gentleman in No. 154 who gargles so frantically and is only a commercial traveler. Even page boy No. 18 has a secret of his own behind his sleekly brushed forehead—an oppressive and horrible secret lies on his conscience. For he has found a gold cigarette case that Baron Gaigern left in the Winter Garden and has not given it up. For fear that it would be found on him when he went off duty, he has left it, for the present, stuffed in between the seat and the back of an easy chair, and in his seventeen-year-old soul Morality and the Rights of the Proletariat wage a bitter war.

Senf, the hall porter, has his eye on the boy—Karl Nispe is his name when he is not merely a number—for he slouches about the entrance with a distracted air and black rings under his eyes. But Senf, too, has other things to think about. His wife has now been for days in the hospital. There can be no question now of a normal delivery. The pains have stopped and strange cramps have set in, but the baby's heart can still be heard beating, and they await the moment for expediting the birth by artificial means. Senf has been out at midday but he was not allowed to see her. She was lying in a drowsed state of exhaustion which the doctors termed sleep. This is how it is with the hall porter, Senf, as he carries on in his mahogany cage, occupied now with the board where the keys hang and now with the railway timetables. Rohna has offered him a few days off, but he does not want time off. He is glad to be in harness and not to have to think. As for Rohna himself, this highly competent Count Rohna, who puts in fourteen hours' work a day, he is a fine fellow, but a hopeless outcast from his own class, and what he thinks about it nobody knows. Perhaps he is proud of his position, perhaps he is ashamed whenever a man of his own class registers his name. His bright and narrow and fair-complexioned face betrays nothing. It has become nothing but a mask.

At two o'clock in the morning seven utterly exhausted, limp, and dejected persons, carrying black cases, left the Grand Hotel by entrance No. II. They were the members of the Eastman Jazz Band going home in their moist shirts, discontented with their pay as all musicians are in every corner of the globe. In front of entrance No. V motor cars were driving off, and a little later the powerful lights of the hotel front were turned out. The lounge was getting cooler, for the central heating had been damped down a little. Dr. Otternschlag, who sat on there almost alone, gave a shudder and yawned. Immediately after Rohna, too, yawned at his desk, closed a few drawers, and retired to his five hours of sleep on the fifth floor. The night porter sorted the next day's morning papers, which had just been brought in by a messenger, who had got wet through in the rain and now went out again with tired and muddy feet through the revolving door. Two loud-voiced American women went up to bed and after that there was a profound silence in the lounge. Half the lights were turned out. The telephone attendant drank black coffee to keep himself alert.

"Shall we go up now?" Dr. Otternschlag asked himself as he drank up his brandy. "Yes, I think we might go now," he replied to himself. He required about ten minutes to carry the decision into execution. Once on his patent-leather feet he was in better form and he embarked upon his customary circular tour of the lounge till he reached the night porter. "Nothing for the Herr Doktor," the porter said unfeelingly, and waved him off with his hand when he was still two or three yards distant. "If anyone happens to inquire for me, I have gone to bed," Ottern-schlag announced. He then picked up one of the moist morning papers and ran over the headlines. "Gone to bed," the porter repeated mechanically, and made a chalk mark on the key board. Through the revolving door there came a chill rush of air smelling of dust and rain. Ottern-schlag turned round.

"Aha," was all he said, after his one serviceable eye had taken in the sight that confronted it. He even opened his mouth in a wry smile. He saw Gaigern come in through the revolving door, large and strong and flourishing as ever, though now looking seriously preoccupied as he pushed the almost senseless Kringelein in front of him. Kringelein was groaning and moaning. Dr. Otternschlag was very well able to distinguish cases of drunkenness from cases of serious illness, in spite of the rather similar state of prostration that accompanies both. The night porter, less expert in these matters, threw a severe and watchful glance on the two arrivals.

"The keys of 69 and 70," Gaigern said in a low voice. "My friend is in a bad way. A doctor, the sooner the better." He supported Kringelein with one hand and took the keys in the other and then propelled Kringelein towards the lift.

"I am a doctor. Hot milk at once to No. 70," Dr. Otternschlag said suddenly in a surprisingly alert tone of voice to the night porter, and then he followed the others without more ado.

"I'll look after Kringelein," he said to Gaigern as they were being taken up. "Don't worry, Herr Kringelein, it's over now."

Kringelein, who did not understand what he meant, stopped groaning and sank in a heap on the lift bench, clutching himself in agony. "Over already," he whispered with resignation. "So soon over? It's only just begun."

"You've gone at it too fast. Everything at once is too much," said Otternschlag. He bore Kringelein a grudge on many grounds, but he held his hand all the same and felt his pulse.

"Nonsense, Kringelein. It's not over yet! You've drunk too much iced champagne, that's all," Gaigern said to cheer him up. The lift stopped with a jerk and put an end to the misunderstanding. Kringelein's knees gave way when he stood in the corridor, greatly to the alarm of the dejected chambermaid. Gaigern picked him up and carried him to bed. While he got him out of his clothes and buttoned him in his new pajamas, Otternschlag disappeared with a busied air.

"I'll be back in a moment," he said, and went out with his stiff shanks galvanized by a new energy.

When he came back he found Kringelein lying rigidly in his bed with his hands pressed to his thighs like a soldier presenting arms. If he was not moaning that was due only to a supreme effort of will. When he had set out in search of life he had promised himself to die like a man and without making a fuss about it whenever the moment came. It was a debt he felt he owed to some unknown power for the extravagant licence of his last days. To this vow he now clung in his brass bed, while pain and the fear of death wrung a cold sweat from his forehead and neck. Gaigern went and fetched his own silk pocket handkerchief from his overcoat pocket and wiped Kringelein's peaked and jaundiced face with it. He carefully removed the pince-nez from his thin nose, and this for the space of a second made Kringelein believe that he was already dead and that all was over. He waited for Gaigern's large warm hand to close his eyes. Instead of that, Gaigern left the bedside and made way for Otternschlag.

Otternschlag took a syringe out of a little black case. From somewhere he produced, like a magician, a glittering ampoule, broke off the end of it with a conjurer's dexterity, and putting his thumb through the ring of the syringe, filled it with extraordinary dexterity with one hand and without so much as looking at it, while at the same moment with the other hand he took hold of Kringelein's bared arm and washed it over with sublimate.

"What's that?" asked Kringelein, though his experiences in hospital had already acquainted him with the beneficent drug.

"Something good. You'll like it," Otternschlag replied in a sing-song voice like a queer old nanny. Meanwhile he pinched up Kringelein's thin flesh between his finger and thumb and drove in the needle under the skin.

Gaigern looked on. "Lucky you had that at hand," he said.

Otternschlag held up the syringe against the light straight in front of his blind eye.

"Yes," he said. "It's my traveling trunk. Always packed up, you see. To be prepared—that's the thing, as Shakespeare so finely puts it. Ready to move on, ready at any moment, do you see? That's the best of this little bit of luggage," he added, as he washed the syringe and put it back and snapped the case. Gaigern took the small black object from the table and felt the weight of it in his hand. An unexpected notion appeared to take him aback. How so? he thought.

"Are you feeling better?" asked Dr. Otternschlag, turning to the bed.

"Yes," Kringelein replied. He sat on a cloud with closed eyes, and it bore him swiftly away. The pain relaxed, and he himself dissolved into a circling cloud. "There, you see——" he still heard the doctor say, while everything became a matter of indifference and the fear of death retreated like a black beast.

"There we are," said Otternschlag, and after a moment he laid Kringelein's head down on the quilt. "He's at peace for the time."

Gaigern, who meanwhile had put Kringelein's new clothes in order, came up now to the brass bedstead and observed the short faint breathing beneath the bright blue pajamas.

"For the time?" he asked in a whisper. "Will nothing—happen? Isn't it dangerous?"

"No, our friend will have to jog along for a bit yet. He has many a caper like this to go through before he is left in peace. His heart, you see, his heart's all there. It's still alive and kicking, and it won't shut up shop yet. It's a machine that's not been much used—Herr Kringelein's heart. A lot has gone to bits round about, but the heart itself insists on its rights. So the marionette must dance on while the last string holds. Cigarette?"

"Thanks," said Gaigern, and absent-mindedly took one. Then he sat down beneath the still-life picture of pheasants and thought hard for a minute or two over what Otternschlag had said.

"And so he's really in a bad way? And can't die all the same? Seems a ghastly business," he concluded.

Otternschlag, who had nodded in reply to each question, replied: "Just so. That's it. That's why I value my little trunk so highly. You cannot really put up with all the pain that being on this earth entails unless you know that at any moment you can make an end of it. Life is a miserable sort of existence, believe me."

Gaigern smiled at this. "But—I enjoy life," he said innocently.

Otternschlag turned his surviving eye on him quickly. "Yes, you enjoy life. Your sort enjoys life. I know your sort and I know you——"

"Me?"

"Yes, you personally, you in particular."

Otternschlag extended his arm and pointed with his heavy, tobacco-stained forefinger at Gaigern's face. Gaigern drew back.

"I once took a nice shell splinter out of your face just there. That charming night you found so interesting; I stitched you up—you don't remember—at Fromelles? Your sort forgets everything. It is another story for me. I forget nothing, nothing."

"Fromelles! In that frightful dressing station? No, I can't remember much. I wasn't conscious of much on that occasion. I was knocked out. I thought in those days you had to faint when you were wounded and so I fainted."

"I noticed you all the same. You were the youngest casualty to pass through my hands. 'Meeting death with a song on his lips' sort of thing. It's quite possible in any case that it wasn't you at all—only one of that sort, you know. And so now you enjoy life? Only to be expected. Glad to hear it. But, you'll grant me this, the revolving door must not be shut."

"What do you say?" asked Gaigern at a loss.

"The revolving door, I mean. Just sit in the lounge and watch the revolving door for an hour. You'd think it was crazed. In and out. In and out. In and out. Droll thing, a door like that. Often it makes you quite seasick to look at it for long. But now listen to me: suppose you come in through the revolving door—well, you want to be sure you can get out again. You don't want to find it shut in your face, leaving you a prisoner in the Grand Hotel?"

Gaigern felt his blood run cold. The word "prisoner" sounded like a concealed threat.

"Of course not," he hastened to say.

"Then we're agreed," Otternschlag went on. He had meanwhile taken the syringe out of its case again and he was playing lovingly with its smooth glass and nickel. "The revolving door must remain open. The exit must always be available. You must be able to die when it suits you, when you please."

"But who wants to die? Nobody," said Gaigern quickly and with conviction.

"Well——" said Otternschlag and swallowed something down. Kringelein was muttering unintelligibly under his drooping mustache. "Well—look at me for example," said Otternschlag. "I am a suicide, you must understand. As a rule you only see suicides after the event—when they have already turned on the gas or pulled the trigger. I, as I sit here, am a suicide before the event. To put it in one word, I am a living suicide—a rarity, you will agree. One of these days I shall take ten of these ampoules out of this box and inject them into my veins—and then I shall be a living suicide no longer. I shall march out through the revolving door, figuratively speaking; and you can sit on in the lounge and wait."

Gaigern observed with surprise that this mad doctor Otternschlag appeared to cherish a kind of hatred of him.

"That may be a matter of taste," he said lightly. "I am not in such a hurry. I have no complaint to make of life. I find it splendid."

"Indeed? You find it splendid? And yet you were in the war. And then you came home, and then you find life splendid? And what, man, have you done about it all? Have you forgotten it all? There—we won't talk of what it was like out there. We all know that well enough. But how can you come back after that, and still say you're pleased with life? Where do you find it—this life of yours? I have looked for life, but I can't find it. I often think to myself: I'm dead already. A shell has torn my head from my shoulders, and I'm sitting as a corpse all the time buried in that dug-out at Rouge Croix. There you have the real and actual impression life makes on me ever since I got back."

Something in Otternschlag's impassioned words touched Gaigern. He got up and went over to the bed. Kringelein was asleep, though his eyes were not quite closed. Gaigern came back to Otternschlag on tiptoe.

"Yes, there's some truth in that," he said in a low voice. "It wasn't very easy coming back. When a man says 'out there,' he means something like 'home.' Nowadays being in Germany is like being in clothes you've grown out of. We've become intractable and there's no place for us. What can any of us start to do with himself? Reichswehr? Drill? Electioneering scrimmages? Thanks! Flying? I've tried it. Toddling off twice daily according to timetable, Berlin—Cologne—Berlin. And as for voyages of discovery, that's all so stale and without danger. That's what it is, you see. Life ought to be a little more dangerous, and then it would be all right. But you have to take it as it comes."

"No. That's not what I mean," Otternschlag said irritably. "But perhaps we only see things from a slightly different angle. Perhaps I should take as amiable a view of things as you do, if my face had been stitched up as well as I stitched yours. But when you look at the world through a glass eye, it has a remarkable appearance, I can assure you—— Well, Kringelein, what's up?"

Kringelein of a sudden was sitting bolt upright in bed. With a great effort he had got his drugged eyes open and he was looking for something. He was feeling about over the quilt with finger tips which the morphine had made insensitive.

"Where's my money?" he whispered. He had come straight from Fredersdorf and a quarrel with Anna, and it was with difficulty that he found his way back to the mahogany-furnished room of the Grand Hotel. "Where's my money?" he asked with parched throat. At first he saw the two men in the plush armchairs only as enormous moving shadows.

"He asks where his money is," Otternschlag repeated, as though Gaigern were hard of hearing.

"He deposited it with the management," said Gaigern.

"You deposited it with the management," Otternschlag repeated after him like an interpreter. Kringelein's dazed head tried to cope with this reply. "Are you still in pain?" Otternschlag asked.

"Pain? Why?" asked Kringelein from his cloud.

Otternschlag laughed with a wry mouth. "All forgotten," he said. "He's forgotten his pain already, and all I've done for him, too. To-morrow he's ready to start again, the— *bon viveur,*" he said with undisguised contempt.

Kringelein did not understand a syllable. "Where's my money?" he persisted obstinately. "All that money? The money I won?"

Gaigern lit a cigarette and inhaled the smoke into his lungs.

"Where is his money?" asked Otternschlag.

"In his pocketbook," said Gaigern.

"In your pocketbook," Otternschlag passed on. "Now go to sleep again. You mustn't get too lively, or it'll do you harm."

"I want my pocketbook here," Kringelein demanded with outspread fingers. He could not express himself clearly in his drugged condition. All that his obscured consciousness was aware of was that he had to pay for every minute of his life in ready money and pay dearly. In his dream he had seen both life and money escaping from him, and carried her up the steps of her house at Tremezzo. He must go to her, he must, he must. But suddenly he was overcome by the unreasoning and irresistible pity that he had felt for Grusinskaya the day before; and he now felt it for Kringelein sitting there on the edge of the bed. He felt pity too for Otternschlag, for the war-wasted face fixed on his own, and pity, remote and unconscious for himself, and this pity was his undoing.

He took two steps into the room and smiled. "Here is his pocketbook," he said. "I took charge of it earlier on in case Kringelein had it stolen at the night club."

"There we are then," said Otternschlag, relaxing again. He took the old worn and bulging pocketbook from Gaigern's hands. It gave him a peculiar forlorn feeling of tenderness to do so. It was so seldom he had occasion to touch the hands of another man. He turned his head and fixed the other eye on Gaigern with an expression that might have conveyed either gratitude or a secret understanding. But he started back at the same moment. Instead of Gaigern's particularly handsome and lively face he saw a mask so blanched, drawn, vacant, and dead, that he was frightened. Are there nothing but ghosts in this world then? he thought with alarm as he made his way along the sofa to the bed and put down the pocketbook by Kringelein's side.

The whole scene had only taken a few seconds and during this time Kringelein had sat plunged in silent reflection.

Now that Otternschlag handed him the pocketbook over which he had made such a piteous lamentation he barely touched it. He let it fall on to the quilt without counting the money, all that money, the money he had won.

"Please, don't leave me," he said, and he said it, not to Otternschlag who had come to his help, but to Gaigern.

He stretched out his arm to Gaigern who stood gloomily by the window smoking a fresh cigarette.

"There's nothing to be afraid of, Kringelein," Otternschlag said meanwhile to comfort him.

"I'm not afraid," replied Kringelein peevishly and with a surprising alertness. "Do you think I'm afraid to die? I am not afraid. On the contrary. Indeed, I ought to be thankful that I have to die. I should never have found the courage to live if I hadn't known I had to die. When you know that you have to die, it's then you get courage—when it's always in your mind that you have to die, it makes you capable of anything—that's a secret——"

"Aha," said Otternschlag, "the revolving door. Kringelein is becoming a philosopher. Sickness brings wisdom. You've found that out, have you?"

Gaigern made no reply. What are you talking about? he thought. Life—death—how can one talk about them? They are not words after all. I live—well then, I live. I die—well then, good God, I die. As for thinking of death—no. And as for talking about it—still less. There is nothing but to die decently whenever the moment comes. If these two were to climb along the hotel front like monkeys, they would soon keep their mouths shut about life and death, he thought proudly. I am ready, too—and I need no help from a boxful of morphine. He yawned and drew in a deep breath of the early morning air that came in through the open window, and at the same time a faint chilliness gave a tremor to his athletic shoulders. "I am sleepy," he said. Then all at once he broke into hearty laughter. "I never got to bed at all last night, and now to-day again it's four o'clock. Come along, Herr Direktor, get under the bedclothes."

Kringelein obeyed at once. He lay down, with his heavy head and the pain, which, though dulled, had not left off, inside him, and folded his hands on the quilt.

had to put things straight with Preysing, otherwise there was no sense or object in anything at all.

Kringelein had a bath and put on the new Kringelein, the one with a silk shirt, a well-cut coat, and a sense of his own worth. His heart was as resolute as a clenched fist as he stood at the door of No. 71. He opened the outer door and knocked on the white-enameled panel of the inner one.

"Come in," Preysing called out. He said it from habit and without thinking, for he had no wish at all that anybody should interrupt his cheerful breakfast with Flämmchen. But as he had called out "Come in," the door opened and Kringelein made his appearance.

He appeared—and it seemed to Preysing as though an explosion had projected him into the Grand Hotel, on to the second floor, the floor of select visitors, and into No. 71. He had put his handsome new felt hat from Florence on his head with the deliberate intention of keeping it on his head, and there he kept it. "Good-morning, Herr Preysing," he said, and carelessly brushed the brim of it with two fingers. "I want a few words with you."

Preysing stared.

"What do you want? How did you get in here?" he asked.

The sight of Kringelein with his hat on his head, this junior clerk from his counting house coming in with this resolute air, amazed him as much as if he had come to announce the end of the world.

"I knocked and you said, 'Come in,'" Kringelein replied with astonishing coolness. "I want a word with you. May I sit down?"

"Please," said Preysing helplessly as Kringelein did so.

"The young lady will please forgive the intrusion," he said next to Flämmchen with address. Flämmchen, with lively amiability, replied:

"We know each other, Herr Kringelein, don't we?
We danced a delightful fox-trot together."

"Quite so. We did," said Kringelein, clearing his throat
of a slight huskiness. His throat was throbbing. After this
there was a silence.

"Well, what is it? I have no time to lose. I have urgent
letters to dictate to Fräulein Flämmchen," the general
director finally said in his general director's tone.

Kringelein, however, showed no sign whatever of
collapsing under it, though he did not quite know where to
begin.

"It's a letter from my wife. The stove has gone wrong
again and the firm refuses to have it repaired. Now that
won't do. The settlement, where I live, belongs to the
firm and we pay the rent punctually. It's deducted from
our wages. Then the firm ought to see that everything
is in good order in the houses on its property and none
of us ought to suffocate because the stoves are bad."
This was how he began. Preysing went a dull red between
his eyebrows and had the greatest difficulty in keeping his
temper.

"You know very well that these matters are no concern of mine. If you have any complaints to make you
must make them to the estate office. It is absolutely unheard of to bother me with anything of this sort."

Full stop. And this might well have concluded what
he had to say. But Preysing must needs add: "Instead of
you people being thankful to have homes put up for you,
you become impudent. It's intolerable."

Though Preysing stood up, Kringelein remained seated.

"Very well, we will leave it at that," he said carelessly.
"You think that you can be as insulting as you like. I
beg to differ. You think that you are something altogether
superior, but you are quite a common man, Herr Preysing,
though you may have married money and built yourself a

house in the country. You are quite common, and there
was never worse said of anybody than is said of you in
Fredersdorf. So now you know."

"That does not concern me. That does not concern
me in the least. I advise you to leave this room."

But Kringelein found unsuspected reserves of strength
within himself. He had twenty-seven years of drudgery
of which to unburden his soul, and he was charged like a
dynamo.

"Yes, it does concern you," he said, "it concerns you
very much. Otherwise why should you have your spies
and informers in the factory, your lick-spittles, like Herr
Schriebes, like Herr Kuhlenkamp, creatures like that who
tread on those below them and cringe to those above? If
anyone is three minutes late, it is reported. They even get
behind the servants. The whole factory knows that. But
we can work the hearts out of our bodies and not a word is
said. We're paid to do that. You don't bother to ask, Herr
Preysing, whether it is possible to live as a human being
on the salaries we get. You sit in your motor car and we
can't even afford ourselves rubber heels. And when we're
old and used up, we can go where we like. Nobody cares.
Old Hannemann was thirty-three years with the firm and
now he sits there with cataract and not a farthing of
pension."

If Preysing had been as black a tyrant as he appeared in
the imagination of a subordinate employee like Kringelein,
he would have chucked Kringelein out of the room without another word. But as he was a self-respecting, well-
meaning, and vacillating man, he let himself be drawn into
a discussion.

"You are paid according to the scale. And we have our
Employees' Fund," he began in an embittered tone. "I
know nothing of Hannemann. Who is Hannemann in any
case?"

"A nice scale! A nice fund!" Kringelein cried. "I was in the paupers' ward in hospital. I was supposed to eat cheese and salami four days after the operation. My wife has made one application after another, but not a penny of extra allowance did I get. And I had to pay for the ambulance to Mickenau out of my own pocket. And I was supposed to eat cheese, with my stomach in the state it was! When I had been four weeks sick, you wrote me a letter saying that I should receive notice if I was sick any longer. Is that so or not—yes or no, Herr Preysing?"

"I can't remember every letter I sign. But, in any case, a factory is not an almshouse, nor a hospital, nor a life-insurance agency. You have now reported sick again and here you are living like a lord or an embezzler——"

"You shall withdraw that. You shall withdraw that at once in this lady's presence," Kringelein shouted. "Who are you to presume to insult me? Who do you think you are talking to? Do you think I am dirt? And if I am dirt you are a great deal dirtier, Herr Generaldirektor. So now you know. You are dirt, dirt!"

Both men now stood face to face glaring at each other in a frenzy of rage and slanging each other as hard as they could go. Preysing was flushed a dark red, almost blue, and big drops of perspiration stood on his shaven upper lip. Kringelein was completely yellow. His lips were utterly drained of blood, and his elbows, his shoulders, and indeed every limb quivered. Flämmchen looked first at one and then at the other. Her head moved to and fro like a foolish kitten's after a swinging tangle of wool. All the same she understood pretty well what Kringelein had it on his mind to say, in spite of his distracted state, and it had her sympathy.

"What do you know or care how people like us have to exist?" he cried, white-lipped under his light, ruffled mustache. "But the way we live is enough to bring one to

despair. It is like climbing up a bare wall. It is like being
shut up in a cellar all your life. You wait on from year to
year, and first you have a hundred and eighty marks, and
when you have waited five years then you have two
hundred, and then you crawl on and wait again. And then
you think: It'll be better later on and later on you'll be
able to afford to have a child—but it never gets to that—
and then you even have to give up keeping a dog, because
the money doesn't run to it, and then you wait on in hopes
of a rise, working like a nigger and putting in overtime
without pay, and then another gets the rise with three
hundred and twenty and family allowances, and you're
left planted. And why? Because the Herr Generaldirektor
doesn't know his business. Because the Herr Generaldirektor promotes the wrong men. Even Brösemann says that.
Anything scurvier than my twentieth anniversary with the
firm was never known in the history of the world. Did you
even congratulate me? Did it enter anyone's head to make
me a donation? There I sat bent over my desk and waited
—but not a sign. Then I thought: It can't be possible. It's
being kept as a great surprise, for it's impossible they
would forget me after I've worked twenty years in their
office—twenty years. And then midday came and then
six o'clock, and I'd put on my best coat, and still waited,
but nothing whatever happened. And so I trudged off
home, ashamed to be seen by my wife and ashamed to be
seen by Kampmann. 'Well,' says Kampmann, 'did they
celebrate the occasion in proper style?' 'Yes,' I say, 'my
desk was covered with flowers, and they gave me five
hundred marks, and the Generaldirektor himself spoke to
me, oh yes, and he knew quite well that I was always the
last to leave the office.' That is what I said to Kampmann,
to hide the shame of it all. And seven weeks later Brösemann had me in and said, 'I hear you have been twenty
years with us. It has been overlooked. Well, is there any-

thing you would like?' And I said, 'I'd like to be dead and done with as soon as possible, that's what I'd like, for there's no pleasure in a dog's life like this.' And then Brösemann went to the old man, and he gave me a rise to four hundred and twenty from the end of May—but that didn't prevent it being a dog's life all the same. And that's when I swore that I'd tell old Preysing the truth one of these days."

Kringelein had begun in a loud voice, but while he spoke his voice sank and took on a note of sadness. Preysing, with his hands behind his back, walked to and fro in the small room. His boots creaked under his weight and the fact that Flämmchen was sitting there all the time listening as her eyes went from one to the other made him furious. Suddenly he came to a stop in front of Kringelein, protruding his corpulent person menacingly towards Kringelein's new coat.

"What do you want of me exactly? I don't know anything whatever about you. You come in here," he said in a chilling nasal voice, "you have the impertinence to come in here and talk like a Bolshevist. What do I care for your twentieth anniversary? I can't bother myself with every single employee in our business. I have other things to think about. I don't sleep on a bed of roses myself, not by any means. Anyone who shows marked competence is paid accordingly and finds an opening. The rest don't concern me. You don't concern me. I know nothing about you. I have had enough of it——"

"You don't know me. Quite so. But I know you well enough. I knew you long ago when you first came to Fredersdorf and lodged in the bootmaker's back bedroom and owed money to my father-in-law for butter and sausage. I remember the day very well when you began to leave off being the first to say good-morning, Herr Preysing, and when you began courting the old man's daughters. I have kept account of you, Herr Preysing, and don't you imagine that anything has been overlooked and omitted. And if any of us made such bloomers in little things as you have made in big ones he would have had the sack long ago. And the insufferable air you have as you go along the passage and look straight through anyone you meet as though he didn't exist. And when in 1912 there was an error in my books for the first and only time, and I was docked of three hundred and ten marks—the tone in which you reprimanded me was something I shall never forget. And the eight hundred workmen you dismissed, they curse you to this day, that's certain. And when you come along in your motor car and open the exhaust so that we get our bellyful of stink, then you think yourself somebody. But I tell you . . ."

Kringelein had got switched on to a side track. He poured out all the experiences and all the hatred of twenty-seven years pell-mell. He mixed up the important with the trivial, the real with the imaginary, and office gossip with what he knew at first hand. This explosion in an hotel bedroom was nothing but the grievance of a sensitive and unsuccessful man against one who had simply made his way with a certain brutality—a genuine grievance, however unjustifiable and absurd. . . . Preysing, on his side, completely incapable of any sympathetic understanding, fell deeper and deeper into ungovernable rage. When Kringelein mentioned the money he had owed in his earlier days to the greasy provision dealer, Sauerkatz, his head positively swam and he was afraid of a stroke. He heard himself gasp for breath. The tiny veins of his eyes were so charged with blood that his vision was red and turbid. In one stride he was on top of Kringelein. He seized him by the waistcoat and shook him like a rat. Kringelein's new hat fell off his head. Preysing deliberately trod it under foot. Strangely enough, Kringelein felt a peculiar pleasure

at this savagery. Yes, he thought with satisfaction, strike
a defenseless man who is at death's door. That's just like
you. Flämmchen, behind the breakfast tray, whispered to
herself:

"Don't—don't do that."

Preysing threw Kringelein against the wall and tore
open the door.

"Enough," he shouted. "Not another word. Outside.
At once. You shall be dismissed. I dismiss you. You're
dismissed, dismissed from this moment——"

Kringelein had picked up his hat and now, with a face
as white as a sheet, he stood between the double doors of
which the inner was open and the outer shut, and, as he
leaned trembling and perspiring against the white enameled wood, he began to laugh with his mouth wide open,
he laughed in Preysing's furious face.

"You dismiss me? You threaten me? But you cannot
dismiss me. You can do nothing to me at all, nothing at
all. I am ill. Dangerously ill, I tell you. I have got to die.
I can only live a week or two. No one can do anything
to me. I shall be dead before you can dismiss me——" he
cried, as he shook with laughter and at the same time
tears smarted in his eyes. Flämmchen got up from the
sofa and bent forward. Preysing, too, bent forward. First
his clenched hands fell to his side, and then he put them in
his trouser pockets.

"Man, are you crazy?" he said in a lowered voice. "I
believe the man is still laughing. I believe he's glad to be
dangerously ill. Are you drunk?"

At these words Kringelein became sober of a sudden
and fell into reflection. He was also a little embarrassed.
He stood where he was between the two doors a moment
longer, and his eyes took in the small hotel suite with a
fleeting glance. He saw Flämmchen standing in a ray of
sun at the window, the corpulent and sobered general

director with his hands in his pockets, and the vista through the open bedroom and bathroom doors. It all trembled indistinctly through the involuntary tears that obscured his eyes and showed his emotional condition. He took up his trampled hat from the floor and made a bow.

"I hope the young lady will forgive the intrusion," he said to Flämmchen once again, in his high-pitched, pleasing voice.

Preysing, with a husband's bad conscience, felt this to be a vulgar and base insinuation. He took his hands from his pockets.

"Get out," was all he said.

But Kringelein had gone already.

Preysing with squeaking tread walked three times up and down the room. His temples throbbed and his forehead was flushed.

"Well?" asked Flämmchen.

Suddenly the general director ran to the door, pulled it open, and, trumpeting like an angry elephant, shouted down the silent corridor.

"You won't escape. I'll have you watched. We'll see where you stole the money to idle about here on. You Communist—you swindler—you impudent cur. I'll have you locked up—locked up——"

But there was nothing more to be seen or heard of Kringelein.

"After all he was decent enough. He was actually crying at the end," Flämmchen said in conclusion.

That was her only comment on the whole scene. . . .

"Leave your stockings on though. It looks so pretty," said Preysing. He was sitting on the sofa in Flämmchen's bedroom, in No. 72.

"No," said Flämmchen, "I should feel horrid. I can't be in nothing but shoes and stockings."

Her body gleamed in the light of the table lamp. There were red shadows on its smooth gold. There were soft reflections on her rounded knees and shoulders where the skin was drawn tight. She sat down on the edge of the bed and first slipped off her blue shoes and then solemnly and carefully her new stockings. The light flowed into the tender hollow between her breasts as she bent down, and her spine rippled smoothly. These were phenomena that Preysing observed with drawn breath.

"You are sweet," he said, but he did not venture to move from where he was. Flämmchen nodded to him over her shoulder with good-natured encouragement. She took her stockings to a chair where she had already laid her dress and underclothing as tidily as a schoolgirl. Preysing now got up and went to her on squeaking shoes. Cautiously he stretched out one forefinger, on which there was a tuft of light-colored hair, and with it he lightly touched Flämmchen's back as though she were a strange, untamed, and dangerous animal. Flämmchen smiled. "Well?" she said amiably. She was a little nervous and impatient. On her side there was nothing but willingness to carry out the unwritten agreement in every particular. After all, a self-respecting person could not take a thousand marks and a journey to England and a new costume and much else besides, and give nothing in return. But this general director was so horribly clumsy. This was now the second evening that he had squirmed around (this at least was how Flämmchen described Preysing's embarrassed and constricted style of wooing). And it was more than unpleasant. It felt like having a tooth stopped by a singularly incompetent dentist. She wished the worst were already well over, but it went on and on, always on the tender spot; and it got on her nerves. She moved her back nearer Preysing's hand, but the timorous forefinger had already moved off and sought a refuge in his waistcoat pocket, where it now reposed itself after the bold adventure, beside his fountain pen. Flämmchen sighed and turned to face the general director. Her complete nakedness at once enchanted and alarmed him.

"You see, now I see you. Now I can see you," he said stupidly. Her body exhaled so inviolable a freshness and cleanness that it affected him more with alarm than with intoxication. "Just as you are. . . . In the picture in the magazine you looked quite different," he said, almost aggrieved.

"Different? How do you mean, different?"

"More coquettish. There was something so fetching about it, you know. . . ."

Flämmchen understood. She was aware of the hidden disappointment over her cool unapproachability and of the repressions in Preysing's sluggish blood, the stagnation of his conventional nature, but she could do nothing to help him. I am as I am, she thought. "Yes," she said, "photographers always put one in some idiotic pose to be photographed. And then they touch it up as well. Did the photograph please you more than I do myself?"

"What do you think—you're sweet," Preysing replied. His vocabulary of endearment was limited. "But won't you say 'darling' to me? Please, do!"

Flämmchen shook her head emphatically.

"Oh, no," she said.

"No? But why not?"

"Just no. I can't do it. I can't really. You are a stranger to me, so how can I call you 'darling'? In every other way—in every other way, I'll do anything you like. But to call you 'darling' is impossible."

"You're an odd creature, Flämmchen," said Preysing,

and he looked at her naked gleaming skin and her painted lips. "You take some knowing."

"Not odd in the least," said Flämmchen with an obstinate pout of the lips. She had her own variety of shyness. "One must think of the future," she tried to explain. "I can go with you to England and all that, but when it's over, it's over, and if I say 'darling,' it isn't over. If I meet you in six months' time, I shall say, 'Good-day, Herr Generaldirektor.' And you will say, 'That is the little typist I took with me to Manchester.' And that will be all right. But it wouldn't be very pleasant, would it, if I met you with your wife and said, 'Hallo, darling, how goes it?'"

The general director positively shriveled up at this. To be reminded at this moment of his Mulle at home was all that was needed to complete his discomfiture. Nevertheless, the sense of forbidden sin and of the taint of vice ran in a hot current through his veins, and added to this was the rather too high blood pressure of a well-fed man threatened with sclerosis of the arteries. He sat down on the nearest chair and sighed. The chair sighed too. Boards creaked, furniture groaned and doors banged at every encounter with Preysing's heavy person. He stretched out his hands, and in an access of courageous ardor, laid them on the fine curve of her body above the hips. He was surprised and disappointed, for instead of the expected softness he encountered a taut, elastic firmness. He drew Flämmchen on to his knees, and controlled their tendency to tremble.

"What muscles you all have. Like boys," he murmured huskily.

"All of us? Who do you mean?"

"You—and the other girls I know," answered Preysing, who was thinking of his daughters, Babs and Popsy, in their bathing dresses. Flämmchen was beginning to feel chilly and the warmth of Preysing's body was comforting.

"There now," she said more familiarly, "he knows girls," and she stroked Preysing's hair to which the Berlin barber had given a stylish cut the day before and a pleasing fragrance. (Well, after all, it is not going so badly, Flämmchen was thinking.)

"Of course I know girls. What do you think? I am not made of pasteboard. I'm a match any day for the handsome young fellows you dance with at your *thés dansants.* Feel how strong I am," he said, and he doubled his arm. He felt that he was getting back the joyful intoxication and all the "go" and pride in which he had emerged from the successful conference the day before, and had rushed on into this incredible adventure. "Just feel how strong I am," he repeated. He held his arm braced for Flämmchen to feel. Flämmchen gratified him by feeling it. And in truth she came upon an astonishingly firm and well-developed biceps under the worsted sleeve.

"Mm," said Flämmchen, impressed. "Iron." She got up from her uncomfortable perch on Preysing's knees and walked back a step or two. She put her hands behind her neck and looked at him through half-closed lids. There were the same light-colored wisps of hair under her arms as there were over her forehead. Preysing suddenly felt a choking sensation.

"Will you be kind to me?" he whispered.

"Oh, yes. Gladly," answered Flämmchen, politely ready to oblige. The next moment the general director threw himself upon her. In his face there was the expression of a man who had burst ropes, broken through walls, and escaped from prison. He was running away from himself, this correct and conscientious and diffident Preysing. He discharged himself like a rocket and landed in Flämmchen's arms. There! thought Flämmchen, a little taken aback by the anxious and passionate surrender that Preysing's distracted state expressed. She put her arms round his neck and he felt her warmth break over him in waves in which he let himself drown, while telegraph forms, innumerable telegraph forms, rioted in front of his closed eyes and became dark red and dark blue and disappeared as soon as his mouth drank in the taste of violets from Flämmchen's painted lips.

It was late in the evening. An echo of dance music from the Yellow Pavilion vibrated in a quiver of melody through every wall of the Grand Hotel. The hall porter, Senf, had handed over his duties to the night porter more than an hour ago. Dr. Otternschlag had gone up to his room and lay with eyes shut and mouth open on his bed. He looked like a stupefied mummy. His small trunk was packed for departure, but now, as before, he had not yet summoned up the necessary resolution for this final formality.

In No. 68 a typewriter rattled on without mercy. The representative of an American film company had taken up his quarters there, and on the brass bedstead, which had witnessed Grusinskaya's night of love, strips of celluloid lay in heaps. The American examined them while he cleared off his business letters. The bell of the machine could be heard in No. 70, where Kringelein sat in his bath and watched the antics of a tablet of bath salts on the white enamel. He was sad, and because he was sad he sang softly and shyly—to cheer himself up. He sang in his bath like a child in a wood. The day had been poor and disappointing. The explanation with Preysing had cost him much and left him prostrate and done up. And, worst of all, Gaigern, the dynamo, this source of energy, this vitalizing and warm-blooded and untrammeled fellow with his 120-miles-an-hour pace had vanished from his sight. Kringelein, as he lay in the pain-assuaging hot water, felt that he had read the last page of his life and turned it over, and that now there was no more to come, nothing, nothing more. . . .

Page boy No. 18, Karl Nispe, crept up the stairs and stopped, crept on, stopped and crept on again. The rings under his eyes were as black as if they had been painted. He swallowed his saliva—for he suffered from those nervous pangs of hunger that afflict most hotel employees. He came from a wretched slum, a backyard, to his duties in the hotel lounge with its pillars, its carpets, its Venetian fountain, and it was to this slum, with its drab poverty, that he disappeared when his time on duty was over. He was a callow youth of seventeen, but he had his girl and she made claims on him that his scanty earnings could not meet. And now he had the gold cigarette case which he had found in the Winter Garden. For four days he had left it buried and hidden away and that was very much the same as having stolen it. Now he had come to the point. He had screwed himself up. He was going to part with it and give it back as though he had just found it. There he stood at the door of No. 69, with beating heart. He took off his cap; at this his face suddenly lost its uniformed air and became human. When he had stood there for some minutes, shaken by the beating of his own heart, he knocked.

Although he had seen Baron Gaigern take his key a quarter of an hour before and go up to his room, there was no reply from within. He hesitated and then ventured upon opening the outer door and knocked on the inner one. On the hooks, however, between the two doors, the Baron's dinner jacket was duly hanging for the valet to take away and brush. The page boy knocked. Not a sound. He waited and knocked again. No reply. He pressed down the handle of the inner door. It was open but the room was empty. The page boy, Karl, who knew something of life, grinned, whistled once high and softly, and put the cigarette case, warm from his hand, on the middle of the table. The room was exceedingly cheerful. The light was on and the air in it was so unusually fragrant and un-hotel-like with menthol, lavender water, cigarettes, and the scent of lilac, that it was a pleasure merely to breathe it. One or two sprays of forced white lilac were in a vase. On the writing table there was a photograph of a sheep dog. In the middle of the room Gaigern's patent-leather shoes were dreaming with a dutiful and self-contented expression. Karl was impressed. He sniffed this atmosphere of bachelor elegance, and grinned. Suddenly with a sharp throb of his heart he took possession of the cigarette case again, stowed it away inside his jacket and under his shirt and went silently out.

A chambermaid was sitting in her little office writing a letter as he passed by the open door. It was very quiet on the second floor. Down below, the miniature propeller of an electric fan was humming. In the Yellow Pavilion a tango was being played.

A faint echo of the music could be detected even in the expensive two-bedded room that General Director Preysing had engaged for his secretary. Preysing emerged from the violet fragrance of his first kiss and said, "Listen!"

"Yes. I heard it a long while. Music," said Flämmchen, "it's nice to hear it in the distance."

"Music? No. Didn't you hear anything else?" Preysing asked. He made a somewhat distraught impression as he sat upright on the edge of the bed and listened. His eyebrows were drawn up in the strain of attention, and his forehead was a complete network of wrinkles—the result of many years of intricate business cares. "I can hear something all the same," he said anxiously.

"What? Where?" Flämmchen murmured. She was getting sleepy and she put her hands impatiently on Preysing's head.

"I heard a knocking of some sort," Preysing pointed and stared fixedly at the door into his bathroom which he had left open.

"I hear something too," said Flämmchen, as she put her hands on Preysing's waistcoat. "I hear your heart beating. I can hear it distinctly. *Tac-tac-tac.* . . ."

Preysing's heart was indeed making an excessive noise in his capacious chest. It beat with a dull and heavy thud beneath his gray suit. He still kept a look-out on the open door on whose painted surface the shaded table lamp cast a pink reflection in the dim room.

"Let me go. I must go and see——" he said. He pushed Flämmchen's hands away from his chest and got up. The bed wheezed as he rose from it. Flämmchen let him go with a shrug of her shoulders. Preysing disappeared with three creaking steps through the bathroom door.

This small white door ought, properly speaking, to have been shut. It separated the general director's suite from his secretary's bedroom. The hotel management had done nothing whatever to do away with this barrier. On the contrary. The little door had no latch, and when it was shut there was no handle to open it by. Preysing, however, had employed a master key, which he always had in his pocket at the factory and had brought with him. With this he had opened the door and forsaken his own tidy room with its boot bags, collar boxes, sponge bags, and all the other paraphernalia of a husband and had stepped through the little door into the boundless and unimaginable realm of adventure. . . .

The bathroom was in darkness and he quickly passed through it. A tap dripped, *pong—pong—pong*, into the bath. Next to the bathroom was the small sitting room, also in darkness and reassuringly silent. Preysing stood still for a moment and felt for the switch without success. He then felt his way on to the closed door of his bedroom

and suddenly came to a stop, dazed and breathless in the
middle of the room. He knew for a certainty that he had
turned off the light, but now the light was on. It showed
like a thread under the door. It quivered over the threshold at Preysing's feet, and then it was gone. Preysing
stood riveted to the spot and stared at the place where a
moment since there had been a streak of light and which
now was dark—as dark as the lighted hotel front and the
arc lamps and electric signs allowed. As he stood there he
was waiting for something extremely unpleasant to happen, though exactly what he did not know. He had a
vague idea that that crazy clerk had forced his way in as
he had in the morning and that he was in there now. He
suspected that this revengeful Kruckelein or Kringelein,
or whatever he was called, had caught him out in a pecca-
dillo and was now in a position to make himself highly
unpleasant by denouncing him or blackmailing him or
making a scandal in one way or another. . . .

It was this that rushed in a dark stupor through Preysing's head as he seized the door handle and abruptly
opened the door.

The room was in darkness. There was not a sound. There
was nobody there. Nobody breathed. But neither did
Preysing breathe.

He put a hand out behind him and switched on the light
by the door. The next moment the room was dark again.
There had been one spasmodic flash of electric light, so
brief that he had seen nothing clearly. A second of the most
extreme and eerie suspense followed. Preysing's brain
worked like mad. There is another switch at the door into
the passage, it told him of its own accord. A man is standing there and as soon as I switch on he switches off.

"Is anyone there?" he said, in a voice unnecessarily
loud and so hoarse that he himself was startled by it. No
reply. Preysing made a dart forward and found the writ-

ing table, knocking his shin against it most painfully. He turned on the table lamp. Then he stared with all his eyes.

Near the wardrobe close to the door into the passage stood a man in silk pajamas. It was not the clerk. It was— Preysing recognized his face in the light of the green-shaded lamp—it was the other fellow, the smart fellow he had seen in the lounge, and in the Yellow Pavilion, dancing with Flämmchen. He stood there in another man's bedroom with a smile—a green grimace.

"What do you want here?" Preysing asked in a forced voice. He was afraid of the beating of his own heart. His knees tingled. His finger tips too.

"Sorry," said Baron Gaigern. "I seem to have mistaken the door——"

"What do you say? Mistaken the door? We shall see about that," said Preysing hoarsely, and pushed his way round the writing table. He held his head low like an animal, and though he saw everything in a haze of red, he came by a miracle on the one significant fact—that his pocketbook was no longer on the writing table where he had placed it with particular care when he went to open the door into Flämmchen's room. "We shall see whether you mistook the room," he heard himself say, and he lurched forward from the table.

At the same moment the Baron extended his right arm and aimed at the middle of Preysing's face. "If you move a step I shall shoot," he said in a quiet voice. For one dizzy second Preysing saw the black mouth of a revolver barrel.

"You'll shoot, will you?" he roared. He made a grab for something and did something with it. He felt his arm swing something heavy through the air with the whole weight of his body behind it. The blow fell with a smashing sound on the man's head and came back like a shock through his own arm.

For a moment the Baron remained standing opposite him with an astonished expression. Then his knees gave under him and he fell against the trunk that stood on the stillage next the wardrobe and down on to the floor, and there he lay face downwards.

"Shoot, would you? Well, there you've got it," said Preysing, when the air streamed down into his throat and he came up out of his access of rage and terror as though out of deep water. "There you have it," he said again to the prostrate man at his feet. His voice already sounded much softer, half apologetic and half reproachful. The man made no reply. Preysing bent over him, but did not touch him. "What's up with you then?" he said, half aloud. Now he heard the music from the Yellow Pavilion. He heard his heart beat and his breath come and go. He even heard the *pong—pong—pong* from the bathroom. The man on the ground, however, made no sound. Preysing looked about him. He now found in his hand the object with which he had dealt the blow. It was the inkstand, the bronze inkstand with the outspread eagle's wings. He discovered black ink marks on his fingers and on the lapels of his coat too. He took out his handkerchief and cleaned himself up after he had gently replaced the inkstand. Then he turned again to the man on the floor. "He's unconscious," he said aloud. He had a dazed and obscure feeling of suffocation as he knelt down beside him and heard the boards creak with a weirdly hissing and significant sound. I shall have him arrested, he thought, but he was still too distraught to ring. He did not like to see the man lie there like that on his face, with his neck that looked as if it was broken and his arms outspread. He looked about over the carpet for the revolver but he could not find it. An oppressive silence now prevailed in the room which a moment ago was full of the noise and the thud of a heavy fall. Preysing had to overcome something in himself before he could take

The next moment, in fact, Kringelein saw to his astonishment Flämmchen's naked, perfect form. It staggered
towards him, fell heavily into his outstretched arms, and
lay there.

Kringelein did not lose his head, nor did his strength
fail him under the burden. She had fainted, and although
the helpless collapse of the warm and golden-brown body
in his arms filled him with a sweet enchanting terror, he
did a number of perfectly sensible things. He put one arm
under the limp neck, the other under her knees, and
lifting her up with an effort, he laid her on his bed. Then
he shut both doors on to the corridor and drew a deep
breath, for the rush of blood from his heart was over-
powering. And now something fell to the floor from
Flämmchen's drooping hand. It was a blue and somewhat
worn shoe with a high heel, which till now she had held
pressed to her naked breast. She had snatched it up and
taken it with her. She had rescued it as though from a
fire or a collapsing house as the only article of clothing that
a catastrophe had left her. Kringelein took hold of her hand
and laid it carefully by her side. He looked round the room
and found the bottle of Hundt's Elixir, and put a few
drops to Flämmchen's lips. A quiver passed over her forehead, but she was too unconscious to drink. But she was
breathing deeply and at every breath the tangle of her
bright hair rose and sank again on the pillow with an indescribable softness. Kringelein ran into the bathroom and
soaked a handkerchief in cold water. He sprinkled it with
eau-de-Cologne (for since yesterday Kringelein was possessed of such refinements) and returned to Flämmchen.
He carefully wiped her face and her temples. Then he felt
for the beating of her heart, and found it under her firm
and rounded breast. He put the cool, wet handkerchief
there and after this he stood beside the bed and waited.

He did not know that his face had taken on an expres-

sion of shy, unfathomable wonder while he stood there
looking down upon her. He did not know that his smile
was the smile of first love on the lips of a boy of seventeen.
Perhaps he did not even know that at this moment he
truly, actually, and utterly lived. But this he did know—
that the feeling which now penetrated him with an almost
painful warmth of appeal, this buoyancy and moltenness
and transparency and release, was known to him only in
dreams. He had never supposed that such a feeling could
be experienced in real life. Under chloroform, something
of the sort had occurred just before the blue, singing haze
went black. And in secret, deep within, Kringelein had
imagined it was like this to die, an unexampled solemnity,
a completion that left nothing unresolved behind it. Certainly, though, Kringelein was far from the thought of
death at this moment as he looked at this girl who had fled
to him for protection.

It really exists, he thought, it really exists. Beauty like
this really exists. It is not only painted in pictures and
imagined in books and trumped up on the stage. It can
really happen that a girl is naked and so wonderfully
beautiful, so utterly beautiful, so utterly—he tried for
another word but could not find one. Utterly beautiful,
was all he could think, utterly beautiful.

Flämmchen frowned, parted her lips like a child waking
up, and finally opened her eyes. The light was reflected
as a round gleam of white in her pupils. She blinked,
smiled politely, took a deep breath and whispered,
"Thanks." Immediately after she shut her eyes again as
though she wished to sleep. Kringelein picked up the quilt
from the floor and spread it carefully over her. Then he
pulled up a chair to the bedside and sat down and waited.
"Thanks," Flämmchen whispered again after a long while.

She was now conscious, but she found it difficult to put
her thoughts in order. A certain confusion was caused by

the fact that at first she mixed up the puny Kringelein
at the edge of the bed with another man, whom she had
liked very much and given up with great sorrow. The
bright blue pajamas and an undefinable tender alertness in
Kringelein's manner led her into this mistake.

"How did I get here?" asked Flämmchen. "What are
you doing here, dearest?" She said "dearest" and this
gave him a shock of sweet surprise, but as he was already
in the midst of wonders he took it as a matter of course.

"You fainted and came to me," he said simply.

Now Flämmchen recognized her mistake. Everything
came back to her and she sat straight up in bed.

"Forgive me," she whispered. "But something so awful
has happened."

She pulled the bedclothes up to her face and screwed
them into her eyes and began to cry. At once Kringelein's eyes filled with tears too, and his lips, which still
smiled, began to tremble.

"It is so frightful," Flämmchen whispered, "so frightful, frightful."

Her tears came in a flood that soothed and appeased
her. She dabbed the sheet against her face and covered
the edge of it with small red heart-shaped transfers of her
painted mouth. Kringelein looked on, and the corners of
his eyes smarted with the pain of his suppressed emotion.
At last he put his hand on Flämmchen's neck. "There,
there, there," he said, "there—there—there."

Flämmchen looked up at him with swimming eyes.

"Oh, it's you," she murmured with relief. Now at last
she recognized in the spruce figure at the bedside the little
man who had danced so timidly with her yesterday and
who had been so courageous that day in his interview with
Preysing. A confiding and pleased sense of security took
hold of her now she found herself in his bed with his hand
gently patting her neck.

"But we know each other," she said, and snuggled up to his fingers with the spontaneous gratitude of an animal. Kringelein ceased to pat her and collected his strength— an unexpectedly large resource of strength and aggressiveness.

"What has happened to you? Did Preysing do anything to you?" he asked.

"Not to me—" said Flämmchen, "not to me——"

"Shall I tell him off? I'm not afraid of Herr Preysing."

Flämmchen looked at Kringelein as he sat erect and collected, and fell into deep reflection. She tried to recall the frightful scene in No. 71 to her memory: the two men on the floor in the green light, the one—dead and stretched out; the other—living and distraught and cowering. But already it was erased from her healthy and resilient soul. Only her lips grew rigid at the recollection and the muscles of her arms tightened with agitation.

"He has killed him," she whispered.

"Killed? Who has killed whom?"

"Preysing. He has killed the Baron."

Kringelein's head swam, but he pulled himself together and kept calm.

"But that's impossible. I can't believe it," he stammered. Without knowing it he put both hands round Flämmchen's neck and drew her face close to his. He stared into her eyes and she stared as fixedly into his. At last she nodded her head three times emphatically without saying a word. Oddly enough, it was only then that Kringelein believed this incredible thing. He let his hands fall.

"Dead?" he said. "But he—why, he was life itself. He was strength personified. How could a fellow like Preysing . . ."

He got up and walked to and fro noiselessly, with his thin feet in new bedroom slippers, blinking in extreme agitation. He saw Preysing going along the passage of pretty for a business post. It's always the same story. The big firms don't like to have girls who are too good-looking, and they are quite right. Then I'm too big for a mannequin. They want forty-two figures or at most forty-four. And as for the films, I don't know what's the matter there. Perhaps I'm not coquettish enough. That doesn't matter later on—on the contrary; but at the start it does. However, I shall pull through somehow. Only I mustn't get old. I'm nineteen already and it's time to see about getting on. Lots of people would say that you shouldn't go with a man like Preysing for money. Just the opposite—it's only for money! I can't see anything wrong in it. I remain just as I was before. Nobody takes anything away from me, even though I am a little nice to him. When you've been a year without a job as I have, running round after film agents, and running round in answer to advertisements, and your clothes go to rags, and you look in the shop windows, I just can't help it—to be well dressed is my dream. The joy a new dress gives me, no one could believe. Often I spend days thinking out the clothes I'll wear one day. And then traveling. I'm mad on traveling, getting right away and seeing new places. At home I have a thin time of it—you can take it from me. I'm not a complaining person. I'm good-natured and can put up with a lot. But often it's enough to make you run away—just to get away, even if it was with the biggest blackguard on earth —only to get away. For money—naturally for money. Money's so important, and whoever says otherwise is talking bunkum. Preysing was going to give me a thousand marks. That's a lot of money. Enough to give one a start in life. But that's over and done with. And now I'm where I was again. And at home it's frightful——"

"I know that. I can imagine that. I understand that very well," said Kringelein. "At home everything is always filthy. Even the very air goes wrong when you

haven't got money. You can't open the window because
the warm air has cost money. You can't have a bath because hot water means coals. Your razor blades are old and
scrape your chin. You have to save over the washing—no
tablecloth, no serviette. You have to be careful with the
soap. Your hairbrush has lost all its bristles, the coffee
pot is broken and cemented together, the spoons are
black. The pillows are hard lumps of old coarse feathers.
What's broken stays broken. Nothing is mended. Your
life policy must be paid. And you can't see that your life's
all wrong. You imagine it has got to be like that."

He was resting his head on Flämmchen's, and thus
they went through the litany of the poor together, rocking
to and fro in time to the monotonous chant. They were
both tired out and over-excited and half asleep.

"Your hand mirror is broken," Flämmchen went on,
"and you can't afford a new one. You have to sleep on
the sofa behind a screen. There's a perpetual smell of gas.
The lodger makes his daily row. The very food you eat and
can't pay for because you are out of a job is cast in your
teeth. But they shan't get me under—they shan't get me
under," she said with energy as she crept out of Kringelein's arms and sat up so straight in the bed that the
clothes fell over on to Kringelein's knees, imparting to
them the warmth of her young body. Kringelein accepted
this warmth as an overwhelming munificence. "I shall get
through," said Flämmchen, and for the first time she blew
the hair off her forehead as a sign that her gayety and vitality had returned. "I can do without the general director.
I shall get through all right."

Kringelein had a string of difficult thoughts to master,
and when he was through with them he tried to put them
into words.

"As for money, I've seen in the last few days just what
it means to have it," he explained with difficulty. "You

same he was afraid. He, too, had Gaigern clearly before
his eyes, in the car, in the aëroplane, at the gambling table,
in the white light of the boxing ring. He saw Gaigern as he
bent over him, as he gave him back his pocketbook, and as
he went through the revolving door.

"Why should they arrest you?" he asked.

Flämmchen gave an emphatic nod.

"As a witness," she said, out of the depth of her igno-
rance.

"Do you mean——?" asked Kringelein vaguely, looking straight through her with his eyes fixed still upon Gaigern. And suddenly he was once more keyed up to the
whirling danger pitch of the day before. "You needn't be
afraid. I'll arrange it all for you," he said quickly. "Will
you stay with me? You will, won't you? You shall have a
good time with me. I only want to give you a good time.
Will you? I have money. I have money enough. It will last
us a long while. And I can easily win some more, gambling.
We'll travel. We'll go to Paris. Where you like."

"My pass has a *visa* for England——"

"Good. England then. Where you like and what you
like. You shall have clothes. One must have clothes and
one must have money. We'll have a gay time of it. What
do you say? I'll give you the money I won—3,400 marks.
You can have more later on. Don't say anything, keep
quiet and stay here. I'll go along now to the other room. I'll
go along to Preysing. I'll see what's happened to him. I
promise you you'll have a better time with me than with
Preysing. Wouldn't you rather be with me than with
Preysing? I'll go now and fetch your things. Trust to me,
and don't be afraid."

Kringelein vanished into the bathroom and dressed
with the utmost speed—black coat and the dark tie of
thick silk. It gave him a strange feeling of fevered excitement to be dressing in the middle of the night while the

street below became silent and the radiators cooled down. Flämmchen sat up in the bed, laid her cheek on her knee and breathed a sigh of relief. Her body now began to ache after her fainting fit and her throat was dry. She longed for an apple and a cigarette. She took the bottle of Hundt's Elixir from the bed table and tried a sip, but she did not like its cinnamon taste. When Kringelein came back he looked quite the fine gentleman. Perhaps he really was a fine gentleman, even though he had split the firewood every day for his wife for twenty years.

"I'm going now. You keep quite still here," he said, and put on his pince-nez. His eyes blinked, but they were bright and gleaming and the pupils were large and black. At the door he suddenly turned back and, going to the bed, knelt down. He put his face in his hands and murmured something Flämmchen did not catch. "Yes, yes, of course," she said. "Yes, gladly."

Kringelein got up, wiped his glasses on the corner of the handkerchief that hung from his breast pocket, and left the room. Flämmchen heard the outer door shut and his steps as he went along the passage. And then, in the distance, the music from the Yellow Pavilion, where the same people were still dancing as three hours before. . . .

Gaigern lay on the carpet in No. 71. He was dead. Nothing more could happen to him. No one now could harass or pursue him. He would never now find himself in prison. And that was good. He would never now keep his appointment in Vienna with Grusinskaya. And that was sad. But he had lived his life to the full in all his outlawed beauty and strength. He had spent his childhood among the fields, his boyhood on horseback. He had been a soldier in the war. He had been fighter, hunter, gambler. He had been a lover and he had been loved. Now he was dead. His hair was moist and matted. There was an ink-

His excessive blood pressure gave him throbbing pains in the back of his head and made his ears ring. Preysing was so crushed that for minutes together he longed to die of a stroke, and expiate his sin. But nothing of the sort occurred. Gaigern remained dead, and he remained alive.

"My God," he groaned. "My God! Mulle, Babs, Popsy. Oh, God."

He would have liked to bury his face in his hands, but he did not dare. He dreaded the darkness in the hollow of his hands.

Thus Kringelein found him when shortly after two o'clock (the music had just stopped) he entered the room after a cautious knock on the door. Kringelein's lips that night were dead white, but there was a fevered patch of red in his cheeks. He was in a strange state of elation, dignified and aloof, and he was very conscious of his appearance in his smart, well-cut black coat, and also of his *savoir faire* in his conduct of the situation.

"I came on the lady's behalf," he said. "I gather that something has happened here. I shall be glad to do anything I can for you, Herr Generaldirektor."

It was not till he had finished speaking that he looked down at the dead Gaigern. The sight did not shock him. He was merely surprised. For on the way from No. 70 the idea had come to him that all this was not true, that Gaigern still lived, that Preysing was no murderer, and that Flämmchen in his room was only dreaming, if indeed her being there at all was not itself a dream. But now he saw Gaigern actually lying there, as actually as Flämmchen was waiting for him in his room. He bent down over the dead man, touched by a familiar warmth of comradeship. He knelt beside him and the smell of lavender and scented Turkish cigarettes in which he had passed so unforgettable and so illuminating a day moved him profoundly. Thank you, he thought, as he caught his breath in a sob.

Preysing looked across with dazed and troubled eyes. "No one must touch him before the police come," he said unexpectedly, as Kringelein stretched out his hand to close his friend's eyes. Kringelein did not bother about Preysing in his corner, he performed the small solemn service. Flämmchen will do as much for me, he could not help thinking to himself. You look so happy. Is it so well with you? It is not so bad, is it? It won't be so very bad. And it won't be long, not long.

"Have you notified the police yet, Herr Generaldirektor?" he asked in a formal tone, when he was on his feet again. Preysing shook his head. "Would you like me to do so for you, Herr Generaldirektor? I am at your service," he went on. Oddly enough, Preysing felt an immense relief now that Kringelein was in the room, politely expressing his readiness to carry out his wishes.

"Yes. In a moment. Not now. Wait," he whispered. There was a semblance to the peremptory but confusing orders with which he harassed his subordinates at the factory.

"It will be imperative to let the old gentleman know of the occurrence. Would you like me to send a telegram to your esteemed family, Herr Generaldirektor?" Kringelein asked.

"No, no," Preysing answered in a quick, hoarse whisper, that sounded louder than a shout.

"Then I should suggest in any case that you put yourself in a solicitor's hands. It is late certainly, but in so exceptional a case one might be able to ring up a solicitor. You will undoubtedly be taken into custody at once on remand. I am very willing to undertake this or anything else that may be necessary, Herr Generaldirektor, before children and all he had—in spite of this, Grusinskaya at her telephone heard quite distinctly, even though faintly, a beloved voice saying:

"Neuwjada? You? My darling!"

"Hallo," called Grusinskaya, "good-evening, good-evening, my dear. Aren't you surprised that I should ring up? You must please speak louder. There's something wrong with the line. I have just come from the theater. It went well. It was splendid, an enormous success. They were crazy over me. I am very tired, but so, so happy. It is years since I danced as I did to-night. Oh, *comme je suis heureuse!* And you, do you think of me? I—I think of you every moment, only of you—I long for you. To-morrow early we leave for Vienna. Will you be there? Speak—speak. Tell me. Hotel Bristol, to-morrow, Vienna. Can you hear? Why, Exchange, Exchange, I've been cut off. I can hear nothing. I want to know whether you will be in Vienna. I'm expecting you. I'm having everything prepared for us at Tremezzo. Are you glad? Only fourteen days' more work and then we shall be at Tremezzo. Do say one word, just one word. I can't hear you. What? Is that Exchange? What do you say? No reply from the Baron? Thank you. Then please give him a message. Say that he is expected to-morrow in Vienna. Good-morning. Thank you."

Such was the conversation that passed between Grusinskaya and the empty room No. 69. She lay in bed in her hotel with her chin compressed in a rubber bandage, her eyes still hot with paint and her heart filled and glowing with tenderness. "But indeed I love you. *Je t'aime,*" she murmured into the dumb telephone, when the exchange at the Grand Hotel had already cut off the connection.

And then, just next door in No. 70, there is that moment, between four and five in the morning, when the drawn curtains were becoming gray and Flämmchen for the first time took Kringelein in her arms. It was that first sweet moment of tenderness when she did not sell but freely gave. Then for the first time she learnt that it was not a mere pleasure, a meaningless gratification, that she had to give away, but something great—an ecstasy, a happiness, a complete fulfilment. She lay there like a very young mother and held the man in her arms like a child that might drink its fill. Her fingers rested in the hollow between the sinews at the back of his neck, which illness and weakness had made. Everything is good now, thought Kringelein, no more pain. I am strong. Tired too, but I shall sleep. I have scarcely slept since I came here. It is a pity time is so short. I don't want to go off. I want to stay here. I don't want to have to stop now when everything is just beginning.

"Flämmchen," he whispered to her warm young body, "Flämmchen, don't let me die, please don't let me die."

Flämmchen at once held him closer, and began to comfort him.

"Die—what nonsense! I won't hear of it. It's not so bad as that by a long way. I'll soon look after you. I know a man in Wilmersdorfer Strasse who can work miracles. He has cured people who were far worse than you. He'll soon fix you up. We'll go to him first thing to-morrow. He'll give you a treatment of some kind, and then you'll be all right again, you'll see. Then we'll set off at once for London, Paris, the south of France. It will be warm there. We'll lie in the sun all day and get sunburnt and be happy. And now you must go to sleep."

She let her unthinking health and strength stream into his exhausted being, and he believed her. He fell asleep blissfully in a blaze of gold that looked like Flämmchen's breast and was also a hill of broom in flower.

And then, two floors higher, there is Dr. Otternschlag

dreaming the dream that comes to him every week. He is going through a dream-town which he knows very well and he enters a dream-house that he has forgotten. A dream-woman lives there and she has had a dream-child while he was a prisoner of war—a horrible child of whom he is not the father. It howls in its neat perambulator whenever it sees his mangled face. And then, as usual, he has to race breathlessly after his Persian cat, Gurbä, all through the dream-town, and to fight on a roof with a stray tom cat with a human face, and finally he crashes down through a burning sky of bursting shells and arrives on his bed in the hotel. When the dream reached this point, Dr. Otternschlag woke up.

"It's enough," he said to himself. "That's done it. How long have I to put up with it? And what's the use? No, we'll make an end of it."

He got up, and fetched his little case. He washed the syringe and broke the tops of one glass tube after another. Ten of them—twelve. He filled the syringe, and washed his arm, which was covered with little inflamed wounds from the needle. Then he paused. He began to tremble. All the strength ran out of his hands. He emptied the syringe without using it, squirting all its precious and surreptitiously acquired contents into the air with the exception of a few harmless drops with which he appeased the craving of his nerves. Then he lay down again, fell asleep, and heard nothing more.

Count Rohna emerged from his room just after half-past three, after being called up by the night porter, noiseless and circumspect and smelling of toilet vinegar, just as though it were broad daylight. He proceeded to room No. 71, took it all in at a glance, and gave the necessary directions. He ordered a cognac for the shattered Preysing and flicked away a winter fly that buzzed round the dead man's body. He stood for a quarter of a minute with folded hands and bowed head. It looked as though he was praying, and perhaps he did indeed pray for the dead man—his equal by birth, and, like him, an outcast. It can't have been easy for him either, perhaps he was thinking, and then he went into his little office and began to talk on the telephone with Police Commissioner Jädicke, whose special duty it was to keep an eye upon hotels.

A little later, when the first street sweepers were at work on the streets, appeared four gentlemen in overcoats, who bore the corporate and unpleasant name of the "Murder Commission." Rohna himself took them up in the lift to the second floor. The mills of justice were beginning to grind. The hotel management begged the police to use discretion in order to avoid a scandal, to hush things up, if possible. . . .

But it was not possible. Soon even Fredersdorf will know what has happened. Soon Frau Generaldirektor Preysing will arrive in Berlin with her apoplectic father, in order to part for ever with her husband in a succession of frightful scenes. That he had killed a man she could get over, in spite of her horror. But the disgusting affair with that woman—and this Preysing, stammering and perspiring and to his own undoing, had to confess at the second inquiry by the magistrate—*that* was utterly incomprehensible to her, and utterly unpardonable.

As for the dead man, Felix Amadei Benvenuto Freiherr von Gaigern, opinions were divided about him, although friendly enough. Not a single person in the Grand Hotel had anything to say against him. There was no previous conviction against him. He lay under no suspicion. He was not known to the police. He had a few debts, and how he had come by his small car (pledged, in any case, as security for a loan) could not be ascertained. But that proved nothing against him. He was a gambler, fond of women, often drunk, but always a good fellow. Some of the hotel staff wept over the whispered news of his death. The page boy, Karl Nispe, with the gold cigarette case in his pocket, wept. This boy was one of the first witnesses to be called and he was able to declare that the Baron was not in his room shortly before twelve o'clock. A lady on the first floor, in No. 18, the room below No. 71, heard the noise of a fall at about the same time. She noticed the time particularly, because the racket above annoyed her. But what had occurred between twelve and half-past three, and why had not Herr Preysing notified the police at once? The story was carried on at this point by the clear, if reserved, answers of the witnesses Flamm and Kringelein—those very answers which were read in the midday papers and gave the final blow to Preysing's moral existence. As for the weapon that Preysing talked about, there was no trace of it, no revolver was found, not even a little pistol such as considerate burglars sometimes employ merely to frighten people with. This told heavily against Preysing. If he lied on this point he was to be distrusted on all others. True, his pocketbook was discovered in the dead man's pajama pocket. But, asked the examining magistrate, worming his way into the matter, may not Preysing himself have purposely placed the pocketbook on Gaigern's person in order to give color to the fiction of self-defense against a burglar? There remained the fact that Gaigern wore socks over his light boxing shoes. There remained, too, a photograph which Baron Gaigern's chauffeur had given the second chambermaid of the second floor, and this photograph enabled the wide-awake police officials to say that this chauffeur at least was a notorious thief and criminal. If they succeeded in laying hands on him, more light would perhaps be thrown on the matter. For the time, however, Herr Preysing remained in prison, under remand, suffering from terrible optical delusions. He was always seeing Baron Gaigern before his eyes, not however as he lay there dead on the floor, but alive and so close that he was seen with extreme distinctness—the scar above his chin, his long eyelashes, every single pore in his skin—just as he had seen him as they collided outside the telephone box. If ever he succeeded in chasing the picture away, it was immediately replaced by a red haze beneath his closed eyelids, and then Flämmchen appeared, Flamm the Second—or rather a part of her only—her hips, as they were shown in a magazine photograph that fell into the general director's hands, when the moment came for Destiny to send him rolling down headlong into the abyss. . . .

It is an odd thing about the visitors in a big hotel. Not one as he goes out through the revolving door is the same as when he came in. Preysing, the pattern of propriety, went out as a prisoner and a broken man, under escort. Gaigern was silently and secretly carried out by four men down the steps by which tradesmen entered— Gaigern the Magnificent, who used to make the whole lounge smile if he merely passed through in his blue overcoat and his wash-leather gloves, with his alert glance and the perfume of lavender and Turkish cigarettes. Kringelein, however, when he and Flämmchen had given their evidence, and they were free to depart, passed out of the hotel like a king. Every back was bent and every hand extended for a tip. In all probability his glory will not last long. Probably within a week or two his next attack of acute pain will end it.

But there is just a chance that this courageous "moribundus" may develop fresh resources and remain alive in defiance of every diagnosis. That in any case is Flämmchen's belief. And Kringelein, borne aloft in ecstasy, wishes to believe it too. And, after all, it is not so very important how long Kringelein has to live. For, long or short, Life is what you put into it. Two full days may be

"No. Nothing, I am afraid," Georgi replied with a politeness copied from the hall porter.

Otternschlag turned about, and went back to his seat, this time in a bee line straight across the lounge—a most remarkable event in his case. The hall porter ran past him. His blond and trustworthy old-soldier's face was wet with perspiration as though after some gigantic exertion. He came to a stop behind his table, as though he had reached a haven.

"It is a little girl. There had to be an operation. But there she is and weighs five pounds. No danger at all now. None at all. Both of them alive and kicking," he panted, and took his cap off—thereby revealing the radiantly happy face of a purely private person, but he put it on again immediately, as Rohna looked over his glass screen. The married couple from the provinces got into the lift, and were taken up to room No. 72, the room with two beds and without a bath. The scent of Flämmchen's violet powder still lingered there.

"Open the window," said the wife.

"Yes, and let in a fine draught," said the husband.

In the lounge, Dr. Otternschlag sat and talked to himself. "It's dismal," he said. "Always the same. Nothing happens. One's always alone, dismally alone. The earth is an extinct planet—no warmth left in it. At Rouge Croix ninety-two men were buried in a fall of earth and never seen again. Perhaps I'm one of them and sit there with the rest ever since the end of the war and am dead and don't know it. If only something worth while would happen in this great big pub. But no, not a thing. 'Left.' Adieu, Herr Kringelein. I could have given you a prescription against those pains of yours. But no, gone without a word. And so it goes on. In—out, in—out, in—out——"

Little Georgi, however, behind the mahogany table

was revolving a few simple and extremely banal thoughts. Marvelous the life you see in a big hotel like this, he was thinking. Marvelous. Always something going on. One man goes to prison, another gets killed. One leaves, another comes. They carry off one man on a stretcher by the back stairs, and at the same moment another man hears he has a baby. Interesting—if you like! But such is Life!

Dr. Otternschlag sat in the middle of the lounge, a stone image of Loneliness and Death. He has his *en pension* terms, and so he stays on. His yellow hands hang down like lead, and with his glass eye he stares out into the street which is full of sunshine that he cannot see. . . .

The revolving door turns and turns—and swings . . . and swings . . . and swings. . . .

THE END